FROM THE MIND OF A WITCH

The Mind Sleuth Series Book 4

Bruce M. Perrin

First Edition

Cover Art by Courtney M. Perrin

Visit the Author at
BruceMPerrin.blogspot.com

Mind Sleuth Publications
ISBN-13: 978-1-955114-00-4 (ebook)
ISBN-13: 978-1-955114-01-1 (paperback)

For my family and
their boundless love and support

Table of Contents

Ordinary morality is only for ordinary people.
ALEISTER CROWLEY
ENGLISH POET AND OCCULTIST

THURSDAY, APRIL 30

6:18 PM, A House in Ste. Genevieve, Missouri

The man on the bed behind her stirred. Della Bergeron tried to remain still, but an uncontrollable shiver passed through her body. She drew her long bare leg under the sheet, wincing with sudden, stabbing pain. A gasp threatened to escape her lips, but she caught it in time.

Her earlier exertions had left her arms and legs trembling, her body covered in a sheen of sweat, but now she was cold and her muscles were cramping with fatigue. That explained the pain and some of her trembling. The larger portion of her shivers, however, came from the indelible images left by a dream. A doctor had been operating. Or maybe it was an autopsy? It was long ago, because his instruments—scalpels and saws, pliers and clamps—were tarnished and crude. And then, with growing horror, she realized that the patient was alive.

The clarity of the grisly scene had pushed Bergeron from her sleep, and now she squeezed her eyes closed, hoping to banish the last remnants from her thoughts. The nightmare, however, refused to release its grip.

Bergeron turned over, finding her lover propped up on an elbow watching. She was surprised. With the energy they had expended earlier she expected to be dragging him out of bed. The direction of his gaze, however, explained all; he was looking exactly where her naked leg had been. But if the man's alertness surprised, his hunger stunned her. She could read the desire in his face. She could sense it in his heartbeat. She could smell it on his skin. It had taken her months to ignite his passion, but now lit, it was an all-consuming blaze. She smiled at her handiwork.

Bergeron wasn't in the mood for a second tumble; she was too tired and sore. But if nothing else, it might remove the last, horrible visages of her nap. She leaned over and whispered in the man's ear. "Again, Victor, my love?"

"Babe, are you trying to kill me?" he asked with a grin.

"Perhaps."

Victor Sims raised his eyebrows and smiled in a way that he probably considered rakish. She thought it made him look childlike and nothing in his physical appearance contradicted that impression. His slightly curly light-brown-verging-on-blonde hair was cut short—almost like the fine hair of a newborn. His face was smooth, round, and unblemished. His eyes were brown and seemed disproportionately large for his head. And being a bit overweight and slightly below average in height only added to the illusion of youth.

But despite Sims's modest physical appearance, Bergeron felt a strong emotional attraction to him, a hunger. It started soon after her daughter had introduced the bumbling, divorced businessman. Almost immediately, Bergeron was interested. Soon, she needed him. It was a passion she had trouble explaining, even to herself. And if the source of her desire wasn't physical, neither was it intellectual. As the founder and president of Meteor Promotions, a booming, full-service marketing company, she might be hailed as the next great mind of the St. Louis business community, but to make that claim for Sims was absurd. He was a mid-level manager stuck in a dead-end job in an electrical supply company.

Bergeron, however, didn't dwell on the mysteries of her cravings, preferring action to pondering. So, she had marshaled her considerable physical charms, and they, along with a love spell, took care of Sims's self-doubts from a first marriage that had lasted mere months. Now, he was hers, body and soul.

"Well, if you kill me," replied Sims, "I could make friends with Peter Johnson, although I don't usually travel in the same circles as murderers from the early 1800s."

"Strange that you mention him," said Bergeron, her eyes blinking as she looked beyond Sims to the images that still lingered in her mind's eye. "I had a nightmare about him. Or at least, about Dr. Fenwick who was given his body for research after he was executed. Although in my dream, the hanging didn't quite finish him off."

Sims's face went blank, then his eyes opened wide. "Sorry, Del. That sounds awful."

Now that Sims had mentioned the local legend, Bergeron's dream made sense to her ... or as much as any dream did. They'd read the story shortly after arriving at the bed and breakfast. Johnson's execution for murder and Dr. Fenwick's receipt of the body for research were a matter of public record in historic Ste. Genevieve, Missouri's oldest town. It was the sightings of Johnson's ghost haunting the former residence of the doctor that were in question. And although Bergeron had yet to make contact with anyone deceased, she was sure the stories were true.

"A bit disturbing, yes, but the dead are part of my expanding world," she said, pausing a moment to consider her observation. "And maybe this is the first step into that new realm." Her expression morphed from thoughtful to playful. "As for making a new friend of Mr. Johnson, we've talked about you expanding your circle of influence. Ghosts need light fixtures and ceiling fans, too."

Sims snorted, one of the man's mannerisms that annoyed her. But before she could respond, he said, "Sorry. I'm still breaking that habit. You know, coming here for this business meeting was pure genius. Or should I say, coming here for the gathering of your coven?"

Victor hadn't even allowed himself a breath between the statements. He probably wanted to avoid another scolding, although she had no intention of doing that. Tonight was too important to be spoiled by minor irritations because, in the last week or so, Sims's place in her evolving world had become clear in Bergeron's mind. He would be the stage on which she demonstrated her new understandings to the coven. He would be the conduit she used to drive her tentacles deeper into their psyches. And tonight was the night it would all start.

She glanced at Sims, his childlike grin now replaced by a wrinkled brow. His eyes moved restlessly around the room, never seeming to find the reassurance they sought. Somewhere along that visual trail, he'd probably seen the clock on the bedside table. It was time for them to get ready.

"So, is Mr. Victor Sims ready to take his rightful place at the head of his company?"

Whatever thoughts that had held him captive disappeared in the wake of her whispered question. "I'm making CEO tonight, am I?" he asked, now smiling.

"In a matter of hours, you'll become one of the chosen. One of the inner circle. After that, your ascendancy is assured." Sims was silent, so she said, "Are you ready to take that step?"

"Hell, yes, I am," he replied. "I'm just sorry there's no time for another ... you know."

Victor raised his eyebrows suggestively, but Bergeron saw through the attempt to cover his unease with false machismo. "Love, do you need to take some of your medication?"

He blew a breath between his nearly closed lips. "I've been trying to cut down on the chlordiazepoxide. Don't you want me clearheaded for the evening?"

"I want you comfortable."

It was true. If Sims lost his nerve, her plans would be spoiled. And make no mistake, it would take all the confidence he had to stand before a group of nameless, hooded businessmen and women who had the power to ruin his life even more easily than they could make it. "How about just one pill, to take the edge off?" she asked.

Sims rose from the bed and shuffled naked to the bathroom. Bergeron felt a chuckle rising in her throat, but held it in. Even from the back, he reminded her of a child. How could a man who spent most of his life on his backside have one that was so accurately described as smooth as a baby's bottom? And just as round?

She threw the sheet aside and stood, catching a glimpse of her long, lean body in the mirror. Her lustrous black hair fell in waves on pale white shoulders. Gray eyes—the color connected with violent swings of energy according to her studies—peered from behind dark curls that fell loosely across her face. She brushed the strands aside. Her cheekbones were high, the only feature noticeable in a countenance so smooth it could be porcelain. The one thing she didn't like in her appearance was her mouth. It was too small. And since she smiled infrequently and never sported a wide-open grin, it seemed like she was forever pouting. But for some reason, men could hardly seem to take their eyes off it. That is, if their eyes made it to her face.

As if to provide a validation of her attractiveness that she didn't need, Sims gave her a thorough, once-over when he came out of the bathroom. "Damn, you are trying to kill me." Bergeron smiled, although this declaration hid his anxiety about the coming evening even less well than the last.

"It's not me who's going to kill you, love. It's your libido. Now, go put some clothes on before we end up being late."

Sims saluted a bit stiffly, then turned to the black tuxedo that had been carefully laid out on a dresser. She went to the closet, removed a long black gown, and laid it out on the bed. It was a simple garment with a neckline low enough and a slit on the side high enough to enthrall any man. That, however, wouldn't be necessary tonight. Every eye would be on her whatever she wore. She started slipping on the dress.

"You don't wear anything under that?" Sims was staring at her again.

"I don't." He'd think she was dressing for his titillation and that misperception was good enough for her purposes. But evidently, that wasn't his thought.

"But these are your ... business associates." The hitch in his speech said he still wasn't sure what to call them, which was good. Their secrecy was by design because strictly speaking, what they did to grease the skids of commerce was of questionable legality. "And your daughter will be there, right?"

There was more to his confusion than she'd thought, but she wasn't going to try to explain. "Yes, she'll be there. But since we've dropped the ritualistic sexual intercourse at the finale of the ceremony, it'll be okay." She smirked lest Sims think her serious.

But the quip failed to reduce the man's tension. His brows were knitted again.

"These gatherings are the path to enlightenment," said Bergeron, sounding a bit frustrated by his growing concern. She took a breath to calm herself. "It'll be over soon and all shall be clear."

Sims drew his mouth into a tight smile, then nodded. "I'm not sure why I'm so nervous."

"You'll be fine. It's a new start and that's a lot for anyone."

"Yeah, I guess so." He paused a beat. "I don't suppose one more pill could hurt." He turned toward the bathroom, then turned back to her. "And that new life?" He waited for her to nod. "I'm hoping you'll spend it with me?"

"Every moment we have. I promise."

* * *

The headlights of their car fought a losing battle against the night as the darkness encroached on the country road. Even in the daytime—the only time Bergeron had been here previously—the area had spoken to her. It was even more haunting now. One moment, the images of fields and fences, farmhouses and trees were shrouded in darkness from a cloud passing in front of the first quarter moon. The next, their spectral images emerged from the void. This dance of ghostly images filled her senses, and her skin started tingling with the energy.

She sensed Victor turning toward her, perhaps because the bouncing of his leg on the car's leather seat had paused. But if he was going to ask her something, he reconsidered. Maybe he had heard, "All shall soon be clear" enough times to know that questions were pointless. His fidgeting returned, accompanied by a long sigh.

After a few more minutes, their driver turned into a pasture. A man in a dark suit stood by the open gate. Bergeron eased her window down. "Everything is prepared, Ms. Bergeron," he said.

"Security?"

"You won't be disturbed."

She raised her window and the driver continued into the field. After a few moments bouncing over uneven ground, he parked the car near a group of trees and turned off the headlights. Bergeron leaned toward Victor because the woods were on his side, but there was little to be seen save the darkened silhouettes of barren branches.

"Why aren't there any leaves on these trees?" Victor asked in almost a whisper.

"All life has fled this place."

"What happened?"

In the moment it took Victor to ask his question, the cloud that had been blocking the moon floated on, revealing a building standing on the edge of the woods ... or what was left of one. Now, the structure was but a skeleton, the black holes of missing windows its eyes, the opening for a door the gaping mouth.

Victor turned in the direction of her gaze and a gasp escaped his lips. "What is this place?"

"Not all of the human experimentation in this area involved bodies that were legally obtained. And now I know from my dream—some weren't even dead."

Human remains had been found nearby, although how and why they had died no one knew. The facts were long lost in history. But in the last hour, Bergeron's dream had taken on the mantle of truth. It was, she was certain, a vision of the past. If Sims couldn't sense it, she couldn't explain.

"Come," she said.

Bergeron exited the car and walked to the back. Sims followed. She opened the trunk and pulled out a black cape. She threw it over her shoulders and lifted the hood, leaving her face in shadow. She removed a red one and held it out. "Yours."

Sims took the cloak but didn't put it on. "We're not going in there, are we? I can't see a damn thing."

"Patience."

He opened his mouth to say more, but she placed two fingers on his lips. He drew back with her touch. "Your hands are freezing."

She said nothing, and after a moment, Sims donned the cloak without further objection. She started toward the patch of trees, their bare branches again cloaked in darkness. The smell of decaying vegetation rose to her nose and left a bitter aftertaste on her tongue. The night was silent, save the song of a lone coyote in the distance. But in the still, the voices of those who had died so horribly in this place came to her like a whisper on the breeze. The tingling of her flesh increased.

"Della?"

She spun around, her connection to the place broken. Sims stumbled backward, nearly falling over something in the dark. She waited, staring into eyes that were moving restlessly over the environs.

"I can't go through with this," he whispered. "Nothing that happens here tonight is going to affect my career."

Bergeron started to protest, but the words didn't come. Though she hadn't thought about it before, she knew how to get what she required in this moment, and pleading wasn't the way. "All would be different after tonight, but I understand. Have the driver take you back to the bed and breakfast. I'll see you there when we're done."

She turned and started walking but took only three steps before his unsteady voice came from behind. "Della?" She looked back. "I guess since you've gone to all this trouble ...."

"Come," she said, continuing toward the woods. Sims trotted a few steps to catch up. When he rejoined her, two bonfires leaped to life just ahead. There was a crude stone altar between them.

Bergeron had designed every detail of this setting, and she looked upon it with approval. The altar faced east, the direction of change. Its stonework was rough. The grounds were cleared of vegetation leaving bare dirt. There would be no tire tracks in the loose soil, no polished stone the work of machines. The setting was a labor of many hours and many hands, hers included.

Around the north end of the clearing stood three long-standing members of the group, those now near or at the pinnacle of their respective organizations. Though she was too far away for her eyes to penetrate the shadows of the raised hoods, the six-foot, six-inch figure had to be Russell Cowan. He and Deborah Fry, with their connections to banking and construction respectively, had done more for the success of the group than anyone except herself. They would be joined on that side by Nicholas Goodwin, the recently named chief financial officer at his pharmaceutical supply company. And since the CEO's health was failing, his stay in that office would be short if all went to plan.

Around the south end were the three who still had several rungs of their corporate ladders to negotiate. Even if Bergeron hadn't known, she sensed her daughter, Lilith Harrison, among that group. It also included Neal London, second and presumptive heir to Cowan in the coven, as Bergeron didn't want to leave the succession plan for finance up to chance. Edward Streeter, director of product development at an aerospace engineering company completed the trio.

Together with Bergeron, these witches made up the sacred number of seven.

The group started chanting, quietly at first, but increasing in volume as she and Sims approached. Now, in the presence of the coven, she knew he would not falter. Like water, he'd take the path of least resistance and that was to do as she instructed. Sims sat on the slab of rock, facing her, then laid down. She walked around to the head of the altar.

Ceremonial implements rested on a shelf—a lit candle, a goblet of wine, and a simple bone-handled dagger. Bergeron retrieved the candle, held it aloft, and repeated an incantation. The witches turned outward, as she slowly moved around the group lighting other candles that had been placed in a ring. Finally, she placed the original candle in a holder, forming a circle of thirteen. Bergeron retook her position at the head of the altar, every eye following her motion. The preparations were complete.

Bergeron's gaze slowly traveled across the faces of the assembled. Those countenances spoke to her, not in the words they were chanting, but in the magical energy radiating from them. Her senses, preternaturally heightened before, now magnified her world tenfold. The tiny sparks from the flames were like blinding flashes of lightning striking the earth mere inches from her feet. The chanting voices became the answering thunder, filling her ears and echoing in the hollow of her lungs and through the surrounding hills. The scent of smoke and the stench of decay mixed with the acrid smell of fear as it rolled off Sims in waves.

Bergeron retrieved the dagger and held it aloft. After repeating another incantation, she poured wine over the blade. The voice of the coven increased in volume. Her gaze again passed over the shadowy eyes of the assembled, coming to rest on a set that was filled with pain and power. In unison, all looked down, dragging her into a deepening spiral of ethereal sensations. Lightning, thunder, the shine of cold steel, the message in those eyes. Again. And again, until all became darkness.

As Bergeron pulled herself from the void, she heard only her voice in the absolute silence that had descended on the clearing. "I kept my promise, Victor. I was with you to the end."

She looked down. She was covered in blood. And Sims was lying on the altar, blood streaming from his throat, the dagger sticking from his chest.

FIVE MONTHS LATER, MONDAY, OCTOBER 5

10:03 AM, Marte Investigative Services

Rebecca Marte's blue eyes and short blonde hair were reflected in the blank screen of the phone in her hand, but she didn't see them. The smell of coffee that had gone cold in the cup on the corner of her desk didn't register either. Not even the sound of her outer office door opening and closing got her attention. Her thoughts were nearby but months in the past.

"Why don't you call him?"

Rebecca jumped, her head spinning around to find retired FBI Senior Special Agent Gus Clements standing at the inner door to her new office. "Quit sneaking up on me like that. One day, it's gonna get you shot."

"That would be pretty tough since you don't carry anymore."

"Yeah, but that policy will change if you don't cut it out."

Gus chuckled.

When Rebecca resigned from the FBI to start her new business, Marte Investigative Services in St. Louis, Missouri, she'd left more than her badge behind. Gone, too, were handguns on the job. It wasn't that she was uncomfortable with them. She enjoyed target practice and still kept her skills sharp. It was just that they were unnecessary, at least for now. No one was going to come after her because they'd failed one of the security screenings she had run for a local business. They wouldn't even know who had conducted it.

And so far, she didn't have to worry about a vengeful spouse either. She'd had inquiries about checking up on a partner—two of them to be exact unless you didn't count the male who walked out after saying, "I thought R. Marte was a man." Without him, there was only the possibly-wronged husband who had spent more time looking at her legs and her chest than the documents she'd given him. Maybe his wife had strayed, but if she had, Rebecca was certain he'd long since blazed that trail.

"So, are you going to call?"

"Who?" Rebecca asked, frowning at her former mentor and current freelance partner.

"Doc, who else? Since you dropped that sleazebag ...."

"Todd."

"Yeah, him," said Gus. "The moron who thought he could date a PI without her finding out he was married. Anyway, with Todd gone, that moon-eyed look of yours has to be about Dr. Sam Price."

"Moon-eyed look?" Rebecca shook her head slowly. "Where the hell do you get these expressions?"

Her question, however, was more about evasion than interest. She understood the words from context. And while she had been thinking about Doc—the nickname almost everyone used for him—she was certain the expression didn't fit. "Narrow-eyed resignation" was a lot closer because Doc was inaccessible to her ... and probably every other woman in the world, save one. And that one he saw only in his memories, a place where she was without flaw and beyond reproach.

"So, how's he holding up?" asked Gus, sidestepping her attempt to change the topic.

"Pretty confident that's what I was thinking about, huh?"

Gus shrugged in reply.

"No change. He's still blaming himself for his fiancée's kidnapping, even though it happened right under the noses of local law enforcement and the FBI." She, too, shared some of that responsibility, since she had been a part of the Bureau's team.

"Maybe I should call him," said Gus. "I don't know him that well, but I hate to hear he's wallowing in pity. Next thing you know, he'll be drinking his meals in some dive bar."

"He's not wallowing in pity." Her tone was sharper than she'd expected. She took a breath. "If anything, it's the opposite. He's hardly sleeping or eating, worried he'll miss some clue buried in the news. Or fail to make some connection in everything he's already dug up."

"But that can change," replied Gus. "If every law enforcement agency in the United States can't find Nicole Veles, he's not going to. And when that happens ...." He held out an empty hand, the shrug coming to his shoulders again.

Perhaps, thought Rebecca, but she doubted that drinking himself to death was where Doc was headed. The question was, did she want to share her hunches about his possible path when she was on such unfamiliar ground? But if Gus was going to call, which she thought was a good idea, maybe there was something he could use in her surmises.

"One day, Doc and I got to talking about school. He had all these crazy stories about being ridiculously anal like he had to keep working on a problem until he had an answer. We saw some of that in the Crusaders for Common Sense case."

Gus snorted. "I thought he was just a wannabe FBI agent."

"Maybe that, too, but I doubt it. Anyway, he has this one-track mind about anything important to him. He even had a term for it. Said he showed the Zeigarnik effect on steroids."

Gus's eyes narrowed.

"Yeah, I'd never heard of it either, so I looked it up ... after about twenty attempts to get the spelling right. It's about how people's thoughts can get filled with all the details of unfinished business. And I guess in the worst cases, like Doc, they can't stop those thoughts until the problem's solved. When we talk on the phone, that's what it seems like. One minute, we're discussing the weather, and the next, he's off on some long story about the evidence he needs and the hunches he needs to check. He knows he's doing it, but he can't seem to stop."

"Is this effect some sort of mental disorder?" asked Gus, raising his eyebrows.

"Not as it was described online but in Doc's case, maybe. Let's face it. There is nothing more important to him than finding Veles. And since that problem's not anything he's going to solve ... well, he's trapped. I think he could ruin his health, not from booze, but from physical and mental exhaustion. Or just plain have a meltdown. I mean, how many famous criminals have been pursued for years by one person who became so obsessed that they lost their job and family?"

"Several, unfortunately," replied Gus.

"Exactly. Doc's pretty bad off and it's only been six months. He's headed for some serious problems."

Gus started nodding slowly as he turned to look at a blank wall. After a few moments, he turned back. "I guess unfinished business nags at most of us, me included. But now that you describe how he's acting? Yeah, I've known a couple of other agents like that. They were great investigators—some of the best I've ever known—but both of them developed problems after a while. They had nightmares and flashbacks, even though there wasn't any specific traumatic event that brought them on. They both left the Bureau, and at least one of them got better in a different job. I lost track of the other guy."

It was good that Gus understood what she was talking about, but at the same time, it was troubling that something like that might be in Doc's future if he didn't ease up. Rebecca could feel a knot forming in her stomach. "So, you'll call him?"

"Sure, although I doubt Doc will listen if I tell him to drop the case." Rebecca shared that opinion, making the knot tighten a bit more.

"You like him, don't you?" Gus asked.

"None of your business, old man," she replied although she was sure Gus knew the answer. He'd spent thirty years in the FBI reading people. "When you call, maybe you could ...." Her ringing office phone interrupted the conversation.

After Rebecca identified herself, the caller said, "Ms. Marte, my name is Rowena Labadie. I'm the sister of Delphine Bergeron. Do you know that name? Or maybe as Della Bergeron?"

Rebecca pointed at a chair, knowing she'd want to discuss this call with Gus when it was over. He sat and unfolded his paper to catch up on the news.

"Yes, of course, Ms. Labadie. I'm familiar with the basics of your sister's case."

"From the media or the FBI?"

Labadie must have seen her company's website, which listed the FBI as a previous employer. "From the papers," replied Rebecca. She doubted that the FBI had been seriously involved—murder was a local matter—but she had already left the Bureau when the killing occurred and didn't know for sure. "What is it you'd like for us to do?"

"Follow up. The police must have missed something because there are just too many things that don't add up. There is no way my sister killed Victor Sims."

Even with her less than two years in law enforcement, Rebecca had heard the phrase "too many things don't add up" dozens of times. Often it just meant the speaker couldn't accept the facts. And that seemed even more likely in this instance as the papers had made the case sound open-and-shut. Headlines such as "Business Leaders Witness Ritualistic Killing" had been plastered on front pages for days.

"Okay. We need to discuss the particulars, both what you suspect and what I can do to help. Can you come by my office sometime today?"

"How about after lunch, say 1:00?" asked Labadie.

Rebecca agreed and hung up. Gus set his paper aside.

"So, a case that made the papers, huh?" Gus said. "You're coming up in the world fast."

"Yeah. You read about the city alderwoman arrested for littering?"

Gus released a single laugh. "That's it, huh?"

"No. I just wanted to point out that making the news doesn't raise the bar all that much. You remember the case of the witch CEO who killed a man during one of her coven rituals?"

"Yeah, I remember. That wasn't her, was it?"

"No. It was her sister. She wants to hire us to look into the case, which is fine with me, except for one thing."

"What's that?"

"I hate to have any association with that witchcraft nonsense."

10:48 AM, A Farmhouse in Western Kansas

The woman called herself Maggie. Maggie Ingalls. And she seemed familiar, although Nicole Veles had no memory of having met her before. But then, Nicole could no longer trust her memory.

According to Maggie, she and her son, Justin, had first laid eyes on Nicole about six or seven months ago. She was near death, lying by the side of a rural road outside of St. Louis, Missouri, and they had stopped to help. Maggie said she'd slept for nearly two days after they got her back to the farm, but eventually, the fever broke and she woke up.

Nicole, too, remembered waking up at Maggie's house. She was exhausted, achy, and nauseous. But she also remembered that one of her first thoughts was "I know this woman." But every attempt to place her since that morning had failed.

That Nicole had simply forgotten the woman was possible, of course. And she might have accepted that explanation except for one thing. When she went back through her memories, there was a period from about a year or two ago until she woke up on the farm that seemed more a chaotic collection of vivid scenes and distorted images than a life she had lived. She knew she had taken a job with a company called Biomedical Engineering Associates out of college. But then, her memories became disjointed. She remembered someone named Worthington, but not who he was. She recalled shattered glass and cleaning up blood in her apartment, but she had no idea whose blood it was. She recalled looking at pictures of military drones, but not why they were important.

And then there were the horrible, vivid images, memories of disease and death by the thousands that had come back to her in the past few months. She couldn't handle thinking about all that suffering for long and wondered if that was why she couldn't remember Maggie. The recollection of that time was simply too painful. Unfortunately, her repression of a shared past, if they had one, couldn't explain why Maggie didn't remember her and that fact weighed on her mind.

Finally, Nicole decided she was just being paranoid. After all, the world had gone through a lot during those months she had lost, and she wasn't the only one with a sketchy mental history. Justin was worse … much worse. He recalled his mom. And he remembered a big house and something that sounded like a one-room school in the country with a group of other children. Or at least, he had memories of recess with them—running, climbing, swinging on ropes, wrestling with the other boys. Those days were sketchy, but between then and a few months ago, his mind was a complete blank.

Fortunately, Justin's memory seemed to be returning. After each session with his mother looking at old pictures, he'd excitedly tell Nicole about another chapter in his life that they had uncovered. She was happy for him, but her recovery was much more piecemeal. She never seemed to recall more than an isolated incident or two, and by chance, most of them were things she wished she hadn't found again. One of the worst was her mother, lying in a hospital bed, slowly dying. She could now picture it like it was yesterday, and it had started appearing in her nightmares.

Nicole leaned back in the armchair where she had been reading and glanced at Justin. He was sitting across the room at a table. His face was scrunched up in concentration as he worked a jigsaw puzzle, his dark brown eyes mere slits below bushy eyebrows. But even before the look, she knew if the goal was to see if she felt the same familiarity toward him that she did toward his mom, she'd fail. He'd been her near-constant companion for the last four months, so now everything about him was familiar.

She knew, for example, if they stood, she'd need to tip her head down a fraction to look into his brown eyes. Despite his small stature, however, he was strong. His hands were calloused and his face was tanned. She knew the small scar on his left cheek that looked something like the state of California, as well as the fact he couldn't remember how he got it. All in all, he looked the part of a boy growing into manhood in a rural setting. But if he had lived here and she in St. Louis, how could she have met his mother? Nicole's feeling of a past connection to the woman was strong, even in the absence of any specific recollection.

"Justin?" He looked up. "How did you and your mom come to take me in?"

"Still can't remember?" he asked with a grin.

"No, not really. That whole time is messed up."

"You were beside the road, maybe 30 or 40 miles west of St. Louis," Justin said.

"No, you told me that already. I mean, how did you come to the decision? Why did you stop? There must have been other cars on the road."

Justin rubbed a hand over his chin, a mannerism Nicole had seen many times. He was brooding over the question. Justin did a lot of brooding because everything was strange and new to him.

His lack of a past also made him very curious, particularly of her. Early in her stay, she'd caught him trying to sneak a peek when she was getting dressed, and her reprimands had little effect. Finally, she had sought help from Maggie. True to the woman's no-nonsense approach to life, Maggie had explained to her son that young women needed their privacy. But then, she took the opportunity to launch into an old-fashioned birds-and-the-bees talk.

It seemed strange to Nicole that they'd never had the chance in the last twenty or so years to do that, but it was even odder—at least in Nicole's mind—that Maggie insisted it be a "family talk." Nicole's feelings of awkwardness became astonishment, however, when the older woman's view of sex seemed solidly rooted in the last century. It even included mentions of the man's needs and the woman's duties. Duties? The word "seriously" had popped into Nicole's head at least a half-dozen times during the fifteen-minute talk, though she kept quiet.

Although unorthodox, the talk with Justin had worked ... at least for a while. But then, the pendulum had swung back, and now things were worse than ever. Justin's behavior had become less about peeping and more about physical intimacy, at least in his fumbling way. He was always rubbing against her, putting a hand on her knee, trying to brush a strand of hair from her face. As before, Nicole had tried firm but compassionate rebukes to his inappropriate advances. And, as before, it wasn't working. Unfortunately, she couldn't count on Maggie's help, as her sympathies had become more aligned with her son.

"You'll have to ask my mom," said Justin, bringing Nicole back to the moment. "But I think she stopped because nobody else was stopping."

"But I was sick. I could have killed you both."

Justin started rubbing his chin again.

Like so many other things in her past, Nicole didn't remember her illness, but she had expectations for it based on experience—specifically, her memory of the coronavirus pandemic of 2020. Who could forget how quickly it had spread across the globe and how completely it had disrupted lives and livelihoods?

From what she could surmise, the virus that had attacked her and Justin moved with similar speed, blanketing the globe in a matter of months. But what was different about it was the mortality rate. It killed with the efficiency of some of the worst Ebola outbreaks, the death rate approaching 90 percent. To make matters worse, it was airborne—not just in the larger droplets from coughs or sneezes, but as much smaller, drier particles that could float in the air for hours. Maggie even kept her and Justin inside when the prevailing wind was coming from the direction of Denver, though she said it was several hundred miles away.

So, in the context of the lethality of the virus, her and Justin's memory losses, while disturbing, were but relatively minor side effects. At least, they were alive while billions of others weren't.

When Maggie had first described what had happened to the world, Nicole had been nearly destroyed. She'd made a mental list of her family—parents, aunts, uncles, cousins. She added her friend, Sam, and did the mental math. With the virus's mortality rate, most of them would be dead. Who among that group had she watched die? How many last words of love and phone calls of encouragement had she heard, only to have the virus strip her mind of the small comforts they provided?

Nicole decided that one, maybe two of her family might still be alive. After all, the virus didn't kill everyone, so she clung desperately to that hope. And though she couldn't stand to ponder who that might be, Sam was always among the living. Why was that? She remembered working with him, but they hardly knew each other. Had they become more? And while everyone else called him Doc, she used Sam. Did that mean anything? But other than a vague feeling that he'd become significant in some way, all of the memories of him were more like the images from a vanishing dream—vague and fleeting.

Eventually, however, even her flicker of hope that some had survived the pandemic also died. It stood to reason that the few who would have escaped the virus would be found in isolated, remote locales. They would live in places like Maggie's farmhouse, which sat amid rolling grasslands that seemed to go on forever. Nicole's kin had lived in Independence, which bordered the larger metropolis of Kansas City, Missouri. And Sam had been in St. Louis. Had he been able to piece together enough information to guess what was coming? Was she 30 miles outside of St. Louis because they had been running together? But then, there would be little reliable data on a virus during the early days of a pandemic, nothing to warn her or Sam about what was to come. She, too, knew that from 2020.

Nicole could feel her eyes becoming moist as her mind retread the vague history of her loss. She shouldn't dwell on it. She couldn't let that empty feeling, that sense of helplessness overcome her again. She turned her focus back to Justin just as he spoke.

"Yeah, we knew you were sick," he replied. "But I was sick, too. Everyone was. And Mom thought if you weren't too bad, maybe she could pull us both through. Why do you want to know so bad?"

"I'm just trying to understand what's happened to me. Don't you want to get back your memories of when you were a kid?" Justin shrugged, which almost made her laugh. Nicole had never met anyone as easygoing as he was.

"And what Mom's doing doesn't help you?" asked Justin.

"Sort of, but not like you." And that fact was frustrating and alarming to Nicole in equal measure.

12:41 PM, Marte Investigative Services

In preparation for her 1:00 meeting, Rebecca had spent most of the morning catching up on the news stories about "The Witch of the St. Louis Business World," as the press had come to call Delphine "Della" Bergeron. With that identifier in the headlines, readers had flocked to the websites and the papers had flown out of the vending machines. And yet, for Rebecca's purposes, the online articles were just reorganized bits and bytes on her computer and the print stories were just wood pulp smeared with ink. It wasn't that the stories were light on content; they weren't. But since Rebecca's purpose was to find proof of Della Bergeron's innocence, they served only to make her quest seem that much more impossible.

The most damning thing was that there was little doubt about the facts. Sims's throat had been slashed before the knife was plunged into his chest and left there as his heart finished its final perfunctory beats. All of the accounts that appeared in the news told that same story, right down to Bergeron standing over the body covered in blood, saying that she'd kept her pledge to be with him to the end. Later, she said she had blacked out, that she couldn't remember anything before mumbling that promise. And even though she recalled making the statement, she had no idea why.

The question in Rebecca's mind was why Bergeron had said anything. Where was her lawyer? And if he hadn't arrived yet, didn't she know any better? Hadn't it almost become common sense to hold your tongue until your lawyer shows up? And claiming temporary amnesia without reason—no blow to the head, no emotional trauma—made Bergeron seem desperate, like a guilty person grasping at straws. But then, Rebecca told herself, rationality didn't come readily to most in the presence of a dead lover.

The second most damaging piece of information was that Bergeron hadn't acted under the influence of any type of drug. Because of the claim she'd blacked out or due to general concerns about her health—different papers cited different reasons—she'd been taken to a hospital after the incident and a blood test had been conducted. And when those results came back, someone had leaked them to the press. Unless the source was lying or mistaken, Bergeron was in perfect health with nothing in her system—not so much as a drop of alcohol. Rebecca would need to verify those results, of course, but she held little hope the papers were wrong.

The autopsy on Sims, on the other hand, had found a high concentration of chlordiazepoxide in his system, a medication that would have made him drowsy and docile. And since Sims and Bergeron had spent the afternoon in their room at a local bed and breakfast, she had ample time to drug him. As for the means to get him to partake, those who had seen them in public said all she had to do was ask; his infatuation with her was that obvious and, apparently, that absolute. This observation, in turn, had led to a series of articles about the authenticity of love spells and potions, but

Rebecca didn't go there. Investigating the possibility of a love spell gone out of control wasn't worth her time.

The only issue in the facts of the case was in the chain of custody of the murder weapon. At some point, the dagger had been removed from Sims's body, perhaps by an overly exuberant paramedic, and it had been dropped on the ground. It was found several hours later, partially covered by some dead leaves. The slipup might make the weapon inadmissible in court, but no one considered that much of an issue anyway. There was simply too much other evidence implicating Bergeron.

In addition to the extensive coverage of the events of that night, several articles explored the idea that Bergeron might plead temporary insanity. And in some respects, the claim that she remembered nothing gave credence to the idea. But there were problems. One was the source of this speculation. Many of the stories quoted other practicing witches who said Bergeron had to be mentally unbalanced; no modern witch performs ritualistic human sacrifice ... if witches ever did. And almost as frequently, the business community had added their weight to the insanity explanation. It didn't take too much digging, however, to find that these insinuations had come from the five business leaders in the coven. That fact, of course, made perfect sense to Rebecca. Caught in a situation rife with the appearance of impropriety, they'd want to distance themselves from their one-time leader. Who knew, they had asked rhetorically, that her team-building ceremonies were just a cover for her homicidal delusions.

But reading between the lines, Rebecca doubted that a plea of temporary insanity was being seriously considered. First, Bergeron had no history of mental disturbance, making this plea much more difficult to prove. Second, no one had identified a precipitating influence, a reason why Bergeron had become unbalanced. There was no evidence, not even a whisper, suggesting that Sims and Bergeron had been arguing. Statements by all who had seen them that day—at the bed and breakfast, the restaurant where they dined, the local shops and museums—told the opposite story. Similarly, their businesses couldn't be blamed. Hers was doing extremely well, while Sims's was stable, if not exciting. There was also the mention in a couple of articles that the family had retained experts on the insanity defense. If their examinations had been conclusive, or even supportive, Rebecca doubted Labadie would have approached her.

After reading and re-reading the media accounts of the incident, Rebecca was left with several nagging questions. For example, one article had mentioned that Harrison had initially been in a pre-medical program in college before deciding to join her mother in business. That casual observation, however, became significant when considering Sims's execution; it had been skilled. Either of the two incisions alone would have been fatal. Finding one of Harrison's old textbooks on human anatomy lying around Bergeron's home would go a long way to explaining how she had become such an efficient killer.

Rebecca realized, of course, that if such a book was found, it would just further bolster an already strong case against Bergeron. In fact, all of her nagging issues, if resolved, would do the same, making her wonder if her predilection for incriminating evidence was a carryover from the FBI? Once focused on finding guilt, could she be effective in proving innocence? But in the end, she decided this problem had more to do with the case—it was nearly open-and-shut—than her acquired tendencies. She just hoped Labadie was bringing more to their 1:00 meeting than "my sister's too nice to kill anyone."

After the fervor of the killing died down and with few of the facts of the case being disputed, the papers had started focusing on the person rather than the crime. The stories ranged, in Rebecca's mind, from mildly interesting to unadulterated muckraking.

In the former category were several stories about Bergeron's personality. They universally portrayed the witch-slash-business tycoon as fearless, self-promoting, and charismatic. She held bold visions for the future and had a willingness to take huge risks, many of which paid off. And likewise, the stories always mentioned her ruthless treatment of the smaller companies she acquired and her no-holds-barred pursuit of new markets. She was, as one article said, typical of the power-hungry, narcissistic business leader of today. Rebecca, however, didn't elevate these stories beyond "interesting" because it wasn't clear that any of these reporters had even met the woman, much less had the training and experience to support their diagnoses.

On the other end of the scale, the stories were alike in the fact that sensationalism seemed the only prerequisite. And perhaps it was a fluke of the order Rebecca had read them, but it also seemed they were into one-upmanship. So, where one story claimed Bergeron was a devoted but recent convert to evil, another said her connection not only ran deep but also well into her genes. She had been raised not far from the New Orleans Royal Street Mansion where Delphine LaLaurie had tortured and murdered her slaves in the 1830s. But since "not far" seemed to mean somewhere in Louisiana to this journalist and inheriting malevolence from a first name was nonsense, Rebecca had abandoned that story early.

Her time reviewing the news, however, hadn't been wasted. She'd come up with a few questions for her client, should she decide to take the case. And at the moment, she was leaning that way. She, too, wanted to be seen as a fearless woman with a willingness to take huge risks for the right reasons. The difference was that she wasn't sure she could pull off these miracles with the regularity that Bergeron had.

Rebecca was reviewing her notes when she heard someone in the outer reception area. She leaned to the side to find Gus making his way to her office. Since this case had the potential to be by far the biggest of her short career as a private investigator, she'd asked for his help, and he'd agreed. Gus stopped at her door.

"You leave your office unlocked?"

"You gonna be my receptionist with what I can pay?" Gus frowned in reply. "It's only open when I'm in here and usually when I'm expecting someone. Are you afraid someone's going to steal the covers off the light switches?"

Gus looked over his shoulder at the reception area. "Yeah, not much in there worth stealing."

"Thanks a lot. So, are you interested in hearing about this case or did you come by early to critique my décor?"

Gus came in and took a seat across the desk from her. "I called Doc."

"How's he doing?"

"About like you said," said Gus. "He's become a living, walking, breathing investigation board for Nicole Veles's kidnapping. He needs to get away from it, except ...."

"Except leaving the hunt for Veles would be like quitting his life," said Rebecca. "It's all he's kept of what he was."

"Yeah," replied Gus softly, then paused a beat. "Anyway, I suggested he find someone to talk to. That got a reaction with every other word having four letters. You never told me he swore like a sailor."

"He didn't use to. I don't think he swore once during the Crusader's case and there was plenty of reason for profanity there. What did he say, other than the swearing?"

"That the last thing he wanted to do was talk about his nightmares when he was awake. He doesn't realize how much he needs to let it go for an hour or two. Or better yet, a day or two. And by the way, he did apologize when he cooled off."

Distracting Doc for a day or two? Rebecca knew that would be a tall order. It couldn't be a woman—there was no room in his thoughts for any female but Veles. It wouldn't be work. He had turned his back on his career, leaving with hardly a word to his boss. Suggesting a hobby would be a joke. That left only one option in her mind. "How about distracting him with this case?"

Gus drew back, his eyes blinking. "First, I didn't know you'd decided to take it."

"I haven't definitely, but I'm thinking about it."

"OK," Gus said slowly. "Then what, pray tell, is in this case for a psychologist? I'm pretty sure he's not an authority on witchcraft."

"No, I have you to cover that part."

Gus guffawed.

"I don't know what might interest him, if anything," admitted Rebecca. "But there are possibilities. For one, Bergeron and Sims were a bit of an odd couple, near opposites in everything from people skills to appearance. Just figuring out the psychology of that relationship might sidetrack him ... for a while."

Gus chuckled. "If I suggested that, he'd probably say, 'Go ask an expletive-deleted relationship counselor'. But given his current state, it's worth a try." Gus glanced at a clock on the wall, then back.

"Your potential client should be here in a few. Wanna tell me what you have so far?"

Over the next few minutes, Rebecca reviewed what she'd learned from the news stories. She had just gotten to the questions she'd compiled for the meeting when the outer office door opened again. She checked the reception area, finding a woman waiting there in a burgundy floral-print dress and carrying a bag almost big enough to stay overnight.

"Good thing we're almost done," said Rebecca, "because it looks like our potential client just came in."

1:02 PM, Marte Investigative Services

Even without reaching the hour of their appointment, Rebecca could have guessed that the woman in her reception area was related to Della Bergeron; there was a strong resemblance to Bergeron's online pictures. But at the same time, everything about Rowena Labadie was just a bit less striking. The hair had lost some of its luster and most of its length. The perfect complexion of the sister showed a few signs of age, even though Labadie was the younger of the two. And the eyes, while similar, were bluer than the startling gray of Bergeron's. After confirming that the woman was indeed Rowena Labadie and introductions all around, the three sat down in Rebecca's office.

"I have a few background questions, Ms. Labadie, if that's OK?" said Rebecca.

"Of course," the woman said, nodding.

"First, I was wondering why you wanted to start an investigation now, before the trial. Your sister's trial lawyer will have his investigators, and if your sister's acquitted, you'd be paying for nothing." It seemed likely that Labadie would have considered this, but Rebecca wanted to be sure.

Labadie slid forward in her chair and stared back into Rebecca's eyes. "I'm not sure how closely you've followed the case, Ms. Marte, but my sister has already been tried in the court of public opinion and found guilty. And while the criminal lawyer she's retained says he's looking for anything that could get her off, he's focusing on technicalities in the arrest and evidence gathering. He'll say otherwise, but he's not seriously considering the possibility she's innocent."

"Innocent?" replied Rebecca, her tone devoid of judgment though she was skeptical. "You mean innocent because she was temporarily incapable of telling right from wrong?" Her research suggested the temporary insanity plea wasn't being considered and this was a chance to confirm that guess. It was also an opportunity to gauge Labadie's feelings about her sister's state of mind. For all she knew, Labadie thought anyone who called themselves a witch was deluded—an opinion that she'd originally favored, although that belief was weakening as she'd studied their beliefs.

"No. Della's not crazy. And while I'm completely confident in that statement, you don't have to take my word for it. We've had two or three experts in to see her and none are willing to testify she didn't know right from wrong that night. If they could figure out why she blacked out, their opinions might change, but so far, that strange fugue hasn't recurred. And to the best of my sister's recollection, it never happened before that evening."

"So, why do you think she's innocent?" asked Rebecca.

Labadie took a deep breath and released it slowly. "It's all the little things. For example, contrary to appearances, she really liked Victor. Possibly enough to marry him, though things hadn't gone that far."

"Contrary to appearances?" Rebecca wanted to hear the woman's take on the mismatched couple.

A nervous smile replaced the slight frown Labadie had worn since arriving. "Well, I'm off to a great start, aren't I? I'm trying to paint this picture of a regular woman who couldn't possibly have killed anyone and I start with her unexpected attraction to the victim. But, frankly, he wasn't typical of her male friends. If I'm being frank, I'd say he was less fit, less handsome, and less well-to-do than any of them. But he was intelligent and she adored him. She was happy."

"And you're confident of this?" asked Rebecca.

Rowena's smile grew fractionally, and she leaned back slightly. "I am. And there's plenty of evidence of it—things like pictures of them out at dinner or the theater. If you look at the calendar on her computer, they had several more dates planned. Sis and I talk, not every day, but often, and she was thinking of a future with him. She wasn't grooming him for human sacrifice."

"The computer was taken as evidence by the police?" asked Gus.

"No, it wasn't. And the last time I asked Della, the trial lawyer hadn't asked anyone to look at it either. As I said, he's not considering innocence as a possibility."

"Okay," said Rebecca. "Anything else make you think she's innocent?"

"Sure. There are several things about that night that don't make sense. For one, Della is a bit of a germophobe, but she didn't have anything to clean the blood from her hands. She would have selected a different knife if she intended to kill. At least, that's what a couple of people have told me. Her last words over the body have been repeated in every story across the internet and in the papers, but after that, she collapsed and had to be rushed to the hospital. No one reports that. Do you want me to go on?"

"That's okay. If we take the case, we'll get into these issues in a lot more detail," replied Rebecca. "The newspapers mentioned that a blood test was conducted at the hospital?"

"Correct. And I have a copy, along with a few other documents I got from Della. You might find them helpful." Labadie dug through her bag, pulling out a thick sheaf of papers and handing them over. "That's her blood test, forensics on several items found at the scene, the initial police incident report, her formal statement to the police, and a list of potential witnesses."

"Thanks," replied Rebecca, setting the paperwork on a corner of her desk. "If we take your case, these will be very helpful."

"Do you have the autopsy report on Mr. Sims?" asked Gus.

"Della doesn't have it. She probably couldn't stand to look at it, so I didn't ask. But I can if you think it would help."

"Probably no reason to upset her at this point," said Gus. "If it becomes important, we'll get back to you."

"About the blood test?" said Labadie. "The fact that they found nothing doesn't mean she wasn't drugged beforehand, does it? Something that could, I don't know, kick in later in the day?"

Rebecca knew that was a stretch. To systematically drug and suggest a complex, murderous plot to a rich and powerful woman would take more than a single dose in the morning. Even something administered over weeks or months might not be enough and that would be very difficult to do and even harder to keep secret. But it wasn't impossible. After all, many of her enemies would be equally rich and powerful. "We'll check it out, which leads me to a question about who might talk to us. The names of the people who were at the ceremony were reported in the papers. You think any of them might cooperate?"

"Not a friggin chance," Labadie said with considerable bitterness. "Sorry, excuse my language."

The apology almost made Rebecca laugh, but she managed to limit her reaction to a smile behind a hand.

"Della and her daughter will talk to you, of course," said Labadie after she swallowed her acrimony. "But the rest of the group will use their money and power to make sure you never get near. But I can get you some background on the group if that helps."

"From a previous member?" asked Gus.

"Correct. His name is David Putnam. At the time he was in the group, he was a VP in strategic business development for a pharmaceutical company. He's a friend. He'll talk to you."

"That would be helpful," replied Rebecca. She paused as a possible connection surfaced in her thoughts. "One of the current members of the coven works for a pharmaceutical company. Any connection between him and Mr. Putnam that you know of?"

"That would be Nicholas Goodwin, but I'm pretty sure they're at different companies. You should ask David."

"Is there anything about the group's objectives that focuses on the pharmaceutical industry in particular?" asked Gus.

"As far as I know, their focus is to harness the positive energy of the group to further their business interests ... or at least, that was how Della described it. Some of those interests undoubtedly involved medicine, but I don't know that they are any more important than any of the others. Basically, they're trying to make money."

Rebecca glanced at Gus and seeing a look that said he was finished with that line of questions, she asked, "Who are Ms. Bergeron's close associates at work?"

Labadie paused, scratching a cheek lightly. "I don't know for sure, but I'd guess there aren't many. My sister likes to work alone. The company lawyer might be an exception. She's known him since college. But Lilith would be able to answer this better than me."

"That's Lilith Harrison?" asked Gus.

"Correct."

"And the company lawyer's name?"

"Tony Fiedler. He's the nicest man. Well, he's got a bit of a temper, but he dotes on Della. I don't know how he knew, but he showed up at the hospital that night to help out. I'd like it a lot better if he was representing her, but he doesn't have the background. Anyway, I'm sure he'll talk to you if you have questions about what happened at the hospital."

"We may," said Gus. His casual sideways glance said the floor was Rebecca's again.

"What about friends outside of work?"

Labadie's frown returned. "I've never been asked to describe my sister's personal life before and now that you have?" She paused, her eyes moving over the desktop in front of her. "If I had to summarize in a sentence, I'd have to say she's something of a loner outside of work, too, but that's going to give you the wrong impression. She can be warm and caring, especially with family. She loves her daughter dearly, and though I'm busy, we make time for each other. She's incredibly active in social and philanthropic causes. But as for close, personal relationships? Victor Sims was really about the only one that I know of. Maybe the only one she's had."

"What about Ms. Harrison's father?" asked Rebecca, checking her notes. "Lowell, I believe it is. What's their relationship like? I couldn't find much about him."

Labadie squeezed her eyes closed a moment before speaking. "I'm sure if you looked, you'd find this out anyway. I mean, back in those days, Della didn't have the money she has now." Labadie paused again. "Della was raped toward the end of her sophomore year in college and became pregnant with Lilith. But, please, don't discuss this with anyone unless you have to. Della's still tormented by the memory. She'd be mad if she knew I told you, but if it helps …."

Her voice trailed off, and Rebecca wondered if she'd need to ask about Lowell Harrison again. But after a moment, Labadie continued. "Anyway, Della was friends with Lowell at the time, but as I understand it, just friends. He proposed and they got married, but he died before Lilith was a year old."

"Do you happen to know the cause of death?" asked Gus.

Was Gus hoping for a pattern, Rebecca wondered? One that suggested that whoever got close to Bergeron also got dead? Wouldn't that be a convenient break in the case, albeit one their client wouldn't particularly like? But they didn't guarantee that the truth would be pleasant.

"Pancreatic cancer," replied Labadie.

Well, damn, no luck on the black widow killer theory. But when Rebecca glanced at Gus, she saw more shock on his face than warranted by the disappointment she felt. That was unusual. Had her partner put that much faith in such a long shot? But after a moment,

Gus recovered. "If he died that quickly after the marriage, I would think he knew he was terminal when he proposed."

Labadie sighed. "He did. So did Della."

"So, it was a marriage for appearances?" asked Rebecca.

"I guess you'd call it that, although Della's never used those words in front of me. And though she didn't love Lowell enough to walk down the aisle with him, she was very fond of him and desperately needed the help. She still speaks of him warmly."

"Did they catch the rapist?" asked Gus.

"Nope, never."

"Sorry for asking you to relive that," replied Gus, then nodded toward Rebecca.

"So, other than Victor, no long-term boyfriends? No engagements that didn't quite last?"

"Long term? Yes," said Labadie. "But close, no. Della would find someone she was comfortable with and they'd date, sometimes for months. But there was never any talk of the future until Victor."

So, no spurned lover, at least that Labadie knew about.

"For background," said Rebecca, "can you tell us how your sister got involved with witchcraft?" Rebecca had only skimmed the considerable literature on the subject, but that was enough to know there was no unified theory or practice. Bergeron's path into this worldview might prove important.

"Frankly, Ms. Marte, I have no idea. There was no talk of the occult or magic when we were growing up. I don't even recall either of us dressing up like a witch for Halloween, although Sis is older. I might not remember if she did. But about fifteen years ago, she became interested and that grew into a passion. She even got Lilith talking about witchcraft and joining her coven. Anyway, however she got involved, her rituals have always been harmless. They've even been .... Never mind."

"What were you going to say?" asked Rebecca.

"I was going to say her rituals have always been positive, but that sounds strange after what's happened. But I'll give you an example. Neither of us has ever been outdoor types. Wrong complexion for one thing and I hate bugs. But Della has developed this communion with nature that I have to admit, I admire. She also claims that the rise of her company is the result of her beliefs. She doesn't say that in the trade journals, but in private she has."

"Did she put spells on competitors?" Rebecca didn't think any businessman would retaliate because a witch had cast a spell, but if it was accompanied by an unexpected downturn in profits, maybe. Some people didn't need much justification to secure their wealth with murder.

"She never mentioned anything like that to me," replied Labadie. "Her rituals were more about timing and the receptiveness of nature ... which I guess includes people? I'm not really clear on a lot of that. And maybe she did other things, but you'd have to ask Lilith or David."

"So, you're not a witch?" asked Rebecca.

"Oh, no. Never saw it as anything real, like Sis and Lilith do."

Gus looked at Rebecca, and from the slight tip of one hand, Rebecca knew he had completed his questions. She pushed a sheet of paper across the desk to Labadie. "This is a general description of our services and our rates. We're going to step out a moment to discuss your case and give you a chance to look that over. Do you have any questions?"

After Labadie declined, they went into the reception area and closed the office door. "So, what do you think?" asked Rebecca.

"I'm just the temp. Let's hear your thoughts."

Rebecca shook her head and chuckled. Gus hadn't left his mentoring ways back at the FBI.

"Most of Ms. Labadie's reasons for innocence are questions about whether the killing was premeditated or not. Bergeron didn't have any hand cleaner. She had plans with Sims in the future. Even if all of them are true, they don't prove innocence. They just mean that Bergeron didn't start out thinking that she was going to kill Sims. But there's an even more fundamental problem. Maybe all of Bergeron's lack of premeditation is a cover. Any prosecutor worth his salt is going to point out that a woman who can run a multi-billion-dollar company is capable of adding bogus dates to her calendar. I can hear the closing argument in my head—Della Bergeron single-mindedly pursued and entrapped Victor Sims in her deadly game of occult rituals."

"Yes, but ...." Gus got only that far before Rebecca held up a hand.

"I think the counter to that is, if Ms. Bergeron is so capable, why did she devise such a half-assed cover?"

Gus chuckled. "Not as eloquently put as the first part, but, yeah. If the killing was planned, she must have thought one of two things. The power she was about to demonstrate to her coven would protect her, in which case the shrinks should find some sort of delusion. Or the clues she planted about the future would raise enough questions to get her off. She's building a case for reasonable doubt."

"So, our role probably becomes finding more evidence that the crime wasn't premeditated and hope that the charge gets reduced to manslaughter?" asked Rebecca.

"I wouldn't put it that way to the client, but, yeah, that's a possibility. What about proving innocence? You give up on that completely?"

"Not completely, but mostly," replied Rebecca. "It could still be a competitor or someone in the coven, in which case they'll be hiding under the cover of wealth and power. That'll be tough to prove without access to them. But since they had to come in contact with Bergeron before that night, probably dozens of times, maybe we can dig something up from the comings and goings at her business or her home."

"So, you want to take the case?" asked Gus.

"Yeah, I'm game. Shall we check on Labadie, see what she's decided?"

They went back into the office, finding the woman pacing in front of the desk. She turned to them. "You're hired, if you still want the job after seeing this text from my sister."

Labadie held up her phone, and Rebecca read the message aloud. "I just realized. The night Victor died, I was possessed by another witch."

WEDNESDAY, OCTOBER 7

5:32 AM, A Farmhouse in Western Kansas

Nicole threw the covers aside, the nights on the plains already cold enough to justify them. She rose and stretched her arms. Days on the farm were long and the work was hard, but they had left her lean and muscled. And unless that missing year or so was different, she had never been this tanned.

She shrugged on a pair of jeans—about the only new garment Maggie had found for her—followed by a shirt that had seen better days and boots that were in similar shape. She removed the chair propped against the doorknob. Perhaps that was unnecessary. Justin hadn't tried to come in during the night so far, but she didn't want to take any chances.

When she entered the living area, he was sitting on the couch. "Morning." He grunted something in reply, clearly in a foul mood. Maybe he had tried the door? He got up and went to the table to work on the puzzle that still sat there half-finished.

For all the concern he caused her, Nicole still felt sorry for Justin. He had few memories to guide his behaviors. And concepts like fairness or sharing that should have come from his early years, whether he recalled the specifics or not, were lacking as well. Nicole renewed her resolve to talk with him, to get this sexual gulf that was growing between them reduced. It was just that she didn't know how to approach it with someone who knew nothing of social norms or personal rights. My body, my choice would mean no more to him than walking on the moon. Well, another day clearing rocks from the new garden plot would give her plenty of time to think.

She walked over to a large, south-facing picture window. It was one of the few panes of glass and easily the largest in the house, an energy-saving measure for what she was told would be a long, harsh winter. Through it, she saw the pale gray of a gravel driveway cut through the monotonous brown of dead prairie grasses in the front yard. This rough gray and brown carpet ran to a ten-foot-high chain-link fence topped with barbed wire. It circled the house, creating a compound of about 40 by 40 yards with the house in the center. The fence was perhaps unnecessary, but there had been rumors that animals could host the virus and Maggie wasn't going to take any chances. Beyond the fence, the gravel road stretched across the endless plains before disappearing over the horizon.

The house itself was large enough with three bedrooms, a kitchen, a bathroom, and the living room. True, the accommodations were made a bit cozier because Maggie used a fourth bedroom—one of the larger ones—as her office. But Nicole couldn't begrudge the woman who'd saved her life. And besides, if Maggie was home, she was in her office. It wasn't underutilized. The only times she and Justin entered that sanctuary were the sessions to help restore their memory. Though the woman's view of sex was rooted in the dark ages, Maggie seemed to know an amazing amount about amnesia and its treatment.

From her vantage point standing at the window, Nicole couldn't see the backyard, but there was no need. She knew that area almost as well as her own face. Scattered around it, in no particular order she could detect, was a chicken coop with a few hens; the new and the old garden plots, both now dormant; a ramshackle toolshed with the shovels, hoes, and rakes they used to work the soil; and a building that had probably once been a granary but was now closer to a pile of decaying wood. There was also a carport with Maggie's old rusty pickup truck. Her equally old four-door sedan had to brave the elements because, unlike the truck, their lives didn't depend on it.

And that was the totality of Nicole's world, her refuge on a planet that was diseased and dying. Perhaps Justin's indifference to recalling his past was for the best. If he never remembered freedom, he wouldn't miss it.

"Justin," shouted Maggie as she rushed out of her office. "There's a rabbit off to the east. If you'd been awake, you could have gotten him before he was out of range."

"I wasn't asleep," Justin replied. He tended to take statements literally, but at least, he was starting to recognize the issue. That seemed the case now as he jumped up from the table and ran to the window saying, "Sorry. I got lost working that puzzle."

"And you, young lady. What's your excuse? Daydreaming again?"

"Wondering how to control your son" was a statement that would only raise Maggie's ire. She didn't want him controlled, so Nicole just said, "Sorry."

Justin moved close to the window to get a view to the east, so close that his nose almost touched the glass. "I'll get him." He headed toward the kitchen where he stored his rifles.

"It's a waste of ammunition," Nicole said, after taking Justin's place looking out. She turned back to Maggie. "That rabbit must be close to a hundred yards away and in some rough terrain. Justin may not even get a shot."

"Bullets we have. Meat, not so much," Maggie replied matter-of-factly.

Justin jogged back into the living room, his rifle in hand. "Can I go outside the fence?"

"You know the rules, son." He nodded and went out the front door.

Maggie's rules said that she was the only one permitted outside their compound because she was immune to the virus. On one of her foraging trips, she'd found an abandoned store with enough canned fruits and vegetables to last them for months. Fresh meat, however, was another matter. Occasionally, she'd return with some unidentifiable cut hastily wrapped in yellowing paper, explaining that she'd been able to barter for the food with an itinerant hunter. But that was rare.

So, Justin hunted from the safety of the compound, leaving the grounds only if he shot something. Then, he'd be permitted a single trip directly to the kill and back. He'd field dress the animal outside the fence while Nicole or Maggie heated water for a hanging-bucket shower. Only after he had bathed and changed clothes would he be permitted back into the compound. Occasionally, the game was dried for the winter and Nicole was getting better at that task. But more often, it went directly into a pot on the wood-burning stove. Nicole was getting used to stewed meat at any hour of the day. If they were lucky enough to have protein, it wasn't going to waste.

"You're looking well-rested this morning," said Maggie.

Nicole bristled. It wasn't the woman's words or her tone. Both sounded sincere, but Nicole knew the statement was just a preamble to what Maggie wanted to say. "I'm going outside to watch."

"Okay, but have you given any more thought to what we discussed?"

What you have been proselytizing was the more accurate term in Nicole's opinion. "Yeah, and I'm still against it."

"Nicole, honey, this is serious. You have to put your feelings aside. The world has been decimated. It must be repopulated."

Nicole didn't reply, hurrying out the front door instead.

She had heard this message from Maggie before, dozens of times in the last several weeks. And from those repetitions, she knew it was pointless to say, "I'd like to get a better understanding of what's happened to the world before I give up on my dreams." She had said this in varying forms, her denunciation of the idea of parenthood finally escalating to, "When we know that Justin is the last man on earth, I'll think about it." That had come out in anger because the woman just didn't listen. Or more likely, she didn't care what Nicole thought.

But in addition to anger, the woman's dogged persistence had raised another emotion in Nicole—unease. Why was Maggie in such a hurry to see her pregnant? Humanity wasn't going to become extinct in the next couple of years. And when Nicole asked, she got various forms of "no time like the present" or "a journey of a thousand miles" in reply. But Nicole couldn't escape the feeling that there was something else going on. And if so, maybe the missing memories would hold the key. She just had to remember.

Nicole turned her attention to Justin, watching in silence as he stood motionlessly at the fence. Five minutes passed. Then, ten. Then, fifteen. Finally, he put the rifle in the crook of his arm, turned away, and walked to where she was standing.

"Got away," he said. "Sorry."

"That's okay, Justin, although I was going to ask your mom if I could help dress this one. It's about time I learned to do that."

"Sure. I can teach you, but you need to put on your old clothes."

That made Nicole laugh. Her shirt was threadbare and the hem at the bottom was pulling loose. "Sorry, but this shirt is as old as it gets. I was wearing it when you and your mom picked me up, remember?"

Justin's eyes narrowed. "No, you weren't. You were wearing a light blue shirt with a dark blue logo right about here." Nicole stepped back, not sure he was going to put his hand on her chest but not sure he wasn't either. If Justin was offended, it didn't show. "I remember the blue shirt like it was yesterday. I never saw this one till later."

Nicole recognized the blue shirt from Justin's description. It was from her past employer, Biomedical Engineering Associates, and the logo was theirs. But she hadn't seen it since waking up at the farm.

"When you found me, was I carrying anything? Maybe a bag or a backpack?"

"Nope."

"And I wasn't wearing my blue windbreaker over this shirt?"

Justin blinked a couple of times. "I think the jacket might have been on the ground next to you," he said.

"So, what happened to the blue shirt? It's not in my room."

"Don't know. I just remember when we got you up and you looked at me, you were wearing the blue shirt. I'm sure 'cause you were the prettiest thing I'd ever seen."

The compliment was touching, but the implications of what Justin had said overwhelmed those feelings. Nicole turned from him and started toward the house, lost in thought.

The shirt she wore now was hers. She recalled buying it before she started work. But more importantly, she remembered waking up in it in Maggie's house with the blue windbreaker hanging on a peg on the wall. Perhaps in the panic of fleeing the pandemic she had thrown on both shirts? Or maybe it was unseasonably cold and she needed three layers? But if something like that was true, then where was the blue shirt? Even if Maggie had removed it before Nicole woke up, someone had to destroy it and Maggie didn't do that kind of menial chore.

There seemed no way Justin had seen her in the company shirt. And if that was true, what the hell was going on?

9:47 AM, Meteor Promotions

The text from Bergeron—that she had been possessed by another witch—had given Gus and Rebecca pause, but it wasn't enough to scare them away. They took the case. And by now, a day and a half later, Rebecca had hoped they would have completed interviews with Della Bergeron and Lilith Harrison, and with a little luck, David Putnam, the past coven member. The fact of the matter, however, was that they'd completed none of those talks.

It wasn't that these individuals were stonewalling, but they had been living with this situation for over five months. Their sense of urgency had disappeared, especially for discussions with a third or fourth set of investigators who had no official authority over the case. And frankly, two of the three individuals—Putnam and Harrison— were busy.

Meteor Promotions was still reeling from the scandal surrounding their founder and CEO, so Harrison was working fourteen-hour days to correct that situation. It had been no secret that she was being groomed for her mother's job, but everyone believed that the succession was fifteen to twenty years in the future, not today. But by all accounts, she was doing well, giving their clients and the public a new face to trust.

David Putnam's scheduling conflicts came as more of a surprise to Rebecca. He was tied up in the Eastern District of Missouri Bankruptcy Court. Weren't the members of Bergeron's coven all rich and powerful? In any case, she was scheduled to meet with him tomorrow afternoon at his office.

And then there was Della Bergeron herself, who had the most to lose, of course, and no job to interfere—she was free on bail and on leave from her job. And yet, she had rescheduled twice, the latest being from tomorrow morning to late in the afternoon after the Putnam interview.

Apparently, after coming to the belief that she was under the control of another witch on the night of Sims's death, she had taken it upon herself to unmask the culprit. Rebecca had been stunned by her decision. Gus, on the other hand, had taken it in stride, asking who better to find a witch than another witch? And when Rebecca laughed at the idea there was anything like a supernatural being to find, he'd simply said, "We might get a lead from her suspects, whether they have magical powers or not."

Rebecca had to admit he had a point.

It had been a last-minute decision to meet with Harrison today, but when an opening in the daughter's day appeared, Rebecca jumped at the opportunity. Now, she was sitting in the Meteor Promotions parking lot, her car windows rolled up against the cool morning breeze. Through the windshield, she could see the company's headquarters, Building 103. It was one of five identical buildings of red brick trimmed in white stone on the sprawling, pristinely maintained suburban campus. Given the rapidity at which this enterprise had appeared in this sparsely-populated setting, one common synonym for the word meteor, a shooting star, was more fitting than the alternative of a falling one.

Rebecca reached across the car seat, picked up her notebook, and leafed back a few pages. During the wait for schedule openings, she had done her homework on Harrison. There was little on her youth until college and then it was the standard social media posts—shots of her and her sorority sisters planting flowers, posing with young men, or raising a little Cain. The latter posts were quite tame compared to the hell-raising Rebecca had done even in high school, so she dismissed them as simple fun. There was no mention of witchcraft and nothing scandalous to be found. In fact, about the only posts not filled with sweetness and light were some harsh words for a couple of young men who had dared to address her as "Lilly." She hated the nickname.

Harrison had joined Meteor Promotions four years ago with a master's degree in marketing and then disappeared into the bowels of the burgeoning business. That all changed, however, five months ago, and now she was plastered all over the pages of the company's website. The same pattern was also true of the social scene, although to a lesser extent. Before Sims's death, she had made appearances at a couple of philanthropic causes, championing one, and had made everyone's "St. Louis business faces of the future" lists. But in the last five months, she had lived in the center of the limelight. Rebecca wondered if the combination of a demanding social scene and an even more demanding work environment was taking a toll; Harrison looked tired in several of the most recent pictures.

Rebecca was startled by a knock on the driver's side window, even though she expected Gus. They'd agreed to team on the interviews with Della Bergeron and Lilith Harrison and conduct the rest solo. He was right on time.

Rebecca exited the car, and she and Gus made the short walk to Building 103, checked in with the receptionist, and were led to a small conference room with a table and a half-dozen chairs. In a moment, Harrison appeared. Had Rebecca known Bergeron but not seen pictures of the daughter online, she would have done a double take. Harrison looked nothing like her mother. Where Bergeron was tall and trim, Harrison was probably six inches shorter and full-figured. Gone was the mother's long black hair and gray eyes to be replaced by curly light-brown hair cut short and brown eyes. Only the complexion matched; both women were fair-skinned. Presumably, most of Harrison's looks came from the man who had raped her mother.

After introductions and both of the investigators declining an offer of something to drink, she and Gus sat across the table from Harrison. Rebecca started by setting the scene for the night of Victor Sims's death. "The night of April 30, your mother, Della Bergeron, met with a group of her business associates on a piece of farmland near the city of Ste. Genevieve, Missouri."

It wasn't a question, but Harrison already had an answer. "You can call them our business associates if you prefer, but that night she was the High Priestess meeting with her coven."

Rebecca nodded, somewhat taken aback by Harrison's response. She'd put her mother's practice of witchcraft before that of her obvious role in private industry. Perhaps she had the wrong mindset because she'd studied Harrison's business persona in preparation for the meeting; she'd seen little of the woman beyond her recent efforts to reverse the course of a floundering company. But with this focus on the supernatural, both mother and daughter appeared in a light Rebecca hadn't considered seriously.

"OK, coven it is," Rebecca replied. "I know this will be difficult for you, but would you go through the events of that evening, starting at the time your mother and Victor Sims arrived and ending when she was taken to the hospital?"

Over the next ten minutes or so, Harrison recounted what she had witnessed, recalling nothing new, nothing that deviated in any substantial way from the other eyewitness statements. Rebecca had expected that. New information that had been overlooked by everyone until this precise moment would be a coincidence of immense magnitude. More likely, it would be an attempt to mislead. But Harrison hadn't spun any new tales, hadn't said anything to implicate her in a cover-up. Things weren't going to be that easy.

"Did you know Mr. Sims well?" asked Gus.

"Not really. I suppose you've heard I introduced him to Mother, and that's true, in a manner of speaking. You see, Mother thought I should know Meteor Promotions from the bottom up, so back then, I was working in our conference support division. Deadly dull work, I might add. Anyway, Victor's company had contracted us for one of their tradeshows and that's where I met him. He was working in one of their booths."

Harrison paused, her head shaking slowly, her gaze far away. "Talk about your fish out of water. Victor was a technical expert, but small talk made him painfully uneasy. I thought I could help, and we went to lunch at the conference center. Mother usually doesn't go to tradeshows, but she showed up and joined us."

"And after that?" asked Gus.

"I'd see them together from time-to-time. He never seemed that comfortable when I was around, but maybe he was different ... when they were alone."

Harrison seemed a bit uncomfortable to Rebecca, but then, what child wants to talk about her mother's love life? The glance from Gus let her know he was done with this line of questioning. "Back to the night of the coven gathering, did you notice anything unusual in your mother's behavior?"

"No, not really."

"How was she acting?" asked Rebecca.

"Hmm, how can I describe this? Perhaps moved by the magic of the gathering? She seemed to float around in the pool of light from the altar's fire as she led us in the ceremony."

"Enough to get carried away?" asked Gus. "Enough to forget that there were implications to her actions?"

"I have no direct experience," replied Harrison, "but I'd expect she had a heightened sense of all that was around her. The dance of light and dark from the clouds and moon. The taste of smoke on her tongue. The bark of a coyote in the distance as the backdrop to the crackle of the flames and the rhythms of our incantations. That is what it was like for me. For her, it was probably even more mesmerizing."

Rebecca had been surprised earlier, but that feeling was eclipsed by the amazement she felt now. Harrison's comments were speculation, of course, but the daughter seemed to be describing someone reveling in the moment, not overwhelmed by circumstances, not troubled by the consequences of what was to come. Could that be true?

"Did your mother hesitate at any point during the ceremony?" asked Rebecca. "Maybe spoke haltingly or paused without reason?"

"No, nothing like that," said Harrison.

"Did she bump into anything, drop anything, spill anything?"

"No."

"Did she ever fail to respond to someone in the group?"

"There was no part of the ceremony where others would speak to her."

Where were the behaviors Rebecca would expect from someone preparing to kill—hesitancy, nervousness, mental bargaining in the final moments? There was nothing like that in Harrison's description. Bergeron hadn't acted like someone coerced by blackmail or forced by threat of harm. Of course, Harrison wasn't trained to look for these clues, but people tend to be sensitive to body language. Coupled with the blood test that ruled out drugs—at least ones that had been used that night—the simplest explanations of Bergeron's actions were temporary insanity or a High Priestess turning to human sacrifice.

"Do you know if your mother's lawyer is considering a plea of temporary insanity?" asked Rebecca. Her reading of the situation and Labadie had indicated he wasn't. Additional confirmation from Harrison would remove all doubt.

"You should ask him, but I don't think so. He brought in a couple of expert witnesses early on, but apparently, they found nothing to support it."

If she wasn't crazy and wasn't being coerced, what did that leave? Rebecca had little besides some type of black magic. Rebecca couldn't suppress the internal shudder, not because she believed in this form of evil, but because perhaps Bergeron did.

"You saw your mother stab Mr. Sims?" asked Gus.

Interesting. Was Gus looking into the possibility of sleight of hand, that someone had made it appear as though Bergeron had done the deed when she hadn't? But as a means to murder, this brand of magic would be extremely difficult to stage and fraught with the risk of detection.

"Actually, no, I didn't," replied Harrison, leaving the sleight-of-hand door open by the thinnest of cracks. "At that point in the ceremony, all eyes except Mother's were cast downward toward the earth. I heard something like a muffled gurgle, looked up, and that's when I saw her standing there covered with blood. The dagger was in Victor's chest."

So, rather than the lovely assistant diverting the audience's attention, the distraction was built into the ceremony. The deception door opened wider, but the crack still seemed razor-thin to Rebecca. In those moments of contemplating the dirt, someone had to take the dagger from Bergeron, slit and stab Sims, put it back in her hands without her remembering the murder, and return to his or her place before anyone realized anything had happened. Seriously? Rebecca certainly hoped they'd come up with a more plausible alternative since she didn't want to have to present this one to her client.

"Your aunt said the other coven members probably wouldn't talk to us," said Gus, "but did anyone happen to mention seeing Sims being stabbed?"

"Aunt Rowena's right. I can't imagine they would talk to you." Harrison paused a moment. "I don't remember anyone saying something like that, but then, I'm not sure why they would. Mostly, they ran back to their cars to wait for the police."

"You mentioned seeing the knife in Mr. Sims's chest," said Rebecca. "Did you know when the police secured the scene, it wasn't there? Later, they found it under a few leaves beside the altar."

"I heard that."

"Did you see anyone remove it?" asked Rebecca.

"No. It was there when I looked up. Then, Mother collapsed on the altar—nearly fell on Victor. I can't say for sure if it was still there when we got her up because pandemonium was breaking out. She might have knocked it to the ground."

The admission seemed incriminating. Perhaps it was a crude attempt to hide the weapon by the killer? But the knife hadn't been hidden—not really. The blood hadn't been wiped off. Bergeron's fingerprints were still on it. If she had dislodged the knife on purpose, why? What did she hope to gain?

"Is there a chance anyone else would have witnessed the stabbing?" asked Gus.

"There was one security guard posted close enough that he might have seen something, although I know the police have talked to him. I don't know his name, but I can get you the name of the company if you want."

"Yes, please," said Rebecca. "Your aunt didn't mention there were security guards there."

"She may not have known, but my mother wanted to avoid being disturbed by the public, or worse, the media."

Nothing in Harrison's recollection of her mother's behavior suggested that she had been coerced, consciously or unconsciously, and corroboration by a second, independent source would help solidify that conclusion. Getting that verification from the guard would be a good job for Gus. A private security guard, especially if he had come directly into the job, would enjoy talking to an ex–FBI agent. And while she was also ex–FBI, the guard would be less likely to embellish his role during the evening if he was talking to another male.

"What about the other ... witches present that night?" asked Rebecca. "Was there anything unusual in their behavior?"

"Mother told me she felt the influence of another witch just a couple of days ago, but I can't imagine it was anyone in our coven."

That, of course, wasn't an answer to her question and Rebecca waited until Harrison continued. "Interaction before the ceremony isn't allowed. We arrive separately and take our places in silence. So, I don't know how they were acting beforehand."

"Not so much as a whispered comment, a wink of an eye before the ceremony?" asked Gus.

"Absolutely not. Our focus is on the High Priestess and the ritual, not socializing. Later, sure, we talk, although that night it couldn't have been anything coherent. We were all in shock."

"What about earlier, in the weeks before the incident? Was there any friction among the coven members?" asked Rebecca.

"No. Business had been good and the signs for the future were positive."

"So, no heated arguments? No factions within the group?"

"If you get a room full of ambitious business people driven to get to the top of their organizations, dissent is a given," said Harrison. "But on the other hand, you probably won't find a group less prone to infighting than us. We focus our energies on positive change, and eventually, that helps everyone."

"Can you think of anyone who would want to harm your mother?" asked Rebecca.

"That question has been asked and answered, at least twice. I'll get you a copy of the same list I gave to the police and her trial lawyer … if you want it."

"Yes, thanks." This, of course, was one of the problems coming into a case late. People tended to remember what they'd said later rather than what they had experienced at the time. But maybe she could break that cycle. "Since you put this list together, have you felt any need to revise it? Maybe someone else popped into your head later? Or maybe someone on the list has started to stand out in your mind?"

"Sorry, but the list isn't mine. I've only been at a level where I'd hear details about competitor rivalries for a few months. So, I had a couple of our long-tenured VPs compile it. If you need to follow up with them, I can arrange it."

"Perhaps later," replied Rebecca. "But you, personally, don't have any specific concerns about someone on this list?"

"Competition in our line of work is fierce, but no, I can't think of anyone who would resort to violence over a lost contract or two. The two individuals who compiled the list added a similar disclaimer."

If the police and the trial lawyer hadn't found good leads here, Rebecca wondered if she and Gus would. But still, they'd look. And even if they found someone with unsavory connections, they'd still need proof that person had coerced Bergeron in a way that didn't show in her actions on the evening of the killing or in her bloodstream. Was that even possible? She'd seen it only once before—on the Crusader case—but its highly unusual circumstances didn't hold here. It had to be something different, something new, but what? There was no better time to start that search than now.

"As I understand it, you'll be taking your mother's place at Meteor Promotions?"

Harrison sighed. "There has been a succession plan in place since the day I started work, but it wasn't written with the idea this would happen so soon. At this point in my life, I don't want all this responsibility. I'm not ready. So, I've talked with senior leadership about a phase-in approach. Gradually, over about three years, I'll fully occupy the CEO position."

"And what about the coven?" asked Rebecca. "Do you take your mother's place as High Priestess?"

Harrison frowned. "It doesn't work that way. You don't just declare yourself the High Priest or Priestess. You have to work, study, teach, and maybe, someday, that title will be bestowed upon you."

"Sounds involved," said Gus.

"It's a lifelong process. There are elevations in most covens to mark your progress, ours included. I'm working on my second degree, preparing for my journey into the underworld to address my shadow self. And so you don't have to ask, Mr. Clements, my shadow self is my negative side, the side I hide from everyone including myself. Psychology has long recognized the existence of this dark side in humans and confronting it can be a soul-rending experience. It's driven some to madness, but it's something I have to do before I'm worthy to teach, marry, and bury others with our beliefs."

"Is it possible your mother was fighting her negative side the night of Mr. Sims death?" asked Gus. Rebecca stole a glance at him. Was he seriously asking if Bergeron was battling her evil self?

"Possibly," replied Harrison, "but not likely. She is third degree, having made the journey into the underworld years ago. More likely, she was fighting the dark side of another. She believes that was the case and I have no reason to doubt her."

"We saw the text to your aunt saying that," said Rebecca, "but possession seems quite a bit different than, say, positive thinking to deal with a business issue. Is possession something your coven accepts? Something that could happen to one of them at any time?"

Harrison paused, taking a deep breath. She slid forward marginally in her chair and laid her arms on the conference room table. "Have you ever been talked into doing something you know is wrong? Have you ever felt manipulated by a good line, a few, casual drinks when you were relaxing?" Rebecca started to answer, but Harrison didn't wait. "Take those rather inconsequential spells and potions, distill and refine them over hundreds of years of practice and thousands of practitioners, and you may gain some idea of the world you hold in disdain."

For an instant, Rebecca's anger flared. She didn't think she'd showed disdain—doubt, perhaps, but not disdain. But after a moment, she knew Harrison's statement contained an element of truth. Because she had trouble accepting concepts like black magic and possession as real, she was willing to ignore much of what the woman had to say. But to ignore Harrison's thoughts might be to discard evidence simply because she had framed it as supernatural. If Harrison had said her mother was driven to win at any cost, Rebecca would have accepted that as probable. But to suggest she was battling her shadow self? That was more likely to generate a harumph in her than a mental note to investigate further, even though the implications of the two statements were virtually the same.

Damn, that sounded like something that Doc might say—the old Doc, anyway. And was it that much different than what Gus had told her two days ago—that they shouldn't ignore the individuals Bergeron suspected whether they had magical powers or not? Rebecca glanced at Gus, receiving another of his slight nods of acknowledgment. She wasn't surprised; they had worked together too long for him to mistake her pause. But when she turned back to Harrison, she saw a similar look on her face. "You've taken a step into a larger world."

This statement also annoyed, but as before, Rebecca knew it held some truth. That fact, however, didn't mean she had to admit it. "So, a spell to possess would require a lot of time and effort. You don't just casually chant it once and that's it, right?"

"Devoted practice is the key to all of our magic," replied Harrison. "Nothing comes from haphazard mumbling."

"And is physical proximity between the witch and the possessed necessary?" asked Rebecca.

"Not necessarily. We seek to influence many we have never met, always in positive ways. But for the type of possession that affected Mother, I'd think proximity and maybe even one of her possessions might have been needed."

"You mean like a lock of her hair?"

"Possibly, Mr. Clements, but a cherished keepsake was what I was thinking." Harrison paused. "Because this seems like something important to you, I should mention I have no direct experience with possession of this type. So, I'm guessing a bit, based on the ceremonies and rituals Mother has taught us."

At best, Harrison's statements were a lukewarm endorsement of the idea that the possessor needed prolonged exposure to the possessed. But in the world of bullets and bad guys that Rebecca knew, anything like brainwashing or slow-acting drugs would require weeks, if not months. "Who do you know who has had relatively long-term physical access to your mother? Staff in her home? Colleagues at work? Members of her coven?"

"No, no, and no," replied Harrison. "Mother doesn't believe in permanent house staff. Her personal assistant hires services for things like cleaning or to cater large events, and she systematically cycles the work among several local businesses. At work, Mother has many difficult decisions to make, so she doesn't socialize with her subordinates. You never know who you may need to fire. Tony Fiedler, Meteor's lawyer, probably comes closest to being a friend; they knew each other in school, but it's mostly or all business now. And the coven? They have some access to her. They meet about once or twice a month, but the interactions are both open to all of the coven and formalized. I'm not sure if that meets your definition or not.

"There are, however, three exceptions to her limited sphere of confidants. One is me, of course. Mother and I talk regularly. Aunt Rowena is the second. They talk probably three or four times a month, perhaps more. And the last is a man named David Putnam. Until about a year ago when Victor Sims came into Mother's life, the two of them were close."

It took Rebecca a moment to process this information, and even then, she wasn't certain she understood. "Your aunt mentioned David Putnam as someone who might give us some background on the coven, but you're saying he and your mother were involved?"

"I am. And, yes, David could provide background. You should keep in mind, however, that he lost his way. His views on the coven will be skewed, perhaps drastically."

"How long were Mr. Putnam and your mother together?" asked Gus.

"Around two years, but my mother could answer that question better."

"Any hard feelings when he left?" asked Rebecca. It would be a longshot for Putnam to have both the means to influence Bergeron and the motivation to do so, but she could hope.

"Frankly, I'm not sure. Mother became interested in Victor Sims when her relationship with David was still relatively new, probably in the first year that they were together. But as I mentioned, Victor was painfully shy and socially awkward. I didn't think much of it, but when Victor eventually got the nerve to ask her out, Mother dropped David. So, from the outside, it looked like a recipe for hard feelings, though Mother never spoke of any."

It would take a bit more digging if jealousy had been Putnam's motive for ... well, whatever he did to get Bergeron to kill Sims. But there was another possible motive. "I understand that Mr. Putnam has fallen on hard times since leaving the coven."

"I've heard that," replied Harrison.

"Did the coven have anything to do with it?"

"Yes, but probably not in the way you're thinking. When someone wins in business, others lose, and David Putnam has been on the wrong side of some of our recent wins. But that's just business."

Rebecca, of course, wasn't interested in whether the coven had gone after him intentionally as much as whether he had thought they had. The problem, however, was that the timeline was complicated. He would have had to establish his influence over Bergeron before the downturn in his fortunes. But perhaps he saw it coming?

Having finished her questions and hearing the same from Gus, Rebecca thanked Harrison for her time. The two investigators stopped by Rebecca's car before leaving the campus.

"I'm calling Doc after lunch. Want to join me?"

Gus rubbed his chin. "Find something in the interview that might interest him?"

"You heard what Harrison said about psychology long recognizing the evil side in humanity."

Gus chuckled. "Sure, I'll join you just to hear him say you need to find a priest for an exorcism. Any other eye-openers in the interview, preferably something more directly related to the case?"

Rebecca exaggerated her smirk. "Well, the talk with David Putnam tomorrow moved up on my scale of importance. He had opportunity and motive—jealousy, money, or both."

"Agreed." But Gus's expression fit better if he'd said the opposite.

"What's wrong?"

"Probably nothing," he replied, "but that was the second thing our client failed to mention to us. Sure, maybe Ms. Labadie didn't know about the security detail and she wouldn't know one of the guards was close enough to witness the ritual. But giving us a contact on the coven and failing to mention he was the former lover of the suspected killer? That's quite an oversight."

"True, but if Labadie is covering for Putnam ... or if they are even working together, why did she give us his name? For that matter, why would she hire us at all?"

"What better way to look innocent?"

1:03 PM, Marte Investigative Services

After the Harrison interview, Gus had joined Rebecca for lunch. They'd stayed away from any talk about the case, giving what they had just learned a chance to settle in their brains. But when lunch ended half past twelve or so, Rebecca had been anxious to get back to work. She'd now been here for almost twenty minutes and still no sign of her partner. So, when he stepped into the reception area, she called out, "Get lost on the way here?"

"Nope. Just making my tires last longer than the three months you get on yours." Gus came in and sat in one of the chairs across the desk from Rebecca. "We gonna call Doc now?"

"In a minute. While you were saving your tires driving slower than I walk, I was back here thinking about the possible motives for the Sims killing. Assuming it wasn't the act of a person with a mental illness, it has to be one of two things. Either someone wanted Sims dead or the killing was designed to discredit the businesswoman."

"Or the witch," added Gus. "I don't know, but is a power struggle within a coven possible?"

"I'm not sure either, but the money vs. magic distinction is one worth keeping in mind. So, let's take the case that Sims was the target. Then, what happened that night would have to be one of the most convoluted murder plots ever devised. The perp would have to come up with a way to force a rich and powerful woman to do his or her bidding without her knowledge. It would be less risky to shoot Sims in the back in broad daylight on the National Mall."

Gus chuckled. "OK, but what if the killer was after two birds with one stone? Then, David Putnam ends up in a bad light. He goes after Sims because he took his place in Della Bergeron's life and he ruins

Bergeron for her betrayal or because of his business losses or both. We still have the problem of how he did it, but we have that problem with all our suspects. How the heck did anyone force Della Bergeron to do something that was against her will? Assuming, of course, that it was against her will."

"During the interview, I also realized there is a timeline issue with Putnam," said Rebecca. "We have to assume he saw his financial or romantic downfall coming because when Sims came along, his means to influence her ended. What kind of drug or mental timebomb could he have planted that went off six months later without any intervening contact between them?"

"Yeah, I had the same thought," said Gus. "So, if Della Bergeron alone was the target?"

"Then, for starters, any of her competitors would have a motive—thin the ranks of the competition. Unfortunately, I'm not sure how strong a motive that is. Estimates of Meteor's gross revenue are a shade over two billion dollars, which is plenty of reason for murder. The problem is, Meteor would still retain some, maybe most of that business after Bergeron is gone, and there are five or six other, similar businesses, some local, some national, that would share in what's left. Now, the windfall from displacing her is pretty small. There's also the question of how someone from these companies got access. It's not like any of them have a standing invitation to Della Bergeron's home. And I checked—there have been no break-ins there in recent years."

"OK," said Gus slowly. "So, we're not going to look at Meteor's competitors?"

"That list of competitors has been out there a while with no apparent leads. And since the motive is weak, I'm thinking not in the first pass ... unless you see it differently."

Gus paused a moment, his gaze unfocused. "No, can't say that I do."

Rebecca nodded. "Then, we have potential suspects with opportunity, while means and motive are the questions. Those would include Bergeron's family, Lilith Harrison and Rowena Labadie. Bergeron also has a brother, but he lives in Alaska and hasn't been around since last Christmas. And even though Harrison said no, I think we need to look at the staff, both in her home and at the office."

"Agreed," replied Gus. "If there's something like a drug slowly polluting Ms. Bergeron's mind, someone with access every couple of weeks might be enough. And I didn't think of it until later, but this cycling through local businesses can't be true of her security company. There almost has to be some consistency there because no company would want to be constantly training new people on her equipment and the grounds."

"Can you look into that? I was going to ask you to talk to the guard present at the ritual anyway."

"Sure," he replied.

"At Meteor, I want to look closer at the company lawyer, Tony Fiedler. His name keeps coming up as a close associate, although how close is not clear. And the fact that he and Lowell Harrison were friends in school? That makes me uneasy."

"All three of them knew each other? Where did you hear that?" asked Gus.

"Fiedler mentions Lowell Harrison on one of his social media accounts. Calls him one of the biggest influences in his early life and names Bergeron in the same context. Anyway, Fiedler would gain influence within the company if Bergeron had to step down. The same is true of Harrison—Lilith that is, not Lowell. But she seems to have all the responsibility she can handle already. As for Labadie, I'm not sure why she would want to harm her sister. Perhaps a sibling rivalry gone toxic?"

"Could be," said Gus. "Maybe we can get Bergeron to elaborate on their history, see if there's anything suspicious there."

"Okay. And finally, on my list, we have the coven. They've been meeting as a group regularly behind a wall of secrecy, giving them the opportunity. As for means, who knows what types of influence they could exert with their potions and spells. And because Della Bergeron believes in witchcraft, magic might be a potent weapon against her, like holding a gun to her head. But like Meteor's business competitors, the coven's financial reasons are weak, even more so because they aren't direct competitors. But like you pointed out, the possibility of a struggle for power within the coven makes them worth a closer look."

The two investigators became quiet, each looking at the other. Finally, Gus said, "Glad we had this little pep talk. Retiring to Florida is looking better by the minute."

Rebecca laughed. "Yeah, loads of suspects, none of which look that good for the crime. And we didn't even discuss the witch hiding out in the shadows who was controlling Della Bergeron from a distance." Though she'd meant the comment in jest, it seemed almost as likely as any of the other scenarios they'd discussed. And Gus wasn't laughing. Rather, he looked thoughtful.

"Something wrong?"

"Not really," he replied. "When I was with the Bureau, I often thought a lot of public defenders would do well to listen to their clients' explanations of why they were innocent. Not that those declarations were true so much as there was often an element of truth if they looked close enough. And the best I can come up with Bergeron is that she was influenced by someone or something beyond her understanding. But what that is?" He held out two empty hands.

"Beats me, partner. Well, I'm ready for that phone call to Doc. Let's see if we can distract him from his nightmare with ours." But the words felt wrong as they left her mouth. "I'm not going to make things worse, am I? Our case may be as unsolvable as his."

"I don't really know," admitted Gus after a moment. "But he won't become as invested in our case as he is with his personal life. And giving him something less critical to ponder doesn't seem like it could hurt and just might help. I say, give it a shot and back off at the first sign of an issue."

Rebecca sighed, wishing she had better insight into Doc's mental quagmire. But the person who might have some idea of a way out was the one caught in it. She put her office phone on speaker and dialed. Doc answered on the third ring.

"You have news?" He sounded out of breath.

It wasn't the greeting Rebecca had expected. "About Nicole Veles?" she asked. The phone remained silent. "No, sorry, Doc. We haven't heard anything about her. Gus is here with me and we're both keeping our ears open. I'll call immediately if we hear anything."

"Hi, Doc."

"Gus," replied Doc in greeting. "So, if it's not news for me, what's this about?"

"Just checking in, seeing how things are going," said Rebecca.

"Fine."

"Are you still in New Mexico?" she asked.

"Colorado."

"How did you decide to look there?" asked Gus. Rebecca figured he was hoping for more than one-word answers, but from a previous call, she knew this wasn't the right approach.

Doc took a deep breath. "My car trunk is filled with information on the kidnapper. If you want to fly out here and spend a couple of days studying it, we can talk search strategy." Gus glanced at Rebecca, and she shrugged in reply.

"I'm sorry, Gus," Doc said after the pause. "I'm just tired."

"I understand," replied Gus. "And I'm sure you know more about the kidnapper than anyone else in the world."

Doc said nothing, so Rebecca took over. "If you have a minute, I thought I'd tell you a little about our latest case."

There was another audible sigh on the speaker, then, "I only have about fifteen minutes."

"We're doing some follow-up on a case involving a woman who calls herself a witch. She killed a man during a coven ritual."

"The witch of the St. Louis business world?" asked Doc.

"Right. So, you've heard of her?"

"You can't read the crime section of any paper in the United States without knowing something. But I thought it was pretty much open-and-shut."

"Hopefully not," replied Rebecca, "since we're looking for evidence of her innocence. Right now, we're getting the big picture, looking for places where we might dig a little deeper. The daughter of the suspect—who, by the way, also considers herself a witch—

mentioned the idea of a shadow self. It's the notion that everyone has a dark side that they keep hidden."

A laugh came over the phone, sounding more derisive than amused. "Ah, a Freudian witch."

"So, the idea of an evil side is Freud's?" asked Rebecca, more to keep him talking than from interest.

"Yeah, among many others. One of Freud's ideas was that we need to subvert our impulsive, amoral id so that society could exist, but I hardly think blaming a witch's id for the killing is going to do anything for her defense." There was a slight hesitation, then, "Hold on. Is this just to distract me?"

Gus started waving his hands, shaking his head, and mouthing the word "no." Months of working together weren't needed to interpret his meaning, but Rebecca felt Doc would see through this ruse sooner or later anyway.

"What gave me away?" asked Rebecca.

Doc laughed, although this time he sounded amused. "Maybe because you implied that I needed a diversion last time." His sigh this time was longer and louder. "OK, give me a rundown."

Gus sat upright in his chair staring at the phone and slowly shaking his head. Rebecca nodded at her partner, then launched into her summary of the case. When she was done, she asked, "Any thoughts?"

"You remember I'm not a clinical psychologist, right?" replied Doc. "I'm not a behavioral profiler like in the FBI. I've never even taken a class in abnormal psychology."

"Yeah. As I recall, you said you studied cognition as it applied to people in general, rather than those with a mental illness."

"Right. So, you know how to take this. I'd say your suspect, the witch of the St. Louis business world, is wacko. Drop the case the first chance you get. But … if anything comes to me in the middle of the night, I'll give you a call. My waking hours, however, go toward finding my fiancée. OK?"

"Of course," replied Rebecca.

"Then, I gotta run." Doc ended the call.

After a moment staring at the phone, Gus said, "I have to admit, you know him a lot better than I do. I thought he'd explode when you admitted the call was a smokescreen. It's just too bad he didn't take the bait."

Rebecca was shaking her head even before he'd finished. "Not true," she said. "He was interested. Those facts will percolate in the back of his head until one night, he calls me at 2:00 AM. You'll see."

THURSDAY, OCTOBER 8

10:22 AM, Yates-Baden Sciences Building 4

Rebecca leaned back against the seat of her car, the sun's rays through the windshield warming her face. She glanced across the parking lot to the Yates-Baden Sciences building, knowing it was owned by the same pharmaceutical research company that had employed Putnam when he was in the coven. The building she was looking at, however, wasn't where he had worked. At that time, he would have been at the company's headquarters, a lavish structure that dominated five acres of manicured grounds. This building, on the other hand, was utilitarian. Save two evergreen shrubs lining the sidewalk to the front door and a black and white sign beside it, the scene in front of her was all glass, brick, or asphalt.

Putnam, however, was still employed, which was perhaps surprising from what Rebecca had found online. He had only made two bad calls, but in the process, he'd cost the company millions. But rather than terminating him, he'd been reassigned as the senior manager for research on high blood pressure medications. Given that this market niche was extremely competitive and that Yates-Baden was seriously lagging their competitors, this job was probably as close to being exiled to Siberia as the company could manage. And since this meeting had been delayed due to Putnam's appearance in bankruptcy court, he hadn't handled his personal finances any better.

Rebecca released a long breath, realizing it had more to do with nerves than oxygen. She couldn't remember feeling this anxious before an interview since the second or third one she'd conducted for the FBI. The problem was that Putnam's possible involvement in Victor Sims's death rested on two major and completely untested assumptions. The first required a significant leap of faith, specifically that Putnam had somehow foreseen his financial or romantic fate some six months or more into the future. But as improbable as this supposition was, it paled compared to the second — that he had found a way to control another person to change that trajectory.

"Who am I kidding?" Rebecca muttered to herself, knowing that these assumptions were virtually indefensible. Perhaps she should advise her client to terminate the contract and save herself some money. That action, while potentially giving her some peace of mind, wouldn't change anything for Labadie ... except by possibly making the situation worse. She would just find another private investigator and the next one might be willing to charge for going through the motions, safe in the belief that the case was a loser anyway. At least Marte Investigations would give their client the best she and Gus could manage. And at this point in the case, their best suspect, however poor of a possible perp he might be, was David Putnam.

Rebecca picked up her notebook from the seat beside her and exited the car. After checking in with a receptionist at the front door and a short wait, she was led to a corner office in the front of the building. It, too, was best described as utilitarian, with a large wooden desk, four five-drawer file cabinets, and four chairs — three for visitors and a desk chair for the occupant. A potted plant and three pictures on the wall were the only adornments to an otherwise Spartan setting.

From his online photos, Rebecca recognized the man behind the desk as Putnam. He stood slowly, as if it took a moment to unfold his over-six-foot frame, then flashed a wide grin. He had the looks to go with his confident expression, with sandy, somewhat wavy hair and hazel eyes in a chiseled face. No stranger to the gym, his muscles rippled under a starched white shirt, the sleeves rolled up to reveal two well-tanned forearms. No wonder people were surprised when Della Bergeron dropped him for Sims.

He came around the desk and extended a hand. "David Putnam, Senior Manager." His grip was firm, the handshake longer than necessary. "And you must be Rebecca Marte of Marte Investigations."

"I am. Nice to meet you, Mr. Putnam."

As he returned to his side of the desk, Rebecca stole a glance at the pictures on his office wall. Grinning was plainly a common expression for Putnam, as he sported the same look in each. None of the photos, however, included Della Bergeron. And none appeared to involve work unless beach scenes and forest trails with beautiful companions were part of his job.

"It's David, please. You're the first PI I've ever met, and I have to say, you've set the bar very high. High enough that I'm wondering what mystery you might help me solve." The grin reappeared.

"Spare me" was the thought that went through Rebecca's mind, but "Thank you" were the words she forced past her lips. "It's extremely nice of you to help Ms. Labadie by meeting with me."

"Right now, I think I'm doing myself the favor. I just have to hope our blood pressure medications work. I'd hate to blow a gasket sitting here looking at you."

For a split-second, Rebecca considered playing the doting female, taken in by the man's sleazy lines. And if there was no other way to get what she needed, she might ... someday. But not today. Putnam just needed a reason to take this interview seriously, and she had several to offer.

"As you know, a man, Victor Sims, has been killed, and my client, Ms. Rowena Labadie, believes the circumstances are suspicious. She thought you might be able to help establish her sister's innocence. But I have to admit, I'm not sure why you'd want to, given your past association with Ms. Bergeron. I'd guess there's no love lost between the two of you. Maybe you're even pleased she's been arrested for the killing?"

It seemed to take Putnam a moment to process her words, but when he did, he sat forward in his chair. Gone was the grin, replaced by blinking eyes and a mouth hanging half-open. "Whoa, hold on, Ms. Marte. I'm not sure what you've heard, but there was never anything serious between Della Bergeron and me. It was more of a no-strings, let's-enjoy-each-other kind of thing. Commitment isn't ... well, I used to say, isn't in her nature. But after she and Victor Sims got together and it seemed serious, I suppose it's me that's not in her nature."

"And that made you angry," Rebecca said more than asked.

"Hell, no. Bergeron's beautiful, no doubt, but she can also be a little scary. The fact is, I was going to break it off with her anyway. But then she got with Sims and it wasn't necessary." Putnam paused a beat, still staring like a deer caught in the headlights. And then, his expression turned to anger. "Jeez, when Rowena asked me to talk to you, she said it would be about the coven, not my personal life. This is bullshit."

Rebecca had wiped the smirk off the man's face, but the change in his attitude was too drastic. She'd never get background on the coven, much less information on his reversals in the business world unless he recovered some of his conceit.

"Yeah, I thought it might be more a matter of optics, you and Bergeron," she said. "But I had to know if I could take what you tell me about the coven at face value and if you still harbored feelings for the High Priestess." Penitent looks weren't Rebecca's forte—she didn't have much practice—but she tried for one now, letting the innuendo hang in the air. Hopefully, the look and the contrived explanation would be enough to keep him talking.

Putnam continued to scowl, but after a moment, he shrugged and said, "Yeah, I suppose."

Rebecca relaxed. She should take advantage of the return of some of his vanity to discuss the coven, but there was something else on her mind. "You said Ms. Bergeron could be a little scary. What did you mean by that?"

Another frown appeared on Putnam's face, but this one seemed more due to concentration than displeasure. "Della can get inside your head. Like she's reading what you're thinking. It's a great business skill but when it was just the two of us? I can tell you, it got a little freaky."

"But don't a lot of couples have experiences like that?"

"You're still thinking of Della and me like an old married couple, and it was never like that. I've known several other women as well or better than I know her, and that never happened with any of them. But when Della did it ... well, I thought she might actually be a witch."

"So, you don't think she's a witch?"

"Hell, no. I don't believe any of that occult, supernatural crap."

"But you were in the coven, right?"

"I play golf, too, but that doesn't mean I'm a pro. I was in the coven for much the same reason I chase a little white ball around the links. That's where the power is. Or was, anyway." He paused, his grin coming back full force. "You know, maybe golf is where my future is. I did get off some massive drives at the range earlier this morning. You play, Rebecca? Or is it Becky?"

Rebecca was starting to think Putnam only had two modes—on the make or on the defensive—and she didn't want to drive him back to the latter again. "Rebecca, and no, I haven't played recently. Hard to find the time." Especially when you don't have a job where you can play hooky most of the morning, she thought, but didn't say. But even if she had wanted to say it, she wouldn't have had the chance because someone knocked on Putnam's door.

"Yes," he called.

Rebecca glanced over her shoulder to find the head of a twenty-something brunette sticking through the doorway. "Mr. Putnam, sorry to interrupt," she said tentatively.

"No problem." Then, turning to Rebecca. "Hayley Minden, my new assistant." Then, back to the woman. "What is it?"

"It's the team looking at ...."

"Come in," said Putnam. "I can hardly hear you."

She did, wobbling slightly on her three-inch bandage heels. She stopped just inside the door to grab the hem of her pleated gray miniskirt and then did what Rebecca could only describe as a shimmy. It was as if she was trying to slip up inside a garment that was too short for the setting. Too short for the setting? Rebecca stifled a laugh at the thought. That dress was too short for sitting.

"It's the Nuverin 320 team," she said with a little more volume.

"Ah, crap," said Putnam. "Not them again. Ms. Marte, would you mind giving me a moment?"

"Of course." They stepped out. Rebecca shook her head, vowing if she could find Hayley when she was finished, she'd tell her that Putnam wasn't worth the discomfort of her attire.

At the Same Time, The Nicholas Goodwin Residence

"Frickin' witch," Nicholas Goodwin muttered to himself, then looked around to see if any of the help had wandered into his study. Not that they would be surprised by his sentiment; they'd heard him rail against Della Bergeron often enough to know his feelings toward the woman. They'd probably only wonder when he had changed from the "B" word to the one starting with "W." That shift was the result of a reprimand from his wife, but even she couldn't complain about him calling Bergeron a witch. She was one.

Goodwin spun his chair from the desk and stared sightlessly out the picture window behind him. The muscles in his jaw clenched and unclenched rhythmically as he replayed his only call to Bergeron since the night Sims had died.

"Hello, Nicholas. What a nice surprise to hear from you."

Her greeting had taken him by surprise. She was talking like it was just another day at the office, not the eleventh hour on a sinking ship. "Cut the crap, Della. I'm sure you've dreaded receiving this call as much as I detest making it. I just wanted to know what you're going to do to end the shit storm you've created?"

"I've created?" Bergeron sighed. "You never were much good at putting yourself in someone else's shoes, Nicholas, but this sets a new standard for low. Do you really think I killed a man who I deeply cared for?"

"And do you expect condolences for a loss when you created it?"

"What do you want?" she had asked, her tone now devoid of all warmth.

"It's not what I want. It's what any leader would do. Take the fall. Plead guilty now so the rest of us can get out from under this microscope of police and media scrutiny. You know if this keeps up long enough, some enterprising journalist is going to find enough to ruin everyone's reputation."

"I'm not pleading guilty to something I didn't do."

"Come on, Della, give your blackout story a rest. No one believes it, and I'm not sure it makes any difference anyway. You still stabbed the guy."

After a pause, Bergeron asked, "Is this you talking or the coven?"

Goodwin didn't think he'd hesitated, but perhaps he had, because Bergeron continued, "I thought as much. Good-bye, Nicholas."

That had been over a month ago, but Goodwin still seethed with the memory. And that surprised him because sometime in the long, restless hours between going to bed that night and dragging himself up the next morning, he had come to several conclusions. That usually calmed him, but so far, it hadn't. So, he went through his reasoning again.

First, he didn't know when or the form it would take, but eventually, the members of the coven would be ruined. Maybe it would stem from the whispers he'd already heard—that the coven didn't play by the rules, calling upon supernatural powers to amass their fortunes. Few, however, would take that insinuation seriously. More likely, it would take the form of an erosion of public trust as this priceless business commodity was worn away by rumors of impropriety. "They shared inside information," his competitors would say. And if one of the coven turned against the rest, today's whispered innuendoes would be tomorrow's unsubstantiated claims. And those assertions were worse than facts.

How could he stop his slow but inevitable slide into irrelevance? Goodwin could think of only one way—discredit Bergeron before her actions discredited them.

So, he had spent the last month digging up all the dirt he could find. He'd listed all her casual mentions of marketing campaigns her company was running to shore up a client's weakness or to get a leg up on some new business. He'd also documented all the times a coven member had swooped in to profit from that client's turnaround. No one would believe that was a coincidence, would they? His list also included the constant stream of "strategic business analysis" contracts she won from the coven members, often after one of these windfalls. Could that be anything other than payback?

Unfortunately, all the information he had against Bergeron fell into a gray area. Because she worked in marketing and promotions, nothing she did remained in the shadows. What good were ad copy, press releases, and new taglines if no one heard or saw them? So, it was more a matter of who knew what and when. And on the occasions he'd found information at that level of detail, he'd discovered that the campaigns had been publicized before she mentioned them at a gathering. True, the first public reference might be an off-hand remark she made to an unknown reporter working for a local rag with a distribution in the hundreds, but that was still public. But in other cases, the campaign had been fully launched before it had made the coven's agenda. The information she had delivered to them wasn't always of the insider variety as she had implied.

Even so, Goodwin felt he had enough to burn the witch ... which he thought a clever turn of phrase. Of course, some of the other coven members would get singed by the incendiary evidence he'd accumulated, but Bergeron was always in the center, always the hub of information. He just had to watch his back in case another of the coven came after him when this was done.

And even though it had to be done, Goodwin still found himself hesitating. It must be the lack of sleep. He wasn't sure he'd had a full night of rest in the last five months and that too needed to change. He'd get a little fresh air and exercise—a slow jog around the block because that was all a man of his age could manage. And when he got back, he'd strike the match to start the fire. Then tonight, he'd sleep like a baby.

After changing into his running gear, he stepped out onto the front steps of his sprawling home and stretched. He'd heard the whispered queries, "How much longer till old man Goodwin retires?" All he needed was to pull a muscle and give the vultures more to talk about. He walked down his drive, then turned to the left. He knew a peaceful section of road along the bluffs—the perfect place to fortify his resolve.

In a few minutes, he'd reached the road and started his jog at a slow trot. The day was warmer than he'd expected. His sweatpants and light jacket were not only unnecessary, but they were becoming unpleasant. He decided he could shed the pants and toss them over his shoulders or tie them around his waist. He found a wider spot on the road and sat.

He had just pulled a foot from the first leg of the pants when he heard a car approaching. It was coming fast. He looked up at the car's windshield, glimpsing shiny black hair on the side of the driver's head. "Look out!" The two-word sentence was the last of his life.

10:48 AM, Yates-Baden Sciences Building 4

The moment Putnam had requested to talk to his short-skirted assistant turned into something more like five minutes, but Rebecca didn't mind. It gave her a chance to review the progress of the case so far, which had left her feeling a bit like a tennis ball at Wimbledon—knocked from one side of an issue to the other and back. And it wasn't just the little things. It was basic questions, like what was driving the coven, business or beliefs?

Initially, she couldn't quite reconcile commerce and witchcraft, the latter replete with vague connotations that she found distasteful—animal sacrifices, devil worship, strange initiation rites. Her research, however, had largely dispelled those misperceptions, allowing free enterprise to be the driving force in the coven. In that light, witchcraft became little more than something like a team-building activity with the added benefit of secrecy. Executives might talk to their friends about the great "ropes course" they'd been in, but chatting about a shadowy occult ritual? No way.

Then, Harrison's apparent devotion to witchcraft drove her thoughts to the opposite side of the question. Perhaps the coven's members, these witches, truly endorsed this alternative worldview.

If so, the business gains they realized would be an outgrowth of the positive focus Bergeron promoted. And can-do attitudes could go a long way toward success.

Unfortunately, Putnam violated that generality. He was a witch only to the degree it benefited him personally. Did the coven, sans Bergeron and Harrison, feel the same as him? Or perhaps Bergeron wasn't a witch either? If so, exposing her act would remove all of the otherworldly explanations for what had happened the night of the ritual and give her a more specific focus—the financial benefits of killing Sims.

That Bergeron didn't consider herself a witch, however, seemed unlikely to Rebecca. After all, the woman hadn't denounced the practice of witchcraft despite all the notoriety it had brought to the case. Rather, she had focused a spotlight on herself and the killing by making her beliefs a matter of public record.

"Sorry," Putnam said as he came back into his office. "That took longer than I expected." He walked around his desk and took a seat. "Now, where were we?"

"You'd just mentioned you didn't believe in witchcraft," said Rebecca, avoiding the last topic, which had been golf. "Is this skepticism common in the coven? Maybe even Ms. Bergeron is a witch in name only?"

"Absolutely not," he replied, ending Rebecca's wishful thinking. "She's convinced she's tapped into a bigger world than you or I see." Putnam paused. "Or, at least, I assume you don't see it."

"No, I'm still trying to take in all this one has to offer before I worry about another. So, how'd it work with her as the High Priestess and you, a nonbeliever? Or maybe she didn't know?"

"Oh, she knew all right. I could never hide something like that from her. Like I said, she's a bit scary that way. But she was OK with it. Said we didn't have to think alike ... which was good, because that wasn't going to happen." He paused, his lascivious grin returning. "Well, we didn't have to think alike on that topic, just on other matters."

Rebecca ignored the obvious insinuation. "What about the other coven members? Do they consider themselves witches?"

"Who knows?" said Putnam with a shrug. "If you're going to coven gatherings to harness cosmic energies to improve your lot at work, you don't go around saying, 'Can you believe this bull Bergeron's feeding us?' Kinda blows your cover, don't you think?"

"But nothing came out later, outside the coven meetings? No idle gossip on the links or over drinks?"

"I never socialized with any of them away from the gatherings ... except for Della and Lilith, that is. And frankly, not even with Lilith that much. But just guessing about the rest, I'd say they were willing to withhold disbelief as long as their businesses grew."

Something less than fully committed also fit Rebecca's opinion of the businessmen and women in the group. All except Harrison had distanced themselves from Bergeron after Sims's death. It was the Wiccans and witches of other covens who had come to Bergeron's defense.

"Did any of the coven's rituals deal with ... I guess the phrase would be, black magic? Was the group working against any businesses, trying to make them fail?"

"Why do you want to know that? I mean, it's all a crock anyway."

"Just trying to get a picture of the coven and what they did."

Rebecca wasn't certain why, but she didn't want to share the real reason for her question—the possibility that a business executive might retaliate if a slump came shortly after a black magic ritual. Of course, her hesitancy was probably because it was pretty farfetched to think someone would kill because of a bad quarterly report, but as she kept telling herself—it wasn't impossible.

"Not while I was there," replied Putnam, further eroding an already slim possibility. "Della had a thing about working with positive energies only, which is pretty strange, considering how ruthless she could be at work."

Putnam made a sound that seemed half-laugh and half-grunt. "I remember one company Meteor bought. There was overlap between the functional departments and everyone expected some give and take over months. But Della had other plans. She cut entire departments in the other company just a week after the acquisition. That was pretty cutthroat even for ... even for the business niche she's in."

Rebecca doubted that "business niche" was what he was going to say, but she didn't particularly want to hear his original thought, figuring it was either sexist, vulgar, or both. "But the coven's positive energies would still have negative impacts on their competitors' bottom lines, right? Isn't that why they practice witchcraft?"

Putnam concurred with something that looked like a mix of nod and shrug. "Sure. They win. Others lose."

"So, do you know of any competitors who were particularly hurt by their wins?"

"Particularly hurt? Not really. I suppose you could find some poor schmuck who went under after losing some contract to them. But, hey, that happens all the time. As for targeting some specific business? For the segments they were in—financial, pharmaceuticals, real estate, construction, engineering—they didn't pick and choose who to beat. They just took on all comers."

"How about inside the coven? Did anyone take exception to how Ms. Bergeron was handling the common business opportunities?"

"You don't dis the High Priestess."

"But no one thought they were being shortchanged, not getting what they deserved?"

Putnam chuckled. "It's hard to imagine a group with a bigger appetite for wealth and power than them. But even so, Della sold them on sacrificing today for bigger gains tomorrow. And she kept pulling it off. Besides, it's not like there was a spreadsheet of all the business we were going to take. Trends were discussed, but the individual members had to act on their own behalf. So, if they failed, it wasn't like they could pin it solely on the group."

"So, why'd you leave if the coven was being so successful?"

Rebecca kicked herself mentally. For a topic that she wanted to handle carefully—Putnam's departure from the group and the subsequent downturn in his professional life—her transition felt more than a bit abrupt.

But the flare of temper that Putnam showed earlier didn't return. "Yeah, why?" he asked somewhat ruefully. "It was a lot of things. The weird rituals. The beliefs I didn't share. A girl who was never close but kept moving further away. It was better that I left."

"Sure," replied Rebecca. "A couple of years ago, Yates-Baden went all-in on some research on high blood pressure medications. It didn't pay off."

Putnam blinked a couple of times, then said, "You've done your homework." He paused a moment. "I suppose we could have pressed a little harder, but I'm not sure it would have helped. The niche was crowded then and has only gotten worse. Now, we have ACE inhibitors, alpha and beta-blockers, calcium channel blockers, and on and on. And each of those types has a half dozen or more specific medications. Yates-Baden just never got a foothold in the area."

"Did you ever think Ms. Bergeron might be behind that?"

Putnam's head jerked back and he stared a moment. "You mean like she hexed me or something?"

"Or she used her connections in the coven to increase the competition you faced."

Putnam waved a hand as if swatting away the thought. "If the coven saw a chance for a profit, they wouldn't care if I was the opposition or not. They look for monetary wins, not moral victories … or whatever beating me would be. And besides, our sluggish performance has nothing to do with them. It's the area. Like I said, it's overcrowded."

"From what I could tell from the information online, your background is business management. An MBA in marketing, if I remember correctly. But I suspect you have some background in the pharmaceutical industry as well."

"Been checking me out, huh?" He raised his eyebrows.

The flirting was back, not that Rebecca was surprised given the question about his background. "Just doing the checks any investigator would."

Her statement that it was standard procedure didn't affect the man as his grin never wavered. He was all too happy to tell his life story now that she'd asked. "Nope. Management is management, and I'm good at it. So, I don't need a background in medicine. I just have to tell these guys to speak English once in a while. Otherwise, it's all chemicals and double-blind protocols with cohort matching in clinical trials, whatever all that means."

"Before taking over this department, what types of drug research did you oversee?"

"The same stuff I do here—high blood pressure medications."

"So, with all the products on the market, it must be tough to keep all the different drugs straight."

"I put in the hours," he said, faking his modesty poorly.

"And all the side effects. Some of them must be pretty bad." It was too much to hope that any of them would be heightened suggestibility delayed by months ... but Rebecca mentally crossed her fingers anyway.

"Mostly minor problems, like fatigue, dizziness, or headaches. Some of them can cause digestive issues, and the beta-blockers can mess with men's equipment."

That last one, of course, would be a side effect he would remember. She'd need to review these classes of medications herself, but nothing in what he'd said sounded promising as a drug used to influence Bergeron.

For the person she'd thought forty-five minutes ago was their prime suspect, this interview had been largely a waste of time. As a once successful but now backslidden businessman, he seemed to lack the drive and disposition necessary for anything like framing Bergeron for the crime. And as a source of information on the coven, he was even worse. He knew nothing about witchcraft and little about the group or its competitors.

The only follow-up to this discussion, besides a closer look at the drug research Putnam oversaw, was a question for her client. Why had Labadie recommended Putnam when he had been an outsider? But then, perhaps she didn't know.

"That completes my questions for now. If you think of anything more that might help us, please give me a call."

"I will," replied Putnam. "And maybe next time, we can make it over dinner?"

"Perhaps," she replied, though not meaning it. She stood, thanked Putnam for his time, and left. Rebecca had almost made it back to her car when her phone vibrated. She checked the screen. "Hey, Gus. What's up?"

There was a pause. "I didn't think I'd get you," he said after a moment. "How'd the interview with Putnam go?"

"About as well as any talk with a womanizing jerk could. And I didn't find anything that leads me to suspect him in Sims's death." She spent a couple of minutes covering the highlights of the meeting.

When she was done, there was another moment of silence from Gus. "Any idea where he was this morning?"

Now it was Rebecca's turn to hesitate. "Yeah. He said something about going to a driving range to work on his golf game. Why?"

Rather than answering, Gus asked, "Do you think Putnam might have been acting, pretending he was planning to leave Bergeron? Or that he took his business failings so philosophically? Or even that he's not a witch?"

"What's going on?"

Gus sighed. "I'm at the North Patrol Division building, meeting with an officer who works part-time for Della Bergeron's security service. The company monitors her alarm systems, does some random patrolling in the area, stuff like that, and this officer picks up work when they need extra manpower. He worked the night of the coven gathering. He was the one closest to the ritual.

"Anyway, I heard something in the halls that you should know about. Nicholas Goodwin, the witch that works in the pharmaceutical industry was killed this morning. It was a hit and run on an isolated stretch of road up north, along the Missouri River bluffs. There were no witnesses, but the police think they've found the car. It's now a burned-out shell, so it's not likely there'll be much in the way of physical evidence."

"And you think it could have been Putnam?" asked Rebecca.

"No more than I think it could have been any of the others we're looking at. Putnam wasn't immediately considered a person of interest, so the police may not even talk to him."

"So, we should try to check out his alibi, if nothing else," said Rebecca. And then, she realized the implications of Gus's statement. "Goodwin was killed up north, along the Missouri River bluffs?" she repeated slowly. "Near where Della Bergeron lives?"

"Yeah, about a half-mile away. The police are picking her up for questioning. Guess you're going to need to re-schedule with her ... again."

12:12 PM, A Farmhouse in Western Kansas

Nicole held up a morsel of meat on her fork. "This is delicious. What is it?" She hadn't meant the question as a joke, but now that it was out of her mouth, it sounded like one.

"Beef," Maggie replied, apparently not seeing the irony in the statements. "I got it from that hunter I told you about a few days ago?"

"Ronnie Johnston?" asked Nicole.

Maggie stared at her a moment. "It's actually Lonnie Johnston."

Nicole frowned, then nodded as if committing the information to memory. In fact, she had known the man's name was Lonnie. But since nothing had happened to dispel her unease about Maggie Ingalls, Nicole had started littering her comments to the woman with small errors. Presumably, if Maggie had bartered for food with the man, she'd remember his name. On the other hand, if she'd invented the encounter for some reason, perhaps she wouldn't.

Of course, even if Maggie failed to catch one of her planned misstatements, the woman wasn't necessarily lying. People's memories could be wrong and Nicole was certain she couldn't tell honest forgetting from dishonest fabrication. She wished that Sam was here. Unless she was mistaken—and that was a phrase that recirculated in her thoughts constantly—Doc had a background in psychology. Maybe he could spot the difference?

But even as the thought came to her, she knew the man occupied a more central position in her thoughts than justified by his education. But why that was true, or even if it was true because of the good or the ill he had caused her, she wasn't certain. He was still a mystery in her forgotten past.

In any case, the need to catch Maggie in a possible lie hadn't materialized. So far, the woman had corrected all of the intentional errors, denying Nicole even a hint of possible deceit to explore. So, she returned to the conversation to cover what she'd been doing. "So,

Lonnie has a source of beef? A herd of cattle roaming across the prairie?"

"A feedlot, actually," replied Maggie. "Most of the cattle were dead because there was no one to take care of them. But a few weren't. He turned most of them loose and shot one. Since it was too much for him and his wife, he agreed to an exchange."

"Lucky us," said Justin.

"True, son, but don't talk with your mouth full."

Justin nodded, then crammed another bite of meat into his mouth.

Nicole looked around the table, checking the fit between the picture before her and her notion of normalcy. Why wasn't this scene exactly what it seemed—a hardworking widowed farm wife and her grown son enjoying a hearty lunch? After all, the sense of familiarity that Nicole felt toward Maggie—the one that had started all this questioning—didn't necessarily mean anything. From time to time, didn't everyone have a déjà vu experience upon meeting someone new? And if that was the case, the fact she didn't feel the same about Justin meant nothing.

For a while, Nicole had been concerned about the physical differences between mother and son. Other than brown eyes and dark hair, Maggie and Justin looked nothing alike. To his small and wiry frame, she was tall and broad. To his naturally dark complexion, she was fair though lightly tanned. To his bumbling innocence and gradual grasp of information, her mind was like a steel trap—it caught everything immediately and never let go. Even their hair, which Nicole had thought of as similar wasn't an exact match. His was curlier than hers. But then, all of this could be explained by one statement—Justin was adopted. Or another—family resemblance could skip years. So, Nicole hadn't even bothered asking.

And then there was the company shirt that Justin felt sure he'd seen but couldn't have. That was a little more difficult to explain away, but not impossible. "Maggie, do you have a picture of me in a blue shirt with the Biomedical Engineering Associates logo on the pocket?"

Before they'd lost electricity several months ago, Maggie had downloaded and printed a few pictures of Nicole's former life—the Biomedical Associates building, the building and park across the street, even one of the buildings where she had lived. Now, Maggie used them as what she called memory joggers, placing each picture in a holder that looked something like an antique stereoscope. As a budding collector, back when such trivial hobbies were common, Nicole had seen several in antique stores.

Maggie looked up from lunch, but before she could speak, Justin did. "Yeah, the blue shirt she was wearing when we found her."

Maggie's gaze went from her son to Nicole and back. "Justin, I forgot to check the rain gauge after the shower last night. Can you go out and see how much we got? And then, dump it out."

"In the middle of lunch?"

His tone wasn't lost on the woman. "Stop whining. It'll only take you a second."

Justin got up slowly and ambled toward the back door as if he was trying to prove her wrong—the job was quite time-consuming. When they heard the door slam, Maggie said, "I do have a picture of you in that shirt from your company's website, I believe. And Justin has seen it. I used it to stimulate his memories of finding you. But we both know you were wearing that old, tattered yellow shirt of yours when we found you."

"Then, why is he confused about it?" asked Nicole.

"What did you and Justin do yesterday?"

Nicole paused, wondering what this had to do with her question. "Cleared rocks from the new garden plot."

"You both changed after lunch, so I could get your clothes into the laundry. What shirt was Justin wearing in the morning?"

Justin didn't have that many clothes, but the ones he had, Nicole had seen over and over. And now that she tried to recall one specific instance, she could see him in all of them. "In the afternoon, it was that dark blue one. I remember because I wondered if it was too hot when the sun got higher. But I'm not sure what he was wearing in the morning. I didn't think anything about it."

"Which is common. People recall the main idea about what they saw or did, like you remembering the work on the garden. But the minor details, things like what Justin was wearing that don't change the overall meaning? That sort of thing tends to get forgotten. So, while I knew you weren't wearing the blue shirt, I also knew it wouldn't make any difference if I used it as a memory jogger for my son."

What Maggie had said made sense but that she had a ready explanation less so. It even sounded a bit textbook. "You know a lot about memory, don't you?"

"I wasn't always a farmer's wife," replied Maggie. "And I've given yours and Justin's problems a lot of thought. Anyway, I gave you that long explanation because his recollections are still fragile. I don't want you to upset him, have him questioning the details of what he's recovered."

The back door opened and closed, so Nicole whispered, "Sure. Sorry."

Justin came into the living area. "How much rain did we get?" asked Maggie.

"Just below that first mark. That's a half-inch, right?"

"No, just a quarter."

The mother-son conversation continued, with Maggie explaining why rain in the fall would help their garden next spring, the snow over the winter even more so. Nicole, however, wasn't listening. Rather, she was going over all the other things she'd asked Maggie over the last few weeks, things that didn't seem quite right in a world devoid of humans.

Why couldn't Maggie find an abandoned propane truck to refill the farm tank? That had to be easier than hauling limbs and cutting them up. Why wasn't there even one radio station broadcasting an emergency message? They had a radio that ran on solar, but it wasn't picking up any stations. How was it that they'd had electricity for several weeks and then it had disappeared?

Maggie always had answers. Finding a propane truck was easy; refilling it without power was probably close to impossible ... or at least, far beyond her. There were still a few radio stations broadcasting emergency messages, but she heard them only when she was miles from the farm. And those signals wouldn't last much longer. They had electricity initially because infrastructure would continue working for a while, but not forever. Yes, Maggie always had the answers, although new questions continued to take their place in Nicole's thoughts. And one she had wanted to ask came to her now.

Nicole mustered some feigned excitement and said, "Oh, I almost forgot to tell you. I saw a contrail this morning."

She wasn't certain she had. It was near the horizon, but for her purposes, it made no difference if she was wrong.

Maggie sat up straight, her eyes blinking. "That's interesting."

"What's a contrail?" asked Justin.

Internally, Nicole groaned, "No, don't give her time to make something up." But it was, of course, too late.

"They're those thin lines of clouds in the sky. Airplanes make them."

"Airplanes? There are airplanes?"

"Sounds like it."

Maggie turned to Nicole. "Must be a flight from some remote military base because no commercial airport would be open. They all became virus hotspots early in the pandemic. I went by the St. Louis airport just before they closed it, and when there was no room for ...." Her voice drifted off and she slowly shook her head. "Sorry. That's not a story for lunchtime, especially when you have such great news. If some military forces survived and someone can find a cure, humanity might be able to reclaim the world ... someday."

"How long?" asked Justin.

"Oh, honey, I can't answer that. What species besides humans are carriers? We believed that some mammals were, but has it affected marine life? Birds? Even under the best of circumstances, it would be a long time before we can clean up this mess."

Maggie paused, then turned her attention back to Nicole. "Maybe in the spring, I can start searching more widely. Maybe up into the Dakotas. I think there were some military bases up there. And if things look good, maybe one or both of you can come with me."

"What about checking ... well, the cities, like Kansas City?" asked Nicole.

Maggie's hand went to her throat as a pained expression crossed her features. "I've met a couple of people with friends or family who took that risk. Only one returned and she died of the virus a few days later and took the rest of her family with her. I'm sorry, Nicole, but there's nothing there but death and decay ... and packs of scavengers whose bodies are teeming with the disease."

Justin looked unhappy but nodded. Nicole, on the other hand, tried to keep her expression blank, but she could feel the black of despair creeping into the corners of her mind again. Was this her life? A forty-by-forty-yard compound with only two human companions—one, by the time she died. And if so, didn't taking Justin as a partner make sense?

But the darkness in her mind passed and Nicole considered the older woman's words. And try as she might, she couldn't believe there was nothing left but the remnants of humanity scattered across the globe. Something still felt wrong.

3:25 PM, Marte Investigative Services

Rebecca Marte leaned over to peer through the open door into the reception area, spotting the husky frame of Gus Clements ambling toward her office. "I thought you said Tony Fiedler wasn't going to be here until 4:00?" she called out.

Gus came in and dropped into one of the chairs across the desk from her. "He's not. But you only hit the highlights on the Putnam meeting and I have the interview with the police officer and parttime security guard to cover. So, ladies first?"

"Yeah, OK," replied Rebecca. "But how the heck did you set up this meeting with Fiedler so fast? I thought we'd have to go to his office, busy lawyer for a struggling company and all."

"Ms. Bergeron's current round of questioning at the police station seems to have opened up a few holes in his schedule." Gus waved a hand, probably to forestall the question Rebecca was about to ask. "Fiedler was at the North Patrol Division, too, and practically waylaid me in the hallway. Kept saying this whole incident was getting out of hand and wanted to follow me over so we could talk. But I figured we needed a few moments first and put him off till 4:00."

"Interesting," Rebecca said, then turned her thoughts to the Putnam interview. During it, she had all but dismissed him as too shallow and too lazy to have orchestrated anything of the complexity of framing Della Bergeron. But when Gus questioned whether it might have been an act, she began replaying the talk in her mind. In retrospect, the consistency of his come-ons amid a murder investigation felt suspicious. So, to take full advantage of Gus's years of experience, she recounted the meeting in as much detail as she could recall. The retelling took almost as long as the interview itself.

"I can't rule out the possibility that Putnam was lying about his relationship with Bergeron," she said when she was finished. "Maybe he wanted revenge for being rejected and covered it with his bad-boy image. But in my opinion, he's a player and didn't give her a second thought until her name popped up in the news."

Rebecca paused, considering her words. "But as for him blaming her and the coven for his financial and professional problems? I'm having a harder time dismissing that outright. Discrediting Bergeron and her cronies by killing Sims is extreme but, perhaps, possible. And if Goodwin had some central role in his downfall, Putnam kills him, too, while everyone's looking the other way."

"Could be," said Gus. "Be good to know if Putnam's alibi for this morning holds up."

"I tried checking it. I called him, said I was thinking about knocking the rust off my golf game and asked him where he'd been hitting this morning. Unfortunately, he was checking out a new place, so when I called them, his name meant nothing. And when I described Putnam, the wiseass on the other end said that sounded like about half their customers. He might have left a trail if he used a credit card or made calls from there but no easy way for me to check that." Rebecca paused a moment. "You know, this would be a lot easier if I had something besides public records."

"Missing the FBI?"

"Missing their long reach ... and the better help I had there," she said, smirking while Gus just shook his head. "But at least the coven's business activities are important enough that the winners and also-rans usually make the news. Oh, I also got a lead on Putnam's personal financial troubles—some real estate deals that went sour. The coven members who might have been on the other side of those ventures are Deborah Fry in real estate and construction and Russell Cowan in banking. It's just ...."

Rebecca wasn't sure how to finish, but Gus waited for her to come to a decision. "It just seems like we're playing some really long shots. I mean, how much money does someone need to lose before two killings and framing for murder make sense?"

"He could probably hire it done for 20K," Gus said with a shrug. "Maybe less, but you're right. His motivation isn't the strongest, even if it is the best of the lot. Anything else from the Putnam interview?"

"Just me wondering if Rowena Labadie couldn't have found someone better than him for background. He was an outsider even when he was in the coven."

"Well, like I said, maybe she picked him to keep us looking the other way."

"Hired by the perp?" said Rebecca, her head shaking slowly. "I'm going to discuss the whole Putnam thing with Labadie when we meet tomorrow."

"Good. One of the things I learned from the officer I met at the North Patrol District station is that there are a couple of people who manage Bergeron's security, but the onsite crew is always different. They have strict instructions to rotate personnel in and out. Wanna guess who gave them that order?"

"Rowena Labadie?"

"Bingo," replied Gus. "So, why is the sister so concerned about the same people being around Bergeron day after day?"

"Easier to spot changes," Rebecca said before thinking the question was probably rhetorical.

But if it was, Gus didn't say so. "The other thing you need to check on is Labadie's relationship with her husband. Some of the guards overheard talk of a divorce in the works."

"Must be pretty boring duty if they're eavesdropping on stuff like that."

"Probably is, but Labadie's still an attractive woman, just a bit older than most of them. Her looks would get most guy's ears open. And if it is true, Labadie and Putnam could be working together. In league with the sister, Putnam would have complete access to Bergeron's life and her home. Labadie, in turn, is motivated by something in her past ... or maybe by the disparity between her lifestyle and that of her sister."

"I don't know, Gus," replied Rebecca. "Framing a sister for murder would be pretty extreme."

"It wouldn't be so far out if Labadie figured her sister would never be convicted. Or worst case, she'd spend a few months in prison and that would be enough to settle the score." Gus tilted his head back, looked up at the ceiling a moment, then back at Rebecca. "There are other possibilities. You said Putnam is a philanderer. Maybe Labadie thinks she's in love."

"Damn," muttered Rebecca, mostly to herself. "I thought she had her act together better than that." She glanced at her watch. "So, before Fiedler gets here, you want to tell me about what you learned from the officer you interviewed?"

With a slight grimace, Gus said, "Unfortunately, not much. He was looking outward for threats, away from the altar, as he'd been trained to do. And he wasn't that close to start with. He only turned around after the commotion started, and by then, Sims was dead. He did mention something a bit strange, and I'm not sure what to make of it. He said Bergeron was walking funny when she entered the clearing."

"Stumbling, like she was under the influence of something?" asked Rebecca.

"No. Almost the opposite, like she was floating. Sims, on the other hand, apparently looked a bit unsteady. But I'm guessing since Bergeron was in black and it was dark that floating ...." He was interrupted by the sound of the reception area door opening.

Rebecca leaned over and looked past Gus's shoulder. "Looks like Mr. Fiedler's here," she said softly.

"I'll get him."

When the men returned, Rebecca wasn't sure Gus had the right lawyer. She'd found Fiedler's head-and-shoulders shot online and her private three-word description of the man had been "virile young lawyer." Now looking at this individual, that description had changed to a wizened old man. Gone was the tanned face and black hair to be replaced by a pale complexion and hair that was nearly white. He was also slight of build and perhaps a bit stooped, something she couldn't have known from the online photo, but that now fit the old-man image perfectly. Only the bushy eyebrows, still mostly black, over piercing brown eyes matched the picture she'd seen. Gus did the introductions and everyone sat.

"It's nice of you to take time at the end of your day to talk with us," said Rebecca, thinking she was just making small talk until she got to the meat of the interview. But Fiedler stared at her like she was speaking a foreign language.

"Hardly the end of my day," the lawyer replied after a moment. "I've left far too much up to her trial attorney, and look where that's got us. A business icon and pillar of society will be confined to her home after this last incident ... which, by the way, is totally irrelevant. Della had nothing to do with Goodwin's death."

"The court is going to change the conditions of her bail?" Rebecca asked, ignoring the last of the lawyer's statement.

"That's what her shyster thinks, probably because he spends all his time on plea bargains and procedural technicalities."

Rebecca managed to suppress the smirk that was coming to her face, hearing one lawyer call another unscrupulous. But she also wondered if Fiedler was either too far out of his element or too involved with the suspect to be dispassionate. After all, he was disparaging two of the mainstays of criminal defense—blame the police and bargain with the opposition. She didn't have to wait long for an answer.

"Della's innocent. She'd never harm another human." To Rebecca, his tone seemed to challenge her to disagree. "I've known her since her sophomore year in college, and I've never so much as heard her say a harsh word to anyone."

"I'm not sure everyone in those companies she's taken over would agree."

Fiedler's head jerked around at the sound of Gus's voice. "Business is business." He delivered the platitude with a glare. "She's decisive but takes no pleasure in reducing excess capacity after an acquisition."

If Gus was going to take the bad-cop role, Rebecca knew where she would go. "Of course. Every job has tough decisions," she said soothingly. Fiedler's expression softened a bit as he turned to her.

"So, you were a contemporary of Ms. Bergeron at school?" Rebecca asked, thinking she was still dead-center in the good-cop role. But Fiedler's frown returned.

"My second degree."

"Same major as Ms. Bergeron?"

"No. I'd gone back to get a law degree after studying history. Della was in marketing and getting into the serious part of her program, but she didn't have any idea where she was going with it. I knew she was artistic. She was always doodling in the margins of her papers and her stuff was good. So, I suggested picking up some background in computer graphics. It wouldn't be the most profound insight today but back then? Well, graphic arts and web design gave her the start she needed for her company. And from there, it's skyrocketed."

"Sophomore year," said Gus slowly. "The year she gave birth to her daughter?"

"Lilith was born between her sophomore and junior years," Fiedler replied somewhat curtly, then turned back to Rebecca.

"I believe you knew Lilith's father, Lowell?" asked Gus.

Fiedler turned toward Gus again, leaning forward into his space. The glare returned. "What's that got to do with Della's case?"

"Just trying to establish background," said Gus smoothly.

Fiedler released a long breath. "Yes, the three of us were friends. Lowell died nearly twenty-five years ago when Lilith was still a baby, but Della and I have remained close."

"Romantic at some point in time?" asked Gus.

Fiedler exploded. "That's none of your damn business!" The once pale complexion of the lawyer was now crimson and a vein was pulsing in his forehead. To Rebecca, however, his reaction said more than most statements would have—their relationship had never been all he desired and, most likely, not intimate.

"I'm sorry if these questions seem too personal," she said. "We're just trying to understand Ms. Bergeron's state-of-mind leading up to the incident near Ste. Genevieve. A close friend, even in the past, might know a lot about that."

Fiedler held Gus in his glare for another few seconds, turning only after he started to speak. "She seemed happy in the weeks before Sims's death. But truthfully, she was shortchanging herself. He wasn't even close to her equal intellectually."

But you are, Rebecca said to herself to finish his thought. "You went to work for Ms. Bergeron after college?"

"Not immediately. Her company was small, a one-person operation for a long time. But I watched her grow it. First, an additional software engineer. Then, another, a person for business development and an office manager. It's only been the last three years that I've worked for Meteor Promotions full-time."

"And before that, consulting as needed?" asked Rebecca.

"Yes, consulting when she had legal questions." He paused a beat, his gaze finding no place to rest. "And sometimes we'd end up at the same Christmas party or the like, catch up on old times. Maybe make plans to get together."

Had Rebecca not decided earlier that he was obsessed with Bergeron, the addendum would have seemed strange. But now, his probable blurring of reality and desire made perfect sense. It was time to move on. "Are you a witch?"

Fiedler laughed, his reaction sounding more like disdain than amusement. "No, I'm not. And Della isn't either."

"Are you certain about that?" asked Gus, causing the lawyer's scowl to return. "Her daughter and sister think otherwise."

"Lilith might believe in witchcraft, but not Della. Look, if you get close enough to her, you'd find it's a ruse, some leverage she can use with people whose idea of cooperation is to grab theirs first. They're all alpha-males, even the women, so leading them means finding some way to influence them. The paranormal stuff is unique and plausible enough, especially coupled with her success. It gets them to listen and that's all she needs."

"And she told you this?" asked Gus.

"Not in so many words, but it only makes sense. I mean, someone doesn't just become a witch, do they? She never said anything about it in school."

That didn't fit with what Rebecca had read about modern witchcraft, which depicted it more as a worldview or religion. Couldn't someone change their beliefs throughout life? They should ask Bergeron about what led to her later-life conversion if that's what it was.

"Did you suggest that Ms. Bergeron take a blood test when she got to the hospital?" asked Gus.

Rebecca had become pretty good at seeing where Gus was going with his questions, but this one was an exception. It seemed to be puzzling Fiedler, too.

"I really don't remember who suggested it," the lawyer said after a moment.

"You didn't want to see if someone had drugged her?" asked Gus, a touch of skepticism in his tone. "I mean, otherwise, she doesn't have much of a defense."

Fiedler pulled back from the investigator, staring. "Della's defense wasn't my primary concern, Mr. Clements. Her health was. So, yeah, I may have asked for the test to make sure she wasn't in any danger. Any moron would. But, like I said, I don't remember." He released a long breath. "Look, this isn't getting us anywhere. It's a lot more likely that the six of them colluded to kill Sims and frame Della than anything you're asking about."

"Including her daughter?" Rebecca asked.

"Della and Lilith are cut from different cloths."

"What does that mean?" asked Gus.

"If you'd done your job, you'd know," Fiedler snapped in reply. But when his gaze returned to Rebecca, he sighed. "Most of the time

I've known Lilith, she's been a spoiled brat. But I suppose I should ease up. She's paying the price now."

"Because of the stress from her mother being arrested?" asked Rebecca.

"No. That doesn't bother her because Della will never be convicted. Lilith is paying the price of trying to fill her mother's shoes when she can't. She doesn't have the same abilities. She doesn't read the business winds the way Della does, and because of that, she and the business will both suffer. Fortunately, Lilith's pain will be short-lived because soon this mess is going to get cleared up."

Rebecca had exhausted her questions, so she shot Gus a questioning look.

"I've covered everything I have," he said to her.

Rebecca nodded, then delivered her standard "thanks and we'll be in touch" message to Fiedler.

"And I'm glad I came in, too," the lawyer said, surprising Rebecca … until she considered that he was probably being ironic. His next words confirmed that guess.

"I've been disappointed in the direction her trial lawyer is taking, but I thought your company might have a more enlightened approach. So, I'm glad I came in to discover that my faith was misplaced, that you and your partner have no clue. I'm going to need to look into this matter myself."

Rebecca ran down her mental checklist of where he stood in this undertaking. No background in investigation. No background in criminal law. Infatuated with the suspect. It didn't sound like the optimal starting point to her. "Best of luck in that undertaking, Mr. Fiedler. And, if you don't mind me asking, any thoughts as to where you'll begin?"

"Very little. Unlike you, I don't have the benefit of several days looking into the case."

Rebecca doubted that statement. She'd bet he'd thought of little else since it happened. And then, almost as if he was confirming her suspicions, he said, "There's the group conspiracy I mentioned before, but I'm going to start by looking at one of the members, Edward Streeter. Something besides the ceremonial knife killed Sims. Something that no one saw. Streeter's company is working on a directed energy weapon for the military, which could have easily completed an action that Della was only pantomiming."

"Well, like I said, best of luck."

If Fiedler was expecting them to embrace his theory, it didn't show. He nodded, stood, and strode from the office so quickly that Gus never caught up to him before he got to the outer door. When Gus returned, Rebecca said, "So, other than the fact that he's infatuated with Bergeron and would do anything to clear her, you pick up on anything?"

"Just a whole lot of wishful thinking. He wants to come to Bergeron's rescue so badly, he's entertaining ideas like Streeter stealing a military R&D project that's probably classified. He enlists an accomplice to fire it and this person remains hidden throughout the ritual and the aftermath. The weapon produces an incision that the coroner can't distinguish from a knife wound. And, somehow, it also deposits Sims's blood on the blade and Ms. Bergeron's hands. He's thinking with his heart, not his head."

"Or another part of his anatomy," said Rebecca. "But I'm not sure any of this clears him of the crime. It just makes his motivation one of obsession and his outrage toward us and the other lawyer a cover."

"True, but then how'd he kill Sims?"

"The directed energy weapon, of course."

Gus chuckled.

"Say, why'd you ask Fiedler if he'd suggested the blood test?"

"Because some of my theories are getting as farfetched as his." Gus shrugged in response to Rebecca's raised eyebrows. "If Fiedler wanted to make sure Ms. Bergeron was pulled from a social and financial stratosphere where he didn't fit, he'd need the charges to stick ... at least for a while. If she was drugged, they probably wouldn't; she was high on something that blocked out the reality of her actions. But assuming he knew she wasn't a user, he'd request the test, knowing the negative results would keep her under suspicion until he could save her. So, that request implicates him except for the fact that ...."

"Any moron would have asked for one?" Rebecca interjected.

"Yeah, it does seem a bit like common sense, doesn't it," Gus conceded. "But so far, straws are all I see to grasp at."

FRIDAY, OCTOBER 9

9:27 AM, Marte Investigative Services

Rebecca felt like her head was on a swivel. Look down at the documents on her desk. Look up at the clock on the wall. Look out through her open office door to the empty reception area. Then repeat. And again. She wasn't sure why she bothered looking at the desk; little she saw there was registering because her client was nearly a half-hour late and that fact was starting to weigh on her mind.

Had Labadie framed her sister? There were certainly several suspicious omissions in what she'd told her and Gus, but it still seemed almost unbelievable. Unfortunately, almost unbelievable was trending toward less so as the seconds passed. Had she and Gus stumbled across something and, in the process, sent Labadie on the run? Had she guessed they were questioning her motives and rather than continuing her lies, she was halfway to Mexico?

Rebecca's stream of speculation, however, dried up at the sound of the outer door opening. It was Labadie, and she was apologizing even before she cleared the outer area. "Sorry. The morning was a disaster and traffic was the pits. If we can't get finished before your next appointment, we can do lunch. I'll even buy."

Most of Rebecca's tension drained away with the woman's apology and offer. "Thanks, but we should be fine with the time we have. Please, have a seat."

Now, Rebecca just needed to get to the truth, and with that objective coupled with her client's tardiness, she felt justified skipping the small talk. "I'm curious. Why did you suggest David Putnam for background on the coven? At least according to him, he was never much of an insider. And not a believer in witchcraft."

A look that Rebecca couldn't quite place had flashed across Labadie's face when she started the question but was immediately replaced by what appeared to be concentration.

"Well, we talked about how none of the current members, other than Lilith, would meet with you. That leaves past members and there aren't that many. The coven hasn't been around that long. Other than David, I only know of two, both now retired and moved away. I could probably get phone numbers and addresses if you want them, but I'm not sure they'd talk to you either. Too much notoriety and someone might question where they got the money to live so high in retirement."

That seemed reasonable and Rebecca started to say so when Labadie added. "Don't misunderstand. I don't know that anything they did or the coven has done is illegal, but rumors are more than enough for people to start digging." Labadie paused, looking down at the desk, then back up. "And I guess I didn't realize that David's lack of belief in witchcraft would be a problem."

"It's only a problem because he didn't know the members of the coven well. And hold off on the contact information for the other two, although I may ask for it later. New question. You're familiar with your sister's security service?"

"Yes, I've talked to them from time to time."

"Do you think someone from that company might have seen what happened the night of Sims's death?"

Labadie's eyes narrowed. "And his story got ignored by the press because it was the same as all the bigwigs? Yeah, I suppose that's possible." And then, her eyes widened. "I probably should have mentioned them to you?"

"It might have been helpful, but it's not a problem. We'll follow up." Rebecca didn't think it necessary to say they'd already followed up and it was a dead-end. Rather, she left the message as "every detail could be important."

"I doubt any of the guards were that close anyway," Labadie volunteered.

Rebecca nodded. "Why is it that you coordinate with your sister's security service? That seems a little unusual. I mean, wouldn't she want to communicate her concerns directly to them?"

Labadie's brow wrinkled. "I guess I can see why you'd think it's strange, but it's not like Sis has a lot of concerns or they have a lot to report. Mostly, they just tell me about kids joyriding on some of the roads out there or defacing a sign. But why I do it? I guess I just fell into that role."

"How's that?"

Labadie rubbed her forehead a moment. "I suppose it started when she had her first security system installed. In those days, her place was smaller ... a lot smaller." Labadie smiled as if recalling those days with fondness. "The whole installation only took a couple of hours. But Della didn't like being around while they were working, so she asked me to come over.

"Then, later at the big house, it was over a week of work and I covered the install again. I got pretty familiar with the company. Even had them put in a couple of cameras at my place. So, yeah, I meet with them when Della has a concern, although I don't remember when the last time was."

To this point in the talk, Labadie's tone had been light, bordering on confusion. But by the look on her face, Rebecca could tell she was about to turn serious.

"Look, I don't know what you think about my relationship with Della. And I admit, it's not like we're best friends like some sisters. There was just too much difference in our ages growing up. But I don't mind helping her out from time to time, like with the security company. But when Victor was killed, I was a wreck. And now, Goodwin? That's the real reason I was late today. I'm so scared for Della I can hardly think."

If this was an act, Hollywood was missing out on an exceptional talent. "That's completely understandable," said Rebecca soothingly. "These questions are just background, seeing how things work."

"Oh, my God," said Labadie, a hand coming to her throat as she slid forward in her chair. "You think I told the guards to stay back from the ritual so ... so someone could kill Victor." Her eyes glistened with emotion. Her open hand closed to a fist and she pressed it to her lips.

"No, no. Nothing like that," Rebecca assured her quickly. "Those kinds of instructions would get reported by the company sooner or later, and nothing like that has turned up. And we've interviewed the guard closest to the ritual, who described a standard type of surveillance." Rebecca hadn't shared this information earlier to make a point, but the woman's distress more than justified the change in plans. "So, no, I don't think you told the guards to hold back."

Labadie nodded, softly saying, "Good."

"Do you want to take a break, maybe get a drink of water?" Rebecca asked.

Labadie took a deep breath, then sat back a bit in her chair. "No, I'm OK. And besides, it wouldn't do any good until Della's safe."

Rebecca didn't like the idea of continuing; the woman was distraught. But she still didn't have an answer to her primary question. Perhaps the best approach was to be direct and get this over with, like ripping off a bandage. "Has the security company been told to rotate the crews they have onsite?"

"Yes, I asked them to do that."

"Why?"

"That was Della's call. I just passed it along. As to why she wants different guards all the time, you'll need to ask her to be sure, but I'd say she's just very private."

Another dead end. The shuffling of the guards wasn't Labadie trying to keep them from noticing slight changes in the house or subtle differences in Bergeron's behavior—things that would happen over time if someone was getting inside Bergeron's head with drugs or lies. There was a possibility Labadie was lying, of course, but it was slight; the fact was too easy to check. But still, Rebecca made a mental note to ask Bergeron about the arrangement.

"Ms. Harrison mentioned there's a similar arrangement with the other services—the gardeners, maintenance people, cleaners, things like that," said Rebecca.

"Similar?" said Labadie slowly. "Not really. She hires different companies, but that's to help the local businesses. You know, spread the work around. At least, that's what I always thought." Rebecca was about to ask another question when the woman added, "But I don't have anything to do with these other companies. I think some assistant at her office schedules them for a week or a month at a time. But again, Sis can answer that question better than me."

Was Labadie overlooking the obvious or was the effect of "spreading the work" clear only to her? With different companies and short-term contracts, no one team of workers would visit the Bergeron home more than a few times. The effect of rotating guards and changing service companies was largely the same, although to explain that to Labadie would only make her wonder why routine or the lack of it was important.

Like every interview on this case so far, Rebecca felt she was getting nowhere. And now, she was down to her last line of questioning—was Labadie divorcing her husband? By itself, a positive response would mean little except it opened the door for a relationship with Putnam and a possible collaboration between them in Sims's killing.

"My last question is personal and the reason I'm asking is probably not going to be clear. But it's important. It has to do with your relationships." Rebecca had pictured Labadie reacting in many different ways to this topic—indignation, remorse, even confusion. But what she read now in the woman's demeanor seemed to be resolve. She nodded slowly, her mouth drawn in a tight line.

"I knew this would come out sooner or later. I even considered not hiring a PI because of it, but I couldn't take the stress any longer. Look, I wish it had never happened, but it did."

"You wish your marriage had never happened?"

Labadie jerked back like she'd been slapped in the face. "My marriage? No, I'm talking about …. You're interested in my marriage?"

"Actually, now I'm interested in what you were about to say."

The look of resignation returned to Labadie's face. "I was talking about an affair with David Putnam … if you can call it an affair." She sighed. "As for my marriage, it's over. We're getting a divorce."

Labadie released a long sigh, then nodded as if she'd made up her mind about something. "Ron, my husband, was cheating on me, and I saw a chance to make him jealous at one of his office get-togethers. But I got a little drunk, and David and I ended up in bed."

"Is it still going on?"

Labadie opened her mouth but then closed it again and pursed her lips. Finally, she said, "You don't exactly break anything off with David because, in his mind, there's nothing to break. I could call him now, and he'd act like we saw each other yesterday, not a month ago." She sighed again. "I can't believe I'm saying this, but frankly, some days meaningless sex doesn't sound that bad."

Rebecca had acted on that impulse from time to time as well, and at least once with a guy who wanted a future while she just wanted the night. She had felt bad the next morning and wondered if waking up next to your sister's former lover might carry some of the same type of guilt … or worse. She'd never know; she had no sisters. But whatever empathy Rebecca gained from the insight was overtaken by what the admission implied. It made the possibility that she and Putnam were working together to frame Bergeron somewhat more plausible. Sure, the change was from nearly impossible to extremely difficult to believe—meaningless sex wasn't much of a motivation for murder. But it was a shift nonetheless.

"Where did this happen?" asked Rebecca.

Labadie turned red. "It's been more than once. Both at my place and his."

The plausibility that Labadie and Putnam were co-conspirators inched microscopically higher. Rebecca was probably hoping for too much, but she had to ask even if these questions were becoming incredibly invasive. "Ever meet at your sister's house?"

"Eww, that's sick," said Labadie, her nose wrinkling. "It's bad enough that David's been with Della but to use her bed? No way."

Yep, too much, she thought. "Do you keep any information about your sister in your home?"

"You mean like stuff on the security company?"

"Yes, things like that."

Labadie pursed her lips for a moment. "Well, there's lots of things like pictures and a few clippings from papers, but I'd guess you aren't interested in those."

"Probably not," said Rebecca.

Labadie nodded. "I don't have anything like passwords or codes for gates or doors. The guards always know when I'm coming and they let me on the grounds. And I have a key for the front door, but it's always with me."

Even when you sleep, thought Rebecca, but she didn't ask. She knew the answer.

"I do have some notes on calls to the security company—some of the work they did for me and some for Della. But most of that is old. I may have even deleted the file. And besides, it was on my computer and it's got a password."

Rebecca considered asking how she selected and managed her passwords but decided it was like asking about the door key—better just to assume Putnam had them if he wanted them.

Having covered all of her questions, Rebecca thanked Labadie for her time. As they approached the front door, Labadie stopped and turned to her. "You don't really think David had something to do with Victor's death, do you? I mean, Della's broken up by it, but as far as I know, he's never even called with condolences. He doesn't have any interest in getting back with my sister."

The comment struck Rebecca as a guilty conscience talking—Labadie wouldn't want to believe she was coming between her sister and a man she had known first. "I'm sure you're right," said Rebecca. "Their relationship is over."

Rebecca, however, wasn't just easing the woman's mind. She meant it. The idea that Putnam felt himself to be a jilted lover had lost all credibility in her mind. He wouldn't work to gain any woman's adoration, at least at this point in his life. But what he might do for money? Well, that was a different question entirely.

10:11 AM, A Farmhouse in Western Kansas

Nicole heard movement in Maggie's office, and she looked up from her book. The door was still closed; mother and son were still busy in their latest session. Nicole would give almost anything to know what was going on in there.

Lately, she had noticed striking similarities between Justin's stories about the pandemic and those Maggie told. In fact, their tales matched too well, and Nicole had started wondering if Justin's recollections were actually his.

Nicole had heard about false memories, running across the concept occasionally in the news or a novel. But mostly, she recalled Sam talking about them. He'd mentioned how things like leading questions, subtle suggestions, or even the adjectives used in a question could influence how someone recalled an event. And, somewhat surprising to her, he'd used the word "reconstruct" to describe what happened during recall. Memories were rebuilt from bits and pieces of sensory information from the original event as well as from the thoughts and feelings associated later at every retelling. Memories were, in a sense, Frankenstein monsters—a collection of parts from the past, from now, and from everything in between.

Those ideas certainly fit with one story she'd read several years ago. According to it, professional therapists who were trying to help adults recover memories of childhood abuse had, unintentionally and unfortunately, created memories for events that had never occurred. And to Nicole, one of the most striking features of these cases was how strongly the adults believed in the falsehood. Given objective proof that the abuse had never occurred, these individuals would ignore or deny it. They'd argue it had to have happened because they "remembered it like it was yesterday."

To her growing disquiet, Justin often used those exact words when recounting what he had recovered during a session with his mother. He now remembered picking up Nicole by the side of the road, the children he'd gone to school with, a past home, all like they had happened yesterday.

Nicole would have concluded Maggie was creating false memories in Justin except for one thing. When she thought about her own time with the woman, there were none of the telltale signs that Sam had mentioned.

In a typical session, she would sit in front of the old stereoscope, put her chin on the rest, and look at a picture. Then she would talk about it—what it showed or who it was. If Maggie was placing thoughts in her mind during these talks, Nicole didn't see how. The woman never said anything besides, "Tell me what you see." There were no leading questions. No elaborations. No comparisons to similar settings. With Maggie staying quiet, how could the source of anything she said or felt be anything other than herself?

And then occasionally, there was separate evidence for something that she or Justin had recalled. These confirmations were either falsehoods that Maggie had carefully crafted over long periods or they were exactly what they seemed—verification of a memory. For example, Maggie had a few photographs of Justin's classmates when he was in school. Those could be counterfeit, of course, but they appeared to be old. So, unless Maggie had foreseen the need for these pictures to remove Nicole's lingering doubts and she had artificially aged them, Justin's immediate recall of a new face wasn't a false memory. It was real.

Justin had also recalled several people dying in a large room of an older building, and he had even described the structure to Nicole in considerable detail. She figured that the room was a makeshift ward set up to treat people with the virus and didn't think any more about it. But then, about a week ago, she was burning some clothes that were beyond repair and found a picture in the inner pocket of an old jacket. It was the building Justin had described. And when Nicole showed him the picture, he said, "I know that place. That's where those people died."

Now, for Maggie to create this fake verification of Justin's memory, it would have been necessary for her to find a picture of the building, plant it in an old jacket, and hope that Nicole found it before she pitched the garment into the fire. No one would go to those lengths without some assurance of success. The deaths were real.

This particular memory had become painful for Justin, so he and his mother were devoting this morning's session to recalling more about it. Nicole was still of the opinion that the room was a ward of sick people, and if it was, the question in her mind became, why was he there? Shouldn't those with the virus be in quarantine?

The door to Maggie's office opened, and Justin shuffled out, head down, with Maggie following.

"Sorry, son. I know that was a rough one, but you're getting there."

He turned to his mother, looked up a moment, then dropped his gaze again. "Yeah, I guess."

Maggie put her hand on his shoulder and squeezed it softly. She returned to her office, closing the door behind her.

"More about the pandemic?" Nicole asked softly.

"The same as before. Just more of it."

"The room with the bodies?" Justin was upset and Nicole hated to ask, but her need to understand what had happened to her world hadn't weakened. If anything, it seemed to grow each day.

"Yeah, same room except this time they were scattered around a bunch of overturned tables and chairs. And I could hear them moaning. And the blood, it was everywhere."

"Blood? From the virus?"

"Yeah." He paused a moment. "Sort of, I guess. I didn't know what suicide was, but Mom explained it. Some woman was shooting them, but then she put the gun in her mouth."

"Justin, that's awful."

Nicole wanted to comfort the young man, hug him, but she also wanted to avoid giving him the wrong impression and that objective was proving elusive. Justin seemed to take everything as an overture for intimacy. And even when she did nothing, he found a way to make it sexual. She had spoken to Maggie about his increasing aggressiveness, but if the mother had spoken to her son, the message wasn't getting through. So, Nicole kept her distance.

"I think they asked for it," said Justin after a few more moments studying the floor. "To die, I mean."

"You heard them ask to be killed?"

"No. Well, maybe. I can't remember. But they were just talking at first, this woman and the others. It was only when she started shooting that they ran."

A mass suicide to escape the pandemic? Nicole had never heard of anything like that before, but it seemed possible given the symptoms of the virus—open sores at first, then massive internal bleeding that left bodies black and blue. Some of the infected drown in their own blood; others perished from widespread organ failure. It was difficult for Nicole to imagine surrendering to a bullet before she was defeated by the illness, but then, she couldn't recall the pain from her brush with it. If it was painful enough, anyone would beg for the end.

"Justin, do you remember the first time you thought about these people?"

He stared at her a moment rubbing his chin. "A long time ago. Before we got here. Even before we found you. Why?"

"No reason. Just curious," she said, though her thought was, it all fits. Of course, recalling that he'd recalled it earlier could be a false memory, too, but at some point, some things had to be accepted as truth. And she'd reached that point in this case.

Maggie's door opened again. "Nicole, ready for you."

"I'm not feeling very well. Do you mind if we skip today's session?" Nicole didn't need to stretch the truth; she didn't feel well. Justin's comments had left her stomach in a knot.

"You're not getting sick, are you?"

"No, I don't think so." Nicole looked over her shoulder, finding Justin shuffling off to his room. "It's just everything that Justin's been telling me."

"Yes, it's horrible. This virus is a ruthless killer without mercy. That's why it's so important for the two of you to be careful." Maggie paused and released a long breath. "If you don't feel up to today's session, that's OK. It's just that Justin mentioned you've been talking a lot about someone named Sam, and I thought we could devote today's work toward recalling something about him."

Maggie was right. She had been talking about Sam a lot and thinking about him even more, though her memories of him were vague. But here was a chance to correct that.

"You know, Maggie, I'm feeling better. Let's do it."

10:56 AM, The Della Bergeron Residence

"Rebecca Marte to see Ms. Bergeron."

"You're expected," replied the guard at the front gate to the Bergeron property. "Just follow the main road. Parking's to the left of the building. Your partner, Detective Clements, is already there."

"Thanks." Rebecca rolled up the window against the breeze that was having trouble making it out of the forties and started up the drive. The grounds were immaculately maintained. The dark brown of the road's pebbled surface was separated from the reds and golds of the fallen leaves on the shoulder by a crisp white line. It looked like it had been painted yesterday. Beyond the shoulders on each side rose a stand of mature trees, becoming more skeletal as winter approached. It would be a bit eerie at night, she thought, until she noticed the street lamps, placed and colored to blend in with the surroundings. Little here, day or night, had been left to the whims of nature.

After a moment, she pulled into a clearing. A knoll with the residence atop was centered in the space. The two-and-a-half-story building was stately, although modest for someone of Bergeron's wealth and position. Bow windows on one side and a large picture window on the other flanked a massive oak door with a set of frosted-glass sidelights. The pattern was repeated on the second floor, except that a stained-glass window replaced the door. The structure was topped with a mansard roof and dormers for the rooms making up the half story. Though large—perhaps 3,000 to 4,000 square feet Rebecca guessed—it was a third the size of many of the homes built near Forest Park for the 1904 World's Fair. And frankly, she'd expected one of those behemoths.

Rebecca followed the drive past the front of the building to a porte-cochere on the left. Through it, she found the parking area and Gus. He exited his car as Rebecca parked and left hers. "Hey there, old man," she said, using her familiar greeting.

"Morning. So, how'd it go with Ms. Labadie?"

It was one of the few times Gus hadn't returned her greeting in kind, favoring comebacks such as "Not too old to kick your butt." But she was unhappy with their progress on this case, so it stood to reason that Gus would be, too. He wanted to get on with business.

She quickly reviewed the Labadie interview as they walked to the home's front door, describing how their client had reasonable explanations for everything that had bothered them save one. "And last, she confirmed that she and her husband are getting a divorce. And she also volunteered that she had an affair with none other than David Putnam. Maybe she thinks it's love and conspired with him to frame Bergeron, but personally, it sounded like it was just sex. Just a friends-with-benefits kind of thing."

"Ongoing?" asked Gus.

"Not for the last month or so, but she implied it could happen again."

"You're right. That doesn't sound like Labadie killed out of blind infatuation."

They had reached the front door and Rebecca rang the bell. After a few moments, the door opened, revealing Della Bergeron. Rebecca was surprised but thought she covered it well as she made the introductions. Gus, however, seemed less concerned about hiding his reaction.

"I didn't expect you to answer the door," he said after the customary, "nice to meet you" greeting. "If for no other reason, it'd be a hike from the top floor."

"It would be, but then, the front gate calls when anyone arrives. I have plenty of time to get to the front, check the video monitor, and answer."

"But no house staff to handle that for you?" asked Gus.

Rebecca took the opportunity to study the door and the structure around it while they talked. If there was a camera hidden there, it was the work of a master craftsman. She didn't see anything that looked like it came from this century.

"No, no house staff. I prefer the quiet," said Bergeron, then turned to Rebecca. "It's the dark circle in the egg-and-dart molding on either side of the door."

Rebecca started, not knowing when the woman had caught her looking. "Very well disguised."

"It is," replied Bergeron. "Please come in and we can get started."

The front door opened onto a center hall. There were pocket doors on each side; only the set on the left was open. Past these doors stood two columns, one on each side, and then another set of doors, also closed. At the end of the hall rose a grand staircase leading to a landing featuring three large stained-glass windows. Rebecca wondered how long it would take her to get used to living in this museum. But when Bergeron led them into the parlor on the left, seating them in front of a lazily burning fire, she decided it wouldn't take that long. The room was quite cozy.

"First, just to set the record straight, I'm not really in favor of Rowena paying you to look into my case. Between the police and the investigators my trial lawyer has retained, I believe I'm in good hands. That's not to say anything disparaging about your services, of course."

"Of course," replied Rebecca. "Your sister's just worried about you—normal for siblings who are close." Rebecca hoped the woman would take the statement as an opportunity to discuss their relationship so she wouldn't have to find another way to ask. Fortunately, she did.

"Comfortable with each other might be a better description than close for Rowena and me. I'm considerably older, and I've been extremely busy with my career since college. But she's always been there for me, and I try to return the favor when I can. It's just that in the case of Victor's death, retaining you seems something of an overreaction."

That coincided with Labadie's description of their relationship, and Rebecca checked that topic off her mental list. And Bergeron's protestation that the investigation was unnecessary? Well, that seemed little more than pro forma to her, but apparently Gus thought otherwise.

"We've been on this case less than a week, but even after that short time, I'm not sure your sister is overreacting. There's no doubt about the events of that night, and frankly, no one has found any extenuating circumstances. Or at least none that your average jury member would buy. That seems like something to be concerned about."

It was as if Gus had decided his "bad-cop" role was needed or at least his unvarnished-opinion role. Bergeron, however, seemed unfazed, perhaps even amused by Gus's evaluation; a slight smile seemed to be playing at the corners of her mouth as she held him in a long gaze.

"You phrased it quite well, Mr. Clements, and not by accident, I imagine. No, the average citizen wouldn't understand."

"Wouldn't understand that you were manipulated by ... another witch?" asked Rebecca.

"Correct, Ms. Marte. And like many, you, too, are finding this a difficult concept to accept."

Her hesitation had given her away. That Bergeron was manipulated by someone was still on their list of possible avenues of investigation. It was just that Rebecca wanted to exhaust all of the non-supernatural influences first.

"Somewhat difficult, I suppose," Rebecca admitted. "And I understand you've never been influenced by another witch before or since?"

"Not exactly," Bergeron replied. "The papers didn't get that quite right. What I said was, I have no evidence of it happening before, but perhaps it has. I imagine you've had the experience of wondering if you've dozed off but weren't sure unless you happened to notice the time."

"Sure."

"The same sort of thing applies to that night. I wouldn't have known anything happened had I not come to my senses and seen the knife in my hands, the blood ... the blood on its blade." For the first time, Bergeron's voice faltered. During this frustrating case, it was easy to forget that she had lost a man she cared for, perhaps even loved.

Rebecca was about to offer condolences when Gus spoke.

"How far away do you think this other witch was to have affected you?"

His matter-of-fact tone came as a surprise. Had Gus missed the woman's loss of composure? That wasn't like him. Or did he think it was all an act?

"Unfortunately, a practice like that is far outside my experience, so I have little confidence in any answer. But I'd guess the witch was close. Close enough to look into my eyes, to share passions."

Could this be a lead? Rebecca was having trouble deciding. She wasn't any closer to believing in the supernatural, but Bergeron did. And during her research, Rebecca had found references to European folk healers using humanoid figures—something like voodoo dolls—to battle witches as recently as the early 20th century. If Bergeron believed another witch had something like that on her, was it possible she would surrender to his or her suggestions? If so, would this mental pressure affect Bergeron differently than threats of physical harm? And how was this mental persuasion delivered? Never before had Rebecca felt so ill-equipped to follow a lead, assuming this was one.

Maybe Gus could follow up? He seemed more attuned to these notions. And yet, passing it off to him didn't feel right. It was her company, her responsibility. She just needed a little more background. It was unfortunate Doc wasn't around; he'd be able to shed some light on this power-of-suggestion stuff. Maybe psychologists didn't study voodoo dolls, but they looked at things like hypnosis or the effect of a placebo, right? So, until Rebecca could have a talk with Doc, she'd muddle through.

Gus must have thought he'd turned the interview back to her because when Rebecca broke free of her thoughts, she found him and Bergeron looking at her. "Sorry. I was just wondering ... wondering if this witch who was influencing you could have been one of the coven?"

"Absolutely not. They are my family. All of them, not just Lilith. None of them would do something like that to me. If you want to look into it, check the guards. Or someone hiding nearby. I've mentioned this possibility to the police and my lawyer, but I don't think they've done much."

"Perhaps their reluctance is because initially, you said you had no memory of the ceremony. It's only been later that you mentioned that another witch was controlling you."

Bergeron regarded Rebecca for a long moment. "You did some reckless things growing up. Cars, boys, alcohol, maybe drugs."

It wasn't a question and it was accurate. But then, Rebecca knew it wasn't much of a deductive leap either. She might have been drawn into the FBI and left for a career as a PI after growing up as a wallflower, but that wasn't very likely. "No drugs," she said simply.

"Now, pick one of those risky acts and imagine what it would be like if the memory of it was gone but the emotion remained."

"You felt exhilarated?" asked Rebecca. She knew Bergeron didn't mean excited, but the way the woman was poking around in her past irritated her. That reaction, however, was unprofessional; she needed to push the pettiness aside.

"No, I felt crushed by warring emotions—shock, horror, pain. But the point is, even if the memory of the act is gone, the emotion may stay. And as my initial feelings dissipated, they left something behind, something I had trouble admitting even to myself. It was a feeling of omnipotence, of destiny waiting, and the feeling wasn't mine."

"And you've told your lawyer this?" asked Rebecca.

"Yes. He said I shouldn't trust my memory of a traumatic event, but he's mostly worried because it makes me look insane, overtaken by delusions of power over life and death. And he's not planning on an insanity defense. In my case, there's no precipitating factor and no history of mental issues before or since that would help validate the plea."

Bergeron knew exactly why a temporary insanity plea had little chance in her case. Apparently, as Labadie had claimed, she and her lawyer had discussed it and it had been dropped. That covered the issue for Rebecca, but she glanced at her partner to see if he had more.

"The police have taken a new interest in you after Nicholas Goodwin was killed," he said. "Is there any reason they should?"

Rebecca was somewhat surprised by the sudden shift in topics. Surely, Gus had more questions about the night Sims had died. She knew she did.

"Me involved with Nicholas's death?" Bergeron seemed to be struggling with the change in topics, too. Was that Gus's intention? Keep abruptly shifting the interview among different events, hoping that the lies wouldn't come to mind as quickly as the truth? That tactic was more appropriate for questioning a suspect, but then, in some sense, she was. Rebecca would have to ask him later what his thinking had been.

"No, Mr. Clements. I had nothing to do with Nicholas Goodwin's death. The police are interested because I'm a murder suspect, he was in the coven, and unfortunately, I was in his neighborhood around the time of his death. I bought gas about a half-mile from Nicholas's home. Gas for my car, I should point out. Not the one that hit him."

"You weren't driven to the gas station?" asked Gus.

Bergeron's brow wrinkled. "I am quite well off now, but it hasn't always been the case, even somewhat recently. I have trouble having everything done for me."

"Just topping off the tank or were you going somewhere?" asked Rebecca.

Before the woman could answer, Rebecca heard the soft buzzing of a phone. Bergeron pulled it from a pocket and checked the display. "Sorry, but I need to answer this."

She took a couple of steps, then turned, apparently more to reduce the volume of her voice than to give her privacy. After, "Hello, Mateo," Rebecca could make little sense of the conversation other than the fact that the man wanted to meet her and soon.

When the call was over, Bergeron returned to the seating area. "Mateo Sanchez, the company's Chief Financial Officer. Have you met him?"

"No, we haven't," replied Rebecca, after seeing Gus's shake of the head. "Not a problem, I hope?"

"He didn't want to get into it on the phone, but it was important enough to him that we're getting together tomorrow. And as a family man, his weekends are usually sacrosanct."

"Mr. Sanchez is coming to you with business problems?" asked Gus.

"He's old school, but I'll call in a few others. Not much reason for a meeting with someone who can't do anything. Me, I mean." Her wistful tone was accompanied by a slight shrug of her shoulders.

"Anyway, back to where I was going when I drove through Nicholas's neighborhood. I'd guess you'd say, I was returning to the scene of the crime. And Nicholas's neighborhood is the quickest way to the interstate."

"You're talking about the farm near Ste. Genevieve?" asked Gus.

Bergeron nodded.

"And did you sense anything?"

"No, I didn't ... well, other than the pall of death, which is even stronger. But I'm not surprised. The place has been torn apart, first by the police and then by my lawyer's investigators."

"Did Mr. Goodwin hold a place of particular importance in the coven?" asked Gus.

"No."

"In your business or personal life?"

"No, neither. As a coven member, he was family. Outside of it, he was a trusted business associate, but no more than the others."

"One possibility, of course, is that both killings are designed to punish you in some way," said Rebecca. "You're being forced to watch as those you value as associates and close friends are being murdered? Do you know of anyone who would be motivated to do that?"

"That possibility has not been lost on me, and I've told family and friends—Lilith, Tony, Rowena—to be careful. But, no, I can't think of anyone who would hold a grudge against me that's worthy of murder, and I've given it a lot of thought. In the end, I've decided that Nicholas's death was nothing more than a coincidence, an unfortunate accident made suspicious because of who he was and where he was killed."

"That's possible," admitted Rebecca. She didn't believe in the dictum that there was no such thing as a coincidence in criminal investigations. Chance occurrences happened on a case as often as anywhere else in life. Rather, to her, it was the odds she had to accept that pushed something from a coincidence toward a staged criminal act.

A sideways glance at Gus told her that he had no follow-up questions, so she moved on. "Back to the night of the coven gathering, you had a security service patrolling the area?"

"I did. If word got out, we'd be interrupted by the curious. And if the identity of the witches in our coven was known, we'd be overrun by the media."

"My partner has talked to some of the people who work for that service, and apparently, they were told they shouldn't get too close."

"Yes, Ms. Marte, for the same reason I mentioned before. The curious have no place in a coven ceremony."

"Sure. I also understand that the security company is supposed to change the personnel they assign to each gathering?"

"That's correct as well, although eventually, there has to be some repetition. They only have so many people."

"Who came up with that requirement?"

"I did, but it's not just the security service. It's all of the staff—housekeeping, grounds maintenance, drivers, everyone."

"Isn't that somewhat inefficient?" replied Rebecca. "You'd have to keep repeating the same instructions over and over. Why go to that trouble?"

Bergeron shrugged as if the practice was common. "If the job changes, these companies would need new guidance anyway. And if not, which is the norm, they know the routine. They just have to instruct their people. That said, I realize there is some additional effort, but I like my downtime. I have to deal with people constantly at work. I don't want to extend that obligation to home. With people rotating through my personal space, they aren't offended by the lack of small talk, and I don't feel guilty not making it."

The woman's reply made sense, but it was a bit too smooth for Rebecca. Even her facial expressions seemed something less than spontaneous as if she had rehearsed them in front of a mirror. Additionally, it didn't match what both Labadie and Harrison had told her—that Bergeron was something of a loner at work.

Assuming the sister's and the daughter's statements were closer to the truth, Bergeron still had personal relationships to offset her detachment at the office and around her home. Rebecca knew of four over the last 25 years or so—Lowell Harrison, Tony Fiedler, David Putnam, and Victor Sims. But other than Sims, the associations appeared largely ... how would she describe them? Superficial? A matter of convenience? Rebecca wasn't sure why the woman's sociability was important, but somehow, her thoughts kept coming back to it.

"One of your past coven members was David Putnam, correct?"

"You know he was. You've talked to him." Rebecca was certain that mind-reading wasn't involved in this statement, and Bergeron confirmed it. "Rowena mentioned she'd given you his name and that you'd met with him. So, what do you want to know about David?"

"Besides being a witch in your coven ...."

"Sorry to interrupt, but David's not a witch. I did bring him along a few times, but he never saw the way."

"Right, I believe he told me that," replied Rebecca. "When you were mentioning the people you'd warned about possible danger, you didn't mention him."

"No, I didn't mention him because I can't imagine he's in harm's way."

"But, like Mr. Sims, you were close to him for what, a couple of years?"

"It's not the same." For only the second time in the interview, emotion crept into Bergeron's tone. But unlike the crack in her composure earlier, this was a slip in her patience. She sighed deeply. "True, David and I went out from time to time, and I liked him. But I liked him because he knew what he wanted and didn't bother hiding it. And, frankly, when his desires lined up with mine ...." She completed the statement by holding out both hands and giving a half tilt of her head.

Rebecca wondered if Bergeron knew her sister currently had a similar no-strings relationship with the man? If she did and had no problem with it, it further bolstered the idea that she maintained a considerable emotional distance from others. On the other hand, if Bergeron didn't know about them, Rebecca didn't want to be the one to break the news. She decided to drop the line of questioning when the woman said, "Of course, someone else in the family may have warned David."

Did she just admit .... But Rebecca's thought got no further as the woman said, "Yes, I know they go out. Rowena asked me if it was all right ... although I think it was probably after their first tryst."

"OK," said Rebecca, although after the fact she realized the response was hardly appropriate. "Let me check my notes, see if there was anything else I wanted to ask."

She knew there was nothing there, but the request provided cover and a moment to think. All told, she wasn't imagining the wall Bergeron had built around herself professionally and personally. But why? And how had Sims been able to breach it? Or was her connection with him no different than her relationships with the rest? Perhaps all the men in her life served a purpose, just not one of a lasting connection?

On the other hand, if her association with Sims was different, did its purpose have to be of her design? Perhaps he had wanted to die and somehow, he had manipulated her into doing the deed?

Rebecca knew better than to accept any of these hypotheses prematurely and, as a result, bias what she found and how she interpreted it. But as suggestions for lines of inquiry, the possibilities she and Gus generated were usually quite helpful. Unfortunately, this time was different. When she considered all her guesses dispassionately, they were somewhat absurd.

She glanced at Gus, seeing if he had more to cover, but failed to make eye contact. "I think I've covered all my questions. Gus, anything to ask?"

"No, I think I'm good."

"In that case, Ms. Bergeron, I'd like to thank you for your time and your candor in our talk."

"My pleasure." The trio stood and started for the front door.

As they walked, Bergeron said, "You'll probably find this hard to accept, Ms. Marte, but the answer you seek will be closer to the supernatural than you expect."

Rebecca cast a sideways glance, but the woman was facing straight ahead, denying her of any chance to read her expression. Was she serious? Finally, Rebecca said, "I've been surprised before."

Then, Bergeron turned to Gus and without breaking stride said, "Unfortunately, the weight on you will be difficult to shed, but don't give up on the power of the positive."

"I won't," he said.

They stepped outside and Bergeron closed the door.

After walking a few yards from the house, Rebecca said softly, "What the heck was that about, that power of the positive stuff there at the end?"

Gus stopped and turned toward her. "All right if we talk about it later? I really need to be somewhere else."

"Sure. At the office yet today?"

"Say 2:00?"

"OK," Rebecca said, but he'd already turned and was halfway to his car.

2:02 PM, Marte Investigative Services

After the Bergeron interview, Rebecca had picked up a sandwich at a local sub shop. She let the lettuce on it wilt as she tapped a pencil on the top of her desk. Something about the Bergeron interview wasn't right. Unfortunately, she couldn't even isolate the source of her unease.

She knew she had felt out of her element. But now, sitting in her office, she couldn't decide why. At the highest level, the principles for this interview were the same as any other. Collect information along the possible lines of inquiry. Verify it to the extent practical. Don't force these elemental facts into a theory, but rather, wait for one to emerge. Hadn't she been doing that? Of course, it didn't help that the emerging pattern might involve dragonwort and eye of newt. She might not even recognize a pattern when she saw it.

Then, there was the whole mind-reading thing. Perhaps Putnam's disquiet had put her imagination into overdrive, but she didn't think so. She'd felt Bergeron's words stir up her past and dissect her present. And if she could do that, was there any truth in her prediction—that the answer she sought would be closer to the supernatural than she expected? Surely, that was rubbish. After all, she had recognized some of the tells that the witch had used to read between the lines. Yes, Bergeron was good at reading people but probably no better than Gus.

And what the hell had been going on with Gus during and after the interview? Raising the question of Goodwin's killing when they had been talking about Sims and the coven ritual? Gus, however, always had a reason for what he did, so she had reserved judgment. But now, in hindsight, she could find none. The interview had been meandering and disjointed. And cues that Gus would have normally noticed—her questioning glances, Bergeron's slip in composure— seemed to have been missed entirely.

At least she wouldn't have to wait long for an answer to these last questions; she'd heard the outer door open. After a moment, Gus appeared at her doorway.

"You need to do something about your reception area. You have no idea who's coming in."

"Sure, I do," Rebecca responded. "It'll be a bill collector or someone lost in the building. On a very rare occasion, it'll be a client."

Gus frowned. "It's not funny, Rebecca. You need to be more vigilant in this line of work."

"OK ... sure," she said slowly, wondering what had brought his protective instincts to the fore. Was he feeling threatened by the witches? That would certainly explain the preoccupation. "You know, I got this place because it was cheap and I figured—make that, I hoped—that the business would grow into it. But if it would make you feel better, I'll move my desk so I have a direct line of sight to the door."

"Better," said Gus, the frown lessening but not disappearing. "What do you think about putting a lock on the outer door, so you have to buzz people in?"

That crossed her frustration threshold. "What is going on? We both worked on cases in the FBI with characters a lot more unsavory than any of these witches and wannabes. Why all the concern now?"

Gus walked slowly over to the desk and sat in the chair beside it. "It's not this case. In the FBI, we had months working together, but since leaving, we've never had much time to talk about what's different. What you need to do differently."

Rebecca had never felt she had caught Gus in a lie … until now. This wasn't the truth, or at least, it wasn't all of it. But she wasn't going to push him. She'd let the story come out when he was ready.

"I've been thinking about a motion-activated camera in the hallway. That work for you?"

"Sure. And couple it with a lock you can open from your desk and it's even better."

"I'll look into it," Rebecca promised with a half-smile. "So, the talk with Bergeron. It was a little freaky the way she kept answering my questions before I asked them. You get that feeling?"

"Not really."

Another half-truth, thought Rebecca.

"Not much, anyway," Gus amended after a moment.

Patience wasn't Rebecca's forte, and besides, dancing around the truth wasn't going to solve this case. So much for letting the story come out when he was ready. "Gus, what is going on?"

"What do you mean?"

"It's like you're not tuning in. I usually follow your lines of inquiry, and it amazes me how well you follow mine, jump in and help when I need it. But not so much this morning."

"Was it that bad?" asked Gus, but then he didn't wait for an answer. "I guess I should let you know, you being the boss and all." He paused several moments. "I was at my doctor's this morning, Sorry, but this will be our last case together."

10:39 PM, Rebecca's Apartment

"Hello, Agent Marte," came Doc's voice from her phone.

Rebecca had given up reminding him that she was no longer an FBI agent. He knew the fact. He would tell you as much if you asked. But in his mind, her identity was linked inextricably to the days before the kidnapping. And the thought that he might use Becca, the nickname she reserved for close friends and had mentioned to him, was beyond her imaginings. Perhaps that would change if his fiancée was found, but that might never happen.

She leaned back on her living room sofa, pulling a light blanket over her legs. Her thermostat had already adjusted the temperature for sleeping and she was a little cold. "I'm sorry to bother you so late," she started, just to hear a chuckle. "Or maybe it's not. Where are you anyway?"

"Nevada, but not for long. And, yes, it's only a little after 8:30 here."

"Nevada? Weren't you just in Colorado?"

"Gotta go where the evidence takes me." It was a platitude she'd heard often during his search, but this time, it lacked his customary enthusiasm. She didn't have to wonder why for long. "This trip, however, has been a complete waste of time. I thought you might be calling to see if you could bail me out of jail."

"What? You need to back up. You were in jail?"

"Just a misunderstanding," Doc said quickly. "I thought I was on to something, but the local police took exception to how I checked it out. Everything's straightened out now, and I was just walking back to my car to start the drive back to Colorado. I keep coming back to the eastern part of the state or western Nebraska or Kansas. Maybe the panhandle of Oklahoma or the northeast corner of New Mexico. You see ...." His voice trailed off.

"Sorry," Doc said after a moment, his voice still low. "It's OK to obsess in my mind, but I need to give my few remaining friends a break. What's up?"

His question was the perfect segue to what she wanted to discuss, but another word he'd used had caught her attention. "Is it OK for you to obsess?"

The sound of a sigh came across the air. "Obsess was probably the wrong word," he said softly.

Rebecca paused, considering her words carefully. "I just mean, maybe you'd make better progress if you took a break, came at it with a fresh perspective."

Doc was silent for several moments, then spoke again in the same soft voice. "I don't know how many times I've said to myself, 'Nicole isn't getting a break from her captors. She's imprisoned, maybe hurt, maybe even being tortured. Why should I get a break?' But during the forced idleness of a night and day in jail, I had a lot of time to think. The whole trip to Nevada was doomed before it started. I can see that now. And, unfortunately, the same is true of a lot I was doing in Colorado. I'm exhausted and I'm making bad calls."

It was the first dispassionate assessment Rebecca had heard in the last six months from a man whose life had been dominated by calm rationality when she had known him before. She had thought long about what she wanted to say when this happened, but now, she hesitated. This could go wrong in so many ways. "There might be a better way to help Nicole."

"Like getting her picture on cartons of milk?" His words were clipped by bitterness.

It wasn't going to be easy, and Rebecca found herself releasing a long breath of her own. "I think milk cartons are mostly for missing children, but, yeah, something like that."

The silence she received in reply was disconcerting, but now that she'd started, there was no point leaving her suggestion half made.

"Your old boss at Ruger–Phillips, Ken? He's called me a couple of times, wondering what's happened to you. If you ask, I'm almost positive you can get your old job back. That would give you a home base where you can plan your effort, keep the case in the public's eye, maybe even hire private investigators to run down some of the leads. And you've got weekends for your searches. I could help."

It was a matter of several more seconds before Doc spoke. "Nicole's folks are already doing a lot of that but ... but maybe you're right. Maybe changing my approach could help."

Rebecca felt some of the tension drain from her shoulders, reminding her that she rarely experienced the proverbial lifting of "the weight of the world." Through high school and most of college, she'd hardly given a thought to anything beyond getting as much enjoyment out of life as possible. Her junior year in college, she entered the criminal justice program, joking that she had because if she wasn't going to chase criminals, she'd probably end up one. Interestingly, she found that the quip wasn't that unique in the department; several of her fellow students said similar things, making her wonder if there was an element of truth in it? But whatever the reason, the saying entertained her friends and set a path for her future.

Once on that path, Rebecca had been serious about it. She wanted to do well in school. She wanted to do even better in the FBI. When she started her own business, she reached an even higher level of commitment. And so far, that dedication had paid off in all regards save one—how her last case at the FBI had ended. It had put this man on a downward spiral. He seemed to have veered from that trajectory, however, with this reassessment of his strategy, and she welcomed the warmth she felt as a result.

"I'll need to tie up a few loose ends in Colorado, collect all my stuff. But I can probably be back in St. Louis in a week or so, start setting up shop."

"You want me to be on the lookout for a place you could rent around here?"

Her phone was silent again for a moment.

"I better make sure I have a job first. And what they're willing to pay me if I do."

But as surely as Rebecca knew her name, she was sure that wasn't what had caused his hesitation. That delay had come because of the question, how far from his and Veles's old haunts was far enough? Her neighborhood was probably five miles from where they had lived in the Central West End, but maybe that was too close.

"So, if you weren't calling to bail me out of jail," Doc continued, "why did you call?"

With his question, the tension that had melted away came back to Rebecca as grief. "It's Gus." She spoke so softly she could barely hear herself. She cleared her throat. "He never said anything to me, but he was diagnosed with pancreatic cancer. He got the initial results about a week ago but wanted a second opinion. That came this morning ... and it's bad. It's spread to his lungs and liver."

"Rebecca, I'm so sorry. Is there any chance it can be treated?"

"I guess there are some treatments that might slow it down, but he's not interested. He calls them a 'painful delay to the inevitable,' so he's just going to take pain meds. He says ...."

Rebecca told herself she wasn't going to break down, but it was no use. The words caught in her throat. She took a shaky breath, then continued. "He says he wants to die at home with as much dignity as possible."

Rebecca could hear a sigh on the phone. "I can understand that. Does he know how long he has?"

"A few months, at best. He says he wants to finish this case before ...."

Again, her words were interrupted by her emotions. Doc, however, didn't wait for her to compose herself and complete the thought. "Well, if Gus wants to see this case through to the end, we'd better get busy. Last time we talked, you'd met with the client and the suspect's daughter."

"Right, that's Rowena Labadie and Lilith Harrison, respectively."

Rebecca wasn't confused by Doc's sudden enthusiasm for the case. It was to distract her. What he was doing was the mirror image of what she was trying to do for him. And in her case, she welcomed the diversion. It was something that would help Doc keep his spirits up, while possibly cracking a case that was starting to keep her up nights.

"We've talked to several others since then," Rebecca said. "Della Bergeron. Her company's lawyer. An old friend named David Putnam. Some of her security service. And I've done a ton of digging on the Internet, identifying the losers in some of her many successful business deals."

Rebecca spent the next half-hour summarizing the investigation to that point, reminding herself to omit anything confidential. That constraint, however, proved minimal as she realized everything she had—save the rape and the marriage of convenience between Harrison and Bergeron—was public information. And even the rape could be discovered with some effort and the nature of their marriage inferred, but she was keeping her promise to discuss it only when necessary. The only additions to what could be found in the papers and online were her and Gus's hypotheses, and most of them seemed to lead nowhere.

When she was done, she summarized with, "Lots of suspects, some with possible but weak motives, and no one with the means to coerce Bergeron to kill Sims that we can see."

"That's ...," started Doc, just to trail off into silence.

"Unbelievable?" suggested Rebecca.

"Close to it, unless you're trying to prove the innocence of someone who isn't. Then, all you're missing is Bergeron's motive. And that could come from a delusion in her beliefs over life and death, even if her criminal lawyer doesn't want to use an insanity defense." Doc paused a moment. "I can't disagree with your and Gus's conclusions about Putnam and Fiedler. But what's surprising to me is the range of personality types Bergeron attracts—the anal infatuated lawyer and the completely shallow Lothario—but maybe there's an element of similarity."

"In her ability to use them?" said Rebecca.

"And the lack of any real commitment from her, as you mentioned. Sims was supposedly the exception, but we have to take that on faith. Yeah, lots of people say they were devoted to each other, but she could have been acting."

"Yeah, I had the same thought," replied Rebecca. "I even went so far as to wonder if he was pretending as well. Maybe he had something like a death wish—he wanted to die and she was happy to help as part of building her influence in the coven or getting new powers or whatever."

"Possibly, though not a perfect fit to what we know," replied Doc. "I mean, why would a fake romance be necessary for that? And the drugs in his system and the nervousness he showed that night are somewhat inconsistent. Of course, it would be easy to start doubting when you're walking to your death. A little chemical encouragement wouldn't be that surprising. So, what do you know about him?"

"Very little, actually," said Rebecca. "And it's time I correct that. I'll dig further into his background tomorrow."

"Good. As for the security service, I agree with Gus. Not much suspicious there. And your analysis of what Bergeron's competitors gain from putting her out of business? The possible gain doesn't seem worth the risk of murder." Doc paused a beat. "That leaves the elephant in the investigation—the means used to commit the crime. How the hell did anyone get Bergeron to kill Sims if she wasn't doing it of her own free will?"

"Yeah, so what's the latest in the psychology world on mind control?"

"Still not possible. Well, after a fashion, I suppose it is with brainwashing or drugs. But both would leave a trail. With brainwashing, she'd be taking on someone else's beliefs. She'd be going around saying Sims was the devil; he had to die. And drugs would leave residuals in her system that would have been found unless it was something new or exotic."

"And when you consider all the connections the coven had to the drug industry, that doesn't seem so farfetched," said Rebecca. "Although ...." She paused weighing the possibilities. "I suppose if someone in the private sector stumbled on something like that, it'd be nearly impossible to keep it secret. Especially if it was established enough that people were starting to use it for private vendettas."

"And another scheme goes from promising to shaky," said Doc. "Hey, what about this ability to read people? Bergeron read you?"

"As much as I hate to admit it, yeah, she did. I mean, aren't PIs supposed to be inscrutable?"

Rebecca heard a chuckle in response.

"Yeah, I glossed over my reaction when I summarized the case before, but I admit—she got under my skin a bit, the way she was often a step ahead in the discussion. But in retrospect, she's probably honed that skill for years in business negotiations, just like Gus has done in his investigations."

"Makes sense," replied Doc. "But you know, I've seen that same empathy in you. I saw the pain in your eyes the night we watched Constance and Conroy on television. Soon, the student will pass the master."

Rebecca felt her face warm, and she was grateful Doc was on the phone, not in the room. She, too, remembered that night. It was rife with emotion—anger, disbelief, and the first inkling of a connection to this man. But she had no idea he'd been watching her so closely, that he still remembered that evening. It made her heart beat a little faster, although she knew it shouldn't. She pulled her thoughts back to the case.

"Empathy in the case of Gus I can buy. But we were talking about Della Bergeron here, and she's a cold-hearted witch, the double meaning intended."

"I guess that depends on what you mean by empathy. If it means understanding another's feelings, then she's definitely empathic. She's just not motivated to act on that understanding. But if you use the word to mean her behavior is changed by what she sees in others, then perhaps not."

"Yeah, I follow the distinction, though I'm not sure it helps us. Empathic or not, I keep coming back to the belief that she was temporarily insane ... or maybe, she has the permanent variety. It's the only thing that pulls everything together for me."

There was no response. "Doc?"

"Yeah, sorry. I got a little distracted by another thought. And you're sure the temporary insanity plea is off the table."

She'd lost Doc. Maybe he was running down disconnects in Bergeron's story. More likely, however, he felt guilty for abandoning Veles for the last 15 minutes and had returned to the kidnapping case in his thoughts. And if it was the latter, hopefully, the return wasn't also a regression to his self-destructive ways. She'd done what she could, and she'd call again in a day or two, continue the process.

"Yeah, it's not being considered. Bergeron would have to change her entire story, say Sims betrayed her or something like that. And then, as a result, she lost it. Unfortunately, there's no evidence of ...."

Rebecca got no farther, brought up short by an insight that fit what she knew about the killing so well that she was amazed she hadn't thought of it before. "Yeah, Bergeron won't change her story now," she said just to complete her statement. She needed to end the call so she could work out the implications of this new possibility.

"Doc, I probably should get going, get some sleep. I think your idea to run your search out of St. Louis is the best thing for both you and Nicole. And if there is anything I can do in the transition, just say the word."

"Thanks ... but what just happened?"

Rebecca hesitated. "What do you mean?"

"We're discussing hypotheses one minute, and the next, you've got to go to bed? I may not be as skilled reading people as you or Gus, but a blind man could have seen this."

"I suppose so," she said with a soft laugh. "And I wish I could fill you in, but I can't. Sorry."

"Sure, client confidentiality," replied Doc. "No worries. Push on with your lead. I'll just add, your killer is probably Della Bergeron. If you look beyond all the distractions of her beliefs, the people involved, the missteps in the arrest and investigation, and on and on, she's still the most likely suspect. But if it's not her, I'd keep an eye on Harrison. Maybe Fiedler, but more likely the daughter."

Rebecca started to say her good-byes, but curiosity got the better of her. "Why those two?"

Doc chuckled. "You're going to think I'm holding out on you to get even for you not confiding in me, but that's not true. It's just that I have this vague memory of something I read a few years ago, and I need to check it out before I say more. I don't want you wasting your time."

"OK. Fair enough. Let's talk in a couple of days."

They disconnected. Rebecca pulled the blanket up higher on her legs, thinking about the two individuals Doc had singled out for scrutiny. Then, she tried placing each of them into the scheme she had deduced.

"It could work," she muttered to herself. "Not as well as with my suspect, but it might just ...."

She got up from the sofa and turned up the temperature on the thermostat. There wasn't going to be any sleep for a while yet.

SATURDAY, OCTOBER 10

9:47 AM, Marte Investigative Services

As the hour approached for her meeting with Gus, Rebecca found that all of the excitement of a new lead in the case had vanished. Now, it was a mere wisp of idea in a mind overcrowded with the ache of an imminent loss. Why was life so ... well, not hostile to our existence so much as just not giving a damn whether we lived or died? She could think of dozens of others more deserving of Gus's fate. Why not one of them?

But her ruminations were interrupted as the door to her reception area opened. She leaned over to spot Gus entering. "Morning, partner."

Gus came into her office, frowned, and said, "Don't start that shit."

Rebecca recoiled. Profanity in Gus's world was saved for the occasional joke or the unanticipated shock, not a rebuke.

"I'm an old man and I expect to be addressed as such," he said, his glower now looking a bit forced. "But not too old to kick your butt."

It made sense. He wouldn't want pity, so Rebecca swallowed her pain, knowing she'd bring it back out when she was alone. "Maybe, but you're clearly too old to tolerate the slightest change in my greeting," she shot back. "So, what's up, old man?"

"That's better," he said, the frown morphing to a grin. "Now, what's this breakthrough on the case?"

"I was talking to Doc last night …."

"How is he?"

"He's better. He's not giving up—not that I would have expected that—but I think he's adjusting. He's coming back to St. Louis, probably in a week or so, to see if he can get his old job back and set up a base of operations here."

"That's good." Gus scratched a cheek idly as if making up his mind about what to say or how to say it. "I look at my wife some evenings and wonder how I would cope with what he's going through. Whatever I can do to help him when he gets back, just let me know."

"Will do" were the words that Rebecca spoke, but the thought she had was, "that's why I'm going to miss you so much, old man." Gus's time was measured in weeks, and yet he wanted to spend some of it helping someone he hardly knew but liked. And he probably wanted to help because he knew what Doc meant to her.

"Anyway, we were talking about the temporary insanity defense, and I said it wouldn't work because nothing had happened to set her off. There weren't any shouting matches, no one took a swing at the other … at least, not that anyone saw. But that got me to thinking— what if it's not something that just happened? What if Bergeron is running a long game, a scam that she's been playing since she met Sims? And why would she do that? What if he is the guy who raped her? What if he's Harrison's real father?"

In interviews with suspects, Gus could go hours without letting a single emotion influence his body language. But in the confines of their friendship, he wore his feelings on his face like everyone else. And blindsided by this disclosure, his eyes went wide, then narrowed in concentration as he considered her words. After a few moments, he asked, "Since the guy was never identified, what makes you think Sims was the rapist?"

"If you mean, what evidence do I have? The answer is none. It's just the way this one assumption puts everything else in a new light. Everyone has told us Bergeron's attraction to Sims wasn't typical. So, what if it's not attraction? We've all assumed that behind closed doors, they're physical. But maybe she's just been dangling herself in front of him, taking cruel pleasure in making him look but not touch. For all we know, she's carrying pepper spray in her purse and has a knife strapped to her thigh to keep him in line."

"I thought she walked a little bow-legged."

"Funny," Rebecca replied with a dramatic, oft-practiced eye roll. "But, seriously, she'd want some protection if she was tempting a man with a history of violence. Of course, this sexual torture couldn't go on forever, so she promised him they'd consummate the relationship after his initiation into the coven. He walks into that ritual worried but willing, not knowing he's going to his death."

"But for Sims to start chasing a woman he raped twenty-something years ago? That's crazy."

"Not if he doesn't know." Gus drew back from the desk, staring at Rebecca.

"With a lot of digging, I found some accounts of the attack. It was night. She had been drinking. She stopped at an ATM, but before she got to it, someone attacked her. She couldn't see him, so it's likely he didn't get a good look at her either. The incident was reported in the media, but nothing about the investigation—unsolved rape cases don't sell papers. But you know they would have checked out all her associates. And apparently they found nothing warranting an arrest. So, this could be one of the thirty percent or so of all rapes that involve a sick creep happening upon a vulnerable woman he doesn't know."

"OK. Dark night and they aren't known to each other. So, how'd she find out he was the attacker?"

"I don't know," replied Rebecca. "Maybe something in Sims's voice when they met. Maybe a creepy feeling. Maybe the physical similarities between Sims and Harrison tipped her off—similar eyes, hair, body type? Hell, for all we know, Bergeron checks out every male that fits the general description of the rapist. And by the way, Sims does fit that description with the assumption he's gained a few pounds over the years."

"You checked all of that out last night after talking to Doc?"

"I didn't sleep much. Anyway, after her suspicions are aroused, she gets some of his DNA and uses her influence to get the test run off the records. Once she's sure Sims is the guy, she starts the long slow process of exacting her revenge."

Gus blew out a long breath. "OK, I can see that even after she had proof, she might not want to leave it up to the courts. The justice system didn't do right by her in the first place."

"Right," said Rebecca. "Since Sims has no priors, the charge might get dropped to sexual assault if she turned him in. Now, he's out in a year. And even if the charge is first-degree rape, he could be out in less than two. Since Bergeron has lived with her pain for more than twenty years, that's not going to sit well with her."

Gus rubbed his chin, his eyes going up to the ceiling for a moment. "OK. Let's say you're right about all of that. She has Sims dead to rights and wants him dead. Then, why be so open about their relationship and kill him in front of a half-dozen pillars of the St. Louis business community? And she follows up the ritualistic slaying with stories about blacking out, later to be replaced by an even less plausible tale of a possession? She's created a mess, not an alibi."

"Exactly, and that's what's genius about her plan."

Gus blinked several times. "She's intentionally turning her case into a media circus?"

"Why else does she emphasize her beliefs in every media story? Why else did she choreograph a ceremony where everyone is looking down during Sims's execution? Why else would she have knocked the dagger to the ground where it was easily found? Why else claim a blackout, which is hard to believe, followed by possession, which is impossible. And why else hasn't her lawyer muzzled her in the last four or five months?"

"Maybe she doesn't listen," replied Gus, obviously taking the easiest issue to address.

"And maybe she's not listening because running her mouth is the easiest way to create doubt about what really happened. And think about her other options. One, she could kill Sims and try to conceal it—create some sort of alibi for herself, hire someone to kill him, whatever. Last I checked, the clearance rate for murders was a bit over 60 percent. From her perspective, that's a six in ten chance of ending up in prison or maybe on death row. Then, there's the temporary insanity defense."

"You don't need to tell me," said Gus. "With no history of mental illness, it's a long-shot."

"Correct. So, if I'm right, what she's doing is a gamble but better than the options. On one hand, she has the witchcraft community. It's not the most influential group in the country, but it's gaining acceptance from the younger generation, from the feminist movement, and in business. It's also been afforded some protection as a religious group."

"But if they are involved only to provide smoke, that would mean Bergeron has been planning this for what ... fifteen years?"

"Something like that. The attack without an arrest would have taken a few years to fester, but after a while, Bergeron would have had enough and she started laying her trap. Practicing witchcraft became the act in the center ring of her circus performance. That explains why her beliefs changed so dramatically and so suddenly."

"And you believe witches will take an attack on Bergeron as an attack on them?" asked Gus.

"They already have. There were several articles about infringements on Bergeron's personal or her religious freedom because she's a witch, though whether that's from grassroots support from the community or just a few activists, I couldn't say. But even if they had stayed quiet, her case gains an aura of mystery from her beliefs, at least to a lot of people. And now that she's claiming possession by another witch, there will be a few jury members with more than a reasonable doubt. Others will think she's insane, even if her lawyer doesn't make the argument. That would certainly be rolling around in my head if I was on the jury."

"So, she has the witchcraft community on one side and her business associates on the other?" asked Gus.

"Right. They'll do whatever they can to save their butts, distance themselves from the whole mess. If Harrison is to be believed—or even if she's lying—they'll all claim they didn't see Sims die. I know, that seems like a technicality in the face of the rest of the evidence, but it makes everything circumstantial. There will be no eyewitnesses."

"That'll fall apart if anyone took a peek," said Gus, rubbing the back of his neck with a hand. "And actually, I'd bet several of them were looking, but that doesn't mean they're going to speak up."

"And then right in the middle of this spectacle is law enforcement," continued Rebecca. "The actions of the police and detectives have been under the microscope from the very beginning and anything at all questionable has made the papers. The gap in the custody of the murder weapon has been the most damning, but everything from when Bergeron was read her rights to the admissibility of the blood test results has made the news. And, of course, we know who has access to everything. Bergeron's stirring her cauldron of reasonable doubt in the pages of the newspapers and the lines on the computer screen."

Gus chuckled. "You come up with that line dropping off to sleep last night?"

"Who said I slept?"

Gus grinned. Rebecca knew she wasn't. "The thing that kept me from anything but dozing last night was the thought that if this is true, we're nothing but pawns in her game. She's had every headline for months, but lately, the press has forgotten about her. And then, we get hired and Bergeron suddenly remembers having her mind controlled by another witch? And guess what made the papers last night?"

"Her sudden recollection?"

"Bingo. We could try to find out who leaked her text message to her sister, except her possession was the reason she gave to the police for going back to Ste. Genevieve. So, dozens of people knew about it without ever seeing the text."

"If we were hired to keep the doubt building in the public's mind, then Ms. Labadie might be in on the scheme," said Gus after a moment. "But she could also be an unwitting accomplice. Bergeron told us she opposed hiring us, but who knows what she said to her sister. A few subtle remarks about how inept her criminal lawyer was might be enough."

"I can ask Labadie where she got the idea and maybe find a way to check the money trail. She's not rich and she's separated from her husband. Cash is probably tight."

"Good idea," said Gus. He looked away a moment, then back. "Killing Goodwin for media coverage and to further muddy the waters seems a bit over the top. But maybe his death is unrelated? Or maybe he figured out her scheme and she had to kill him?"

"That makes sense to me," replied Rebecca. "If we can't find what we need looking at the sisters, the daughter, and their activities, coming at the case from his hit-and-run death is another possibility. I also wondered about Bergeron's trial lawyer. Could he be involved? After all, he's the one who has been hammering at the details of the arrest and investigation. Trouble is, that approach is common, and he can only use what Bergeron's giving him. And, as far as I can tell, they'd never met until after Sims's death. So, currently, I'm thinking he's not directly involved."

"Probably not," agreed Gus. "Politicking for public opinion is one thing, but actively obscuring the facts to create doubt? That's probably a reach, though we should keep the possibility in mind."

Gus's hand shot up to his forehead. "Oh, shoot. I almost forgot. I didn't stay up all night on this case like you, but before I dropped off last night, I noticed something in the forensics report on the murder weapon. Something that might increase the doubt in the jury's mind."

"Besides the gap in the chain of custody?"

"Yes, something that makes that gap even more suspicious. Bergeron's fingerprints are all over the knife according to the report, but none of them are in blood."

"So?" But why this was important hit her almost the moment she asked the question. "Of course. Two cuts—a slash to the neck and a stab to the chest. Both were expertly made and apparently without the killer changing grips. Is that as difficult as it sounds?"

"It ain't easy," Gus replied. "A good forensic examiner can show how awkward it would be. Sims is prone on the altar. She's standing at his head. For the wound to the neck, the most common grip would be with the butt of the handle near the little finger to make a slashing motion. To stab him in the chest without changing the grip, she would have had to lean out over the body to get her hand directly above his chest. And even then, she wouldn't have much leverage. On the other hand, the natural grip for a stab to the chest from her position would have the butt near her thumb, so the blade comes directly down from above. The neck could be slit with this grip, but even so, she'd have to lean to the side so the blade was coming from an angle."

"I'm impressed," said Rebecca. "You got all that from the forensics report?"

"I saw the same thing on a case a long time ago. That guy got off, but the evidence against Bergeron is much stronger. If I was on the jury, I'd say all the examiner proved was that she's very agile. But along with all the other nagging issues, she might have a good chance of walking."

Rebecca couldn't help herself and yawned. The lack of sleep was starting to catch up with her.

"Sorry if I'm boring you."

"Ha, ha. I'm going to the shop next door to grab a coffee. Wanna come along or should I bring something back?"

"Thanks, but no. I'm good. I'll just let my old bones relax."

Rebecca stood and started for the door, then turned back. "And, by the way, I know exactly how we're going to break the spell this witch is casting on the public."

"I know, another line from when you couldn't sleep."

At the Same Time, A Farmhouse in Western Kansas

"Your mom's coming," Nicole called to Justin from her spot in front of the picture window in the living room. The woman in her rusty, old pickup had just crested the horizon in the distance.

Other than the sanctuary of her bedroom, this spot in front of the window was Nicole's favorite in the entire compound. Here, she could sit and wonder if there was life beyond the sea of brown prairie grass—that is, more life than the scattered remnants Maggie described. Nicole could even picture herself finding out, knapsack on her shoulder, striding up the driveway toward the blue sky to answer that question. True, her wanderlust was laced with sadness, tainted with the possibility that everything she knew was gone. But it also promised finality. It had the lure of closing the book on the vague memories and dreams that filled both her waking and sleeping hours.

The last time she'd sat here daydreaming, her pleasant though ghostly images of bygone days had included Sam. Now, however, those imaginings were gone from her thoughts and instead were banned to her nightmares. It was also clear why his essence had lurked on the fringes of her consciousness for so long. In the last few sessions with Maggie, she had found that he was important to her past—important in the cruelest, most sadistic, and evil ways she could imagine.

First, Sam had drawn her in with quiet, affectionate warmth and a bit of nerdy studiousness. She found his curiosity about all things scientific appealing; after all, she shared some of that proclivity. And his dogged persistence to crack every riddle? That, too, she showed, although to a much lesser degree. Perhaps it wasn't the mix of traits most women sought, but she found the combination alluring. And the physical part of their association? The warmth of his arms around her, the taste of his lips, the smell of his skin was an intoxicating concoction. She had found herself wondering if he could be "the one."

And then, Sam changed.

It started one night when his dinner wasn't ready when he got home. He'd struck her in the stomach hard enough to knock her to the floor. Then, he stood over her laughing, saying he wouldn't want to leave a mark on her pretty face ... unless he had to.

Later that evening, he had made romantic overtures. She'd demurred, saying she didn't feel well—her stomach was sore although her damaged psyche was the bigger problem. At first, he seemed to understand, but that instant of feigned compassion was followed by a brutal slap across the face. He even berated her for his action, saying that if she ended up disfigured, it was her fault. Then, he had grabbed an arm, dragged her into the bedroom, and raped her.

The memory of that night had been a rude awakening, but it paled compared to the three repetitions of largely the same events over the next month. Nicole wondered when she had become so passive, so helpless. Why was she crawling back to Sam, again and again, just to be beaten and abused?

The pain of those recent revelations surged through her body, bringing Nicole back to the moment. She raised an arm and clenched a fist in front of her face. Perhaps her tan was starting to fade a bit but not her muscle. The tone she'd developed tending the garden and doing household chores over the summer was becoming even more pronounced by cutting wood and preparing their home for winter. And now, she had the perfect use for them because if she ever found Sam, she was going to kill him.

"Mom here yet?" Justin asked, rushing into the room.

"Almost."

Justin hurried over toward where Nicole stood, but when he was about four feet away, he stumbled. He caught himself by placing both of his hands on her chest. Nicole slapped him hard. "Stop that."

Nicole knew her feelings toward Justin were confused, but then, how could they not be? In most ways, he was innocent and naïve. He also showed affection and loyalty to her that was beyond question. In turn, she liked him, but like a brother, not a lover. And unfortunately, his obsession with getting her into bed was hurting—if not killing— any chance that her feelings grew beyond fondness.

"What? I tripped."

Had Nicole doubted his act was anything but intentional, that concern was removed by Justin's smirk.

"Hasn't your mother told you how bad that is?"

"It's not bad. It's ...." Then, realizing he'd all but admitted he did it on purpose, he turned to the window. "Come on. Mom will need some help. Looks like the back of the truck is filled with wood."

Justin left by the front door, leaving Nicole to simmer in her anger. After a moment, she followed.

The day was warm for October, and the sun felt good on her face. She joined mother and son as they tossed the limbs and old boards from the bed of the pickup. Neatness wasn't important at this step because everything needed to be cut to a length that would fit in their stove. Justin did nearly all of that because sawing wood was grueling work.

"I'll split up everything when you're done," she said to the young man.

"All of it?" he asked, looking surprised and impressed at the same time.

"Yeah. I can handle it."

When Nicole had first been given the task to split some of their firewood, it had seemed like a joke. Wasn't that what all the burly men in the movies and romance novels did to impress their women? But after a little practice, she found it was more about a smooth, easy swing, avoiding the knots, and letting gravity do most of the work. And besides, she had a wealth of pain and anger to work off. She only had to picture Sam's face on every piece of wood and she'd never miss, never fail to split the log in a single swing.

"Good haul," said Justin when they were finished unloading the truck.

"Thanks," replied Maggie. "I got lucky. And I saved the best part for last. We have more beef for supper."

"Lonnie Johnston come through for us again?" asked Nicole. She used the correct name, not only because it would be risky to reuse the same misinformation twice, but because she had stopped using the ploy entirely. She had the feeling that Maggie knew what she was doing. "So, what did you have to barter this time?"

"Probably sex," said Justin. Both women spun around to gape at him, and this time, his smirk wasn't subtle.

"That's an awful thing to say about your mother," snapped Maggie.

"Sorry, Mom."

But as Nicole watched, she read embarrassment on Maggie's face. Her own emotions, on the other hand, ran toward shock and disbelief. How and when had Justin discovered this seamier side of life? If the earlier talk from his mother had been what it appeared—Justin's introduction to the connection between his body and a woman's—it would be quite the intuitive leap to go from human anatomy to women selling their bodies. Maybe it was the world's oldest profession, but that didn't mean the concept came to young males out of the blue, did it?

Without realizing it, Nicole had continued to stare at Maggie, and now she realized that the woman was staring back. Maggie said nothing, but the defiance in her eyes spoke volumes. And that boldness could mean only one thing—she was Justin's source for more than just the medical version of reproduction. She was whipping his growing sexual interest into an unhealthy addiction.

Or was it possible that the evil of Sam Price was bleeding over into Nicole's understanding of mother and son? She didn't think so, but she couldn't think with the two of them standing just a few feet away. She turned toward the house, calling over her shoulder, "I'm going to my room. Back in a few."

Once there, Nicole locked the door and sat on the edge of her bed, trying to make sense of her situation. But after a moment, she realized that there was no way living here would end happily. At best, she'd be trapped, raising a house full of children fathered by a man she didn't love. And all the while, she would be wondering what was out there beyond the hill.

Someone knocked on her door.

"Please, I need a few minutes."

Nicole heard a key go into the lock and Maggie opened the door.

"Sorry, but in my house, it doesn't work that way." She walked over to the bed and sat. "Justin's just a confused young man. He didn't mean to upset you."

Maggie's shift from defiance to conciliation caught Nicole off guard, and her head jerked back in confusion. But if she was fortunate enough to catch the woman in a generous mood, she should take advantage of it.

"I'm going to leave before the weather gets worse. I have to see for myself what's become of my family and the rest of the world. You even said yourself that maybe we'd go north next summer. I just want to start sooner ... and maybe head south, where it's warmer."

"Nicole, honey, you can't do that. The plague is everywhere. You'll kill yourself. Or worse, you'll bring death back to this house."

"I'll be careful," said Nicole. "I don't remember studying much about infectious disease, but I know enough about medicine to minimize the risk. And if I get sick, I promise. I won't come back here."

Maggie stood from the bed, paced a couple of steps away, and then turned and came back. She idly rubbed her chin with a hand. But in the next instant, the hand lashed out in the form of a fist, catching Nicole on the temple. Stars exploded in her darkened vision, and she fell backward on the bed, momentarily stunned.

When her senses returned, Nicole sat up to find what were probably handcuffs for a large man clamped around her ankles. She didn't think they were restraints for legs because they were too narrow and the chain between them too short. They'd cut into her skin with every shuffling step.

"What ...?" Nicole struggled to put her growing panic into words. "What are you doing?"

"Protecting you from yourself."

"You can't do this. This is slavery. Sex slavery, the way you're forcing Justin on me."

"Don't be so melodramatic, Nicole. We have a responsibility. I'm not going to let the world die because you're confused."

"Confused? To hell with confused."

Maggie had an answer for all of Nicole's concerns, and they all came back to the pandemic. Her memory was sketchy and her mind confused because of the pandemic. She had nowhere to go because of the pandemic. She had to have children because of the pandemic. It was always the pandemic, but what if ....

"There isn't any pandemic, is there?" Nicole hissed. "The people dying. The scavenging and bartering for food. Even picking me up at the side of a road. It's all lies, isn't it?"

"But you've recalled a lot of this yourself," said Maggie soothingly.

"Have I? I've been questioning my memory for weeks, wondering why everything doesn't line up quite right. The past year or two is a jumbled mess most likely because ...." Nicole was going to say, "because of all the conflicting stories," but suddenly, her thoughts were overtaken by a different reason. It was based on something she'd heard in graduate school. And it explained her current mental chaos perfectly.

The class, if this memory was real, had dealt with ethical issues in medicine and the lesson Nicole recalled involved research on chemicals—xenon, propofol, and others—that could be used to suppress traumatic memories. The objective of the work was laudable, possibly world-changing. If painful memories could be specifically targeted and removed, then anxiety, stress, and depression might be substantially reduced, perhaps even eliminated. But currently, the effects of these chemicals could not be controlled precisely. They were not scalpels wielded by a skilled surgeon, but blunt instruments that would disrupt any thought they touched. The research was, simply put, an ethical landmine waiting for a misstep.

But what had happened to her wasn't a slight misstep. It wasn't a minor miscalculation in the application of these treatments. It was the result of malicious intent. At Maggie's hand, she had become a living walking example of the mental devastation that could be unleashed by these drugs. During her sessions with the woman, she had brought a memory back into the spotlight of her attention from a picture, where Maggie destroyed or bent it with innuendo and suggestion. And afterward, Nicole recalled only the newly minted falsehoods.

It was as if the bed, the floor of the house, even the earth below her vanished with the thought and Nicole was in freefall. Memory was the only thing a person brought forward through life. Her recollections were who she had been and who she had become. And even though she knew memories were flawed—many details were gone; other misimpressions had been added—they were still what made her who she was. And now a stranger was playing in her private vault of stored faces and feelings, sights and smells, dreams and fears. Her mental existence was being killed. Perhaps it would be better if her physical one followed the same path?

But, no, she wouldn't kill herself, if for no other reason that she wouldn't let Maggie win that way. She'd hold on to what was left of herself and fight back.

"Yes, I suppose I have recalled a lot of the sickness and death. And my mom ...." Nicole sighed and slowly shook her head as if accepting Maggie's version of reality. "So, what are you going to do to me?"

"I've wasted weeks trying to make this easy, but you wouldn't have it that way. And now, I can't trust you. So, from this moment forward, we'll do it the hard way. We'll start tonight. And if you're thinking you'll fight Justin, forget it. You won't be in any shape. Hopefully, after you're pregnant, you'll adapt to your new life. Now, take off your shoes."

"What?"

"You heard me."

Seeing no option, Nicole complied. When she was done, Maggie said, "You're free to move around the house ... even to try to climb the fence, although I think you'll find that impossible. You're on a water-only diet for a day, then half rations since you can no longer pull your weight. Maybe that will make you a bit more docile. When you need food for two, you'll get it."

Maggie turned and left the room.

Nicole knew that a part of her past was irrevocably gone, but all of her memories of Maggie, Justin, and the farmhouse were intact. There had to be a weakness in Maggie's plan. And she had to find it.

10:33 AM, Marte Investigative Services

"You need a couch in here," Gus said when Rebecca returned with her coffee.

"No, you need a couch. I'm fine." Though she'd said it, Rebecca found it harder to joke about such things with Gus. A couch for him to rest, if he was going to insist on coming in, was a good idea. "I was thinking about getting one, spruce up the place a bit."

"I doubt that, but even you'll need to crash here once in a while. Just don't go looking for one designed for an old man." Gus waved a hand like he was shooing away the topic. "I forgot to ask. What did Doc think about your new theory?"

"I didn't tell him. I promised Labadie I wouldn't mention the rape to anyone unless it was necessary. And, in his case, it didn't seem like it was. Think I went overboard?"

"Seems a bit of a gray area since, technically, anyone could find that information. But keeping to the letter of a promise is never a bad thing. So, catching Bergeron?" Gus started, just to see Rebecca raise a hand.

"Before we get into that, I should mention Doc had his suspects — Harrison primarily, but possibly, Fiedler. Well, they were second and third to Bergeron, who he thinks probably did it. But why those two, I couldn't say. He wanted to check something before getting into it."

"Harrison and Fiedler, huh?" Gus said, rubbing a chin. "Of course, if it is Bergeron, then he's on the same page as you with your rapist theory. But I suppose one of the other two could also be involved. If so, businesswoman and lawyer exact revenge on a rapist sounds more likely than mother and daughter do the same. So, I don't see why he thought Harrison over Fiedler."

"Like I said, I have no clue. But I don't believe he was talking about a partnership between one of them and Bergeron. I had the impression he thought one of them could be the killer, although that just gets us back to where we were stuck before—how did either of them get her to act against her will? That's why I think he's barking up the wrong tree. Anyway, back to catching Bergeron. You had an idea?"

"Same as yours, I suspect. Run a test of Sims's DNA against that collected from the rapist."

"Not bad," said Rebecca. "And that's my backup plan. But the problem I see is that even if we find a match, Bergeron will just deny she knew anything about it. 'Oh, my God. I was sleeping with my rapist?'" Rebecca's impersonation of Bergeron was spot on, right down to the hint of a Southern drawl, and Gus guffawed.

"When that happens, the truth becomes just another act in her three-ring circus, and we spend our time searching for evidence that she knew who Sims was. And my guess is, she's buried that information deep."

"So, what's the primary plan?" he asked. "Flush her out with the threat of detection?"

"Exactly. Maybe you noticed it in the forensics report, but along with the fibers and footprints and everything else that led nowhere, there was a trace of blood on one of the stones in the altar. It was on a corner, near the top. It wasn't Sims's or anyone in CODIS," said Rebecca, referring to the law enforcement's local, state, and national DNA databases. "After that, the police stopped looking at it. The victim was known and the suspect was solid. They figured it was just a worker who scratched a finger during construction or something like that."

"But being the diligent investigator that you are," said Gus, taking up the story, "you're checking further. Your theory is that Sims was still alive after receiving a few superficial ceremonial cuts from Bergeron, but he was stunned by whatever was hidden in the altar. Maybe some sort of knockout gas. Bergeron collapses on him because she thinks she's killed him ... or maybe, she got a whiff and passed out. The real killer steps in during the confusion to finish off Sims. Is that the kind of thing you're thinking?"

"Actually, that's better," said Rebecca. "I'll use it. I just need something good enough to justify asking for DNA from Harrison. All the other requests—to Bergeron, Fiedler, Putnam, Labadie—will just be a smokescreen. Then, with all those DNA profiles laying around, the risk that we notice the match between Sims and Harrison is too great for Bergeron to ignore."

"And you're thinking she'll just admit she knew?"

"Wouldn't that be nice, but no," replied Rebecca, answering the feigned skepticism in his voice with a touch of fake sarcasm in hers. "I think Bergeron will either lobby for everyone to withhold their samples or try to switch the real reports for doctored ones. In the first case, she'll need some good reasons to ignore a possible lead and abandon her sister's effort to clear her. We just need to keep the pressure on when she makes those arguments. And in the second case, I know someone at a lab who can do the work and watch for anything underhanded. Catching her trying to switch reports should put an end to her games."

Gus paused a moment, nodding. "Yeah, I can see that. And because of it, you need to watch your back, partner."

"Which is why I took my firearm out of retirement," said Rebecca. "I'm carrying till this is over. I suppose you're never without yours?"

"Seldom and definitely not now," replied Gus. "When are you going to get this plan rolling?"

"As soon as we're done talking."

"Good. Try for a meeting with Bergeron on Monday. That'll give her the weekend to sweat after everyone else is already spitting on a swab." Gus scratched behind an ear. "There's just one thing I don't understand. Why ask for DNA from Putnam? I thought he was all but off our list of suspects."

"He is, but with his lifestyle, I can't think of a better consciousness-raising experience for him than opening himself up to all kinds of paternity suits."

MONDAY, OCTOBER 12

5:23 AM, A Farmhouse in Western Kansas

When Nicole awoke from her recurring nightmare—the pain, the rough hands, the crushing weight on her chest—she knew it wasn't just a scenario fashioned by a sleeping mind. It was real and her imprisonment was complete.

First, Maggie had taken her mental life, forcing her self-image into a corner defined by what she hadn't thought about when meeting with the woman. Every memory that had been retrieved in those sessions was now distorted by suggestion, producing a kaleidoscope of drug-induced images, sensations, and emotions that had no basis in her past.

Then, the woman had moved on to limit her physical life, restricting her freedom of movement for months. That, however, wasn't enough. So, for the last two nights, her son had stolen the sanctity of her body as well.

They had raped her, mind and body. And they would do so again and again until Maggie got what she wanted.

Nicole got up from the bed, hobbled into the living room, and sat in the armchair. Her gaze traveled from the picture window, its view merely a backdrop for her thoughts, to Justin's face across the room.

He stared back. He had nothing to say, perhaps feeling that what he was doing was wrong despite what his mother said.

After the first night of this abuse, depression had started to appear at the corner of Nicole's mind. It would be easy to surrender to helplessness because she was powerless, but she fought against the feeling. And in its stead, she welcomed the white-hot light of hatred. If hope couldn't sustain her, loathing would and it was focused on Maggie. She was the architect and warden of her prison.

Justin, on the other hand, was merely following her dictates, unencumbered by a past that would set limits. Nicole wished his mind was not so damaged, but it was, and that fact sheltered him from the full force of her fury.

Many others, however, did not escape so easily. Where were her parents? Why hadn't they prepared her better? Of course, they were older. They had lived in a kinder, gentler world and might not understand how dangerous things had become. But her sisters, her friends? They would know. And now, the affection she had felt toward them drained from her being to be replaced by revulsion. They were doing nothing, leaving her to be slowly destroyed by the evil living in this house.

But more than any of them, Nicole hated herself. Why hadn't she prepared herself better? She had worked hard for what she had—an advanced degree in biomedical engineering, a good job—but with a mind closed to what she so desperately needed now. She needed to know how to hunt, how to survive, how to defend herself. She knew none of that, and she feared the shortcoming would be the death of her.

Nicole looked over at Justin. His eyes were still on her. She looked away without a word.

She had already decided she would kill Sam, should the opportunity arise. But Maggie and Justin? The answer to that question was surprising in its speed—just a matter of an instant—but not in its content. She would kill, if necessary, to gain her freedom. And in every way, Maggie was as worthy of that fate as Sam.

But what constituted an opportunity to escape wasn't a simple question. If she overpowered Maggie, she'd still have to subdue Justin. He'd assume she was irrational, and so, keeping her safe on the farm until she came to her senses would be his answer.

And even if she killed Maggie, how long would he hold her hostage, operating under the illusion of a virus-infested world? He might go months, even years avoiding others while hunting the nearby grasslands. But then, wasn't freedom after years better than dying in her current hell? She knew it was.

Though Nicole only now realized how far she would go to escape, it seemed that Maggie had anticipated her resolve much earlier. But then, the woman had been a step ahead of her from the beginning and she was continuing to adapt. Most likely, she'd told Justin that this was an especially dangerous time—it was the depth of depression before pregnancy restored her to the loving wife he deserved—because his surveillance had increased dramatically the last few days.

But many of the other changes were more obvious. Every door to a space that held a potential instrument of escape—Maggie's office, the toolshed—was secured by a key and a combination lock. Stealing the keys was only half a solution. Maggie had even installed a lock on the inside of her bedroom door; no one was going to slit her throat in the middle of the night. But even more noticeable than this precaution was the knife she had started carrying. And when it wasn't strapped to her waist, it was in her hand as she patiently worked the blade over a whetting stone. Nicole didn't believe that it was only for show.

Justin stirred and the movement caught Nicole's attention. "I'm going to get something to eat. You want something?"

"No." Nicole was off her water-only restriction and on half-rations, so she was hungry, but she wasn't going to give Justin even the illusion he was being compassionate. He shrugged and went into the kitchen, leaving her unsupervised.

She got up from the chair and started searching the living room, although it was almost undoubtedly wasted effort. She'd been through the room dozens of times in her mind and had scoured it repeatedly with her eyes over the last couple of days. She'd seen nothing that she could use to secure her freedom other than the crudest, makeshift weapons—the blunt end of a log for the fireplace, a candlestick holder that might have the heft necessary to stun. But with the noise any attack like that would make, Justin would come running or Maggie would appear at her office door, knife in hand.

Justin returned from the kitchen, a plate in his hand with a hunk of bread and a piece of meat. It made Nicole's stomach growl. She got up to leave so she wouldn't have to watch him eat.

"Where are you going?"

Nicole didn't answer, but rather, stepped into the kitchen. What she saw there, however, brought her up short. The knife Justin had used to prepare his meal was sitting on the counter near the sink. That was in clear violation of Maggie's standing orders—anything that could be used as a weapon, from rolling pins to knives, was to be cleaned and locked away after use. But these laws of the house were new and not yet habits. Justin had forgotten.

At maybe four or five inches, the knife wasn't that long. Nor was it that sharp, but pressed to Justin's neck, she might get the keys and the combinations she needed. Nicole retrieved the knife and started for the door. When she reached it, she stopped, needing a moment to steel her nerves. She'd never done anything remotely like this before, and she'd have but one chance. Failure would bring severe retaliation from Maggie, might even result in her death if things went poorly. But she'd already made her decision. After a deep breath, she curled her wrist, bringing the knife next to and behind her arm. She stepped through the door.

Justin turned and seeing only her arms hanging loosely by her side said, "I thought you were going to get something to eat?"

"Maybe later." Her words caught in her throat, but Justin didn't seem to notice. He turned back to his food.

Nicole walked over to stand behind him, moving casually. But even so, her nearness was unusual, and Justin started to turn around. Nicole's empty hand flashed forward, grabbing his collar. Simultaneously, the knife came up to his throat. She bent down, putting her mouth next to his ear. She wasn't certain this was the best maneuver. If he backhanded her with his fist, she'd be stunned, maybe even knocked unconscious, but the proximity seemed more intimidating, as long as she controlled her voice.

"Move a muscle, and I swear, I'll slit your throat." It came out as a hiss, filled with rage and lacking the anxiety she felt.

"Nicole, what are you doing?"

"Getting the hell out of here. Now, call your mom."

"Are you sure? She's going to be really mad."

Nicole pressed the knife tighter against his throat, and she heard him gasp. "Call her now!"

"Mom." Nicole heard nothing for a moment, and she jerked Justin's collar. "Mom," he called more loudly.

Maggie's office door opened, and she stepped out. It took her a moment to assess the situation, but when she had, she said, "What do you want, Nicole?"

"The keys to the toolshed and the truck. And the combination to the lock on the toolshed door."

Maggie stared a moment. "Or what?"

"Or I'll kill him."

Maggie stared a moment longer. "OK. But clean up the mess when you're done. I don't want blood all over the floor and walls. We'll talk about your punishment later." She went back inside her office, closed and locked the door.

Nicole was dumbfounded and dropped her guard. That was a mistake. Justin grabbed her wrist and twisted. A sharp pain shot up her arm and into her shoulder. She dropped the knife. Maggie came back out of her office.

"You were going to let her kill me," said Justin.

"Don't be silly, son. Nicole's mind is clouded, but behind all that confusion, she loves you. She'd never hurt you. I've told you that, over and over. I've also told you to lock away all the knives. You get another two hours chopping wood to improve your memory."

"Yeah, give me another chance and I'll show you," Nicole snarled, hoping to reverse the damage of her indecision, but it was too late. Maggie had turned to go into her office. Justin stood to clean and lock away the knife, and neither turned back when she spoke.

All Nicole had accomplished was to further convince Justin that his mother was right. She was only to be pitied until motherhood cleared her mind. The rage within her grew.

11:47 AM, The Mateo Sanchez Residence

Sanchez swirled the last of his single-malt scotch in the glass, the ice tinkling, then swallowed it in a single gulp. His wife wouldn't approve of him drinking over lunch. He didn't much like the idea of it either, but he needed the shot of liquid courage.

It would be easy to blame his wife for his current nervousness; she wasn't here for him. But he knew better than that fiction. The visit with her sister in Kansas City had been planned for months. He'd even encouraged her to go, reasoning that her fretting wouldn't help him. But now, he wondered if that thinking was flawed. He needed someone to tell him he was doing the right thing. He needed someone to say Della Bergeron wasn't the shrewd businesswoman he had thought. Rather, she was just a common embezzler, caught in the act by her Chief Financial Officer.

He could, of course, just cancel the meeting. Bergeron was practically gone from the company anyway; witches who performed ritualistic human sacrifice weren't CEO material. But he couldn't. She might get off. She might even come back to work to continue her misappropriation of company funds. That would never do. And even if she was convicted, the company should know what had happened so that it could tighten its financial controls. He was going to honor his commitment to his position while giving Bergeron the courtesy of knowing the charges against her before the rest of the world.

He had first suspected something nearly four months ago when he noticed a slight discrepancy in the books. You had to be at his level, sitting at the top of the financial empire looking down to even notice it. And he wouldn't have spotted it except for the downturn in business after the Sims killing. The shortfall had been allocated across projects, as per policy, except for one, innocuously named Advanced Marketing Technology. Its funding had increased, and it was spending at an unusually high rate.

He'd researched the anomaly, of course. First, he'd thought it was an effort elevated to priority status on one of the few days he'd missed a staff meeting. So, he had checked the logs, and indeed, Bergeron had mentioned the project. But a mention by name was all it was—not a schedule, nothing about staffing, not even anything about its products. But most puzzling, he couldn't see that it had ever been given privileged status, allowing it to grow as the rest of the business eroded.

At the next financial review—Bergeron's last before the scandal of Sims killing sent her into exile–he'd asked about the work. At first, she'd been disinterested, dismissing his question with the wave of a hand. She had a lot on her mind, and he had almost dropped the issue at that point. But even though it was just a trickle in a two-billion-dollar business, it was his job to understand their cash flow, and in this case, he didn't. He persisted and eventually, she asked, "How much are we talking about?" When he gave her the number—something less than a half-million—she'd practically started laughing. Perhaps seeing his consternation, she'd refrained and said, "You don't need to be worrying about a little money ending up in the wrong pot inside the company when we're losing more than that every week."

The decline in business had eventually leveled out, but the spending of the Advanced Marketing Technology project never receded to the new baseline. Someone was keeping it well-funded, and no one, save Bergeron, seemed to know anything about it. There seemed only two possibilities to Sanchez. First, the company had some confidential technology development that was being kept from his office. Practically and legally, that approach was questionable. And since Meteor Promotions wasn't an R&D company, it was also highly improbable. More likely in his mind, the boss lady was lining her pockets for her getaway, figuratively, and perhaps, literally.

After Sanchez compiled the data on the money flow, however, he wasn't sure what to do with it. He'd considered bringing in the police but decided it was a waste of time to even ask them. They were pursuing Bergeron on one, maybe two murder charges. And on the scales of justice, murder always outweighed embezzlement. He'd also thought about involving the company lawyer, Tony Fiedler, but he didn't trust the man. He and Bergeron were too close; they had even gone to school together. For all he knew, Fiedler could be involved in the diversion of funds.

In the end, he'd set up a meeting at her home today to be followed by a discussion with the board of directors in two days. He'd give her an opportunity to explain because, however slight it might be, there was still a chance the project was legitimate. But her calmly explaining the rationale for the project's secrecy wasn't the image he saw in his mind's eye. Rather, he saw her trying to buy him off, then threatening to ruin him when that didn't work. In fact, he was certain he'd be fired before today's meeting was over, assuming she still had the power. But eventually, that wrong would be corrected, too.

His doorbell rang, sending his heart racing. Who the hell could that be? He wasn't normally home at this hour on a Monday, but his wife would be. Perhaps it was one of her friends. He checked the video feed on his phone, frowning at the face he saw there. He opened the door. "What are you doing here?"

The barrel of a shotgun as it came up toward his face was the last thing he ever saw.

1:27 PM, The Della Bergeron Residence

Rebecca had been on her best driving behavior since leaving the office, but it was no use. Gus was still jamming his foot into the floorboard every time she got within 20 yards of another car and putting a hand on the dashboard with every corner they took. She had to say something. He'd notice the omission if she didn't and chastise her for showing pity he didn't want.

"I hear that causes arthritis."

Gus pried his stare from the road for an instant, then back, as if he had to watch or she couldn't negotiate a turn. "What does?"

"Clinging to the door handle so hard your knuckles turn white."

"Ha, ha," Gus replied with feigned derision. "I just want to know what video arcade you used for driver training."

"Video? Who needs video when country roads were just minutes from my house when I was growing up? It's amazing how many hills you can find out in the boonies where you can go airborne at 70 miles an hour."

"Thank God we finally made it," Gus said when the front gate to Bergeron's home appeared. "And with most of the car, too." Gus paused. "So, you got Ms. Bergeron a bit worried about a hidden knockout drug in the altar?"

"Actually, she seemed pretty calm about it when we talked this morning," Rebecca replied, then rolled down her window to identify herself to the guard. Pulling away from the gate, she said, "Her words were, my afternoon's screwed up anyway, so come on out."

"Screwed up, huh? For someone as refined and elegant as her, that's almost gutter talk. Any idea what else ...." But the thought was interrupted by who he saw in an approaching car. "Is that Rowena Labadie?"

"It was," said Rebecca, now sharing time between the rearview mirror and the windshield where she saw a second oncoming car. "And that's David Putnam. What the hell were those two doing here?"

Gus glanced sideways at Rebecca. "You baited both of them, right?"

"Yep. I talked to Putnam on Saturday. He panicked ... as expected. Got to admit, I enjoyed that call. And Labadie was Sunday afternoon. She just seemed confused but was willing to give us a DNA sample. I also talked to Harrison on Sunday. She sounded like she might be partaking a bit, but then, with what her weeks must be like, that's understandable. She agreed to us taking a swab. The Fiedler call was on Saturday. He started quoting laws about the right against self-incrimination. Of course, I pointed out that there was no law against me asking and then said good-bye before he could start a new rant."

Rebecca parked her car in the lot beside the mansion, and the two got out and started for the front door. "What about the plan for this talk?" asked Gus.

"Just keep running the game—mention everyone who's giving us a sample, paint a picture of us sitting around with all those DNA profiles spread out on the table. Oh, and most important, mention that we're adding Sims's profile. The forensics report said his blood wasn't a match to the sample on the stone, but we're adding it as a double-check. Assuming that Sims and Harrison are related, it almost seems a given we'll spot the overlap."

"Hopefully, that's what Ms. Bergeron thinks, and she makes a mistake."

They arrived at the front door. Rebecca pushed the button and stared up at the camera, now that she knew where it was. In a moment, Bergeron answered. "I have half a mind not to invite the two of you in with all the trouble you're causing me."

It was exactly the welcome Rebecca had hoped to receive. The woman was feeling the pressure. Rebecca put on her best innocent look. "I'm sorry, but this seemed the best way to narrow the field. We figured we'd start with the people who've been cooperating with us—your sister and daughter, Tony Fiedler, a couple of the guards, David Putnam."

Actually, she hadn't gone to the security company, but the falsehood fit her story well.

"So far, everyone's going along except Mr. Fiedler and Mr. Putnam," Rebecca said. "And, by the way, we're also including Victor's profile in the sample. The forensics report said his blood wasn't a match to the drop on the altar, but as important as this one rock has become in this investigation, it's worth another look."

Bergeron folded her arms over her chest but made no move to clear a path. "And just what do you hope to accomplish with this stunt?"

"There are only so many people who knew about the ritual. I believe you made up that list for the police?"

Bergeron stared for a moment, then said, "My sister's not on it, but you asked for her DNA?"

"Right, we took that liberty. It's always good to remove your client from all suspicion." Rebecca paused, giving Bergeron a chance to comment, but apparently, she had nothing more to say. "Anyway, we'll eliminate those I named, then get samples from the workers who built the altar. Eliminate some of them and we're down to those who wouldn't provide samples plus the four witches in the coven. And maybe you and Ms. Harrison can get some of them to go along?"

Bergeron cocked her head, then slowly shook it. "Doubtful. I think most of them would rather see me rot in prison." She stared at Rebecca a moment longer, then stepped to the side. "Well, at least you kept the appointment. I guess I'll be true to my southern roots and let you in."

Rebecca had somewhat expected the invitation, mostly because turning them away at the door would look suspicious. Bergeron would want to appear accommodating. She would want to look like she was seriously debating the pros and cons of providing her DNA when she was probably pondering how to keep Harrison's or Sims's profile out of their hands.

"At least we showed up. Does that mean someone else didn't?"

"It does." Bergeron led them into the parlor where they had spoken before, and they took the same seats. "My one o'clock never showed, though David Putnam filled in unexpectedly. You sure put him into a panic. He was railing against Rowena, cursing her for hiring you two. I got her to come over, and together, we talked him down. For some reason, he never considered that any woman who seriously wanted to check paternity would just collect some of the hair he leaves all over the place."

"I'm sorry," said Rebecca. "We didn't mean to cause you …," but she was cut off by the hand Bergeron was thrusting toward her face.

"You need to cut the crap, Ms. Marte," Bergeron said leaning forward.

Rebecca pulled back, the woman's transformation from social aristocrat to self-made, hard-nosed survivor completed before her eyes. Bergeron could call on her roots when the situation demanded it.

"Let's look at the facts, shall we?" Bergeron said, biting off each word. "The list of twenty or so names that I gave to the police were the people Lilith or I spoke to about the ceremony. The five others in the coven would have told their staff and family. The workers probably mentioned the site, if not the date, to all their drinking buddies. And the guards told their coworkers. And on and on. The list you're whittling down with these four or five DNA tests is in the hundreds, maybe the thousands. At this rate, we'll die of old age before you scratch the surface. Second, you don't need DNA from me because, by Missouri law, they took a sample when I was arrested. Even you would know that. And last, do you really expect me to believe that there was some type of hidden toxin or gas that knocked out Victor and confused me, but no one found any evidence of it until you came on the case nearly a half-year later? Give me a break."

"It's a long shot," said Gus evenly, his first words since arriving. "We're just trying to put some pressure on whoever's behind Mr. Sims's killing and being able to place someone at the altar who shouldn't be there is a start."

It was good that Gus had spoken because all of the responses that came to Rebecca's mind had been laden with ire and sarcasm. True, their scheme wasn't perfect, but she felt they had played it well. It had certainly gotten Putnam's attention. But then, the man probably had half the intellect of Bergeron and a personal life replete with indiscretion. Of course, the ploy had scared him. And the rest of the people they'd asked? They'd probably gone along out of confusion and a sense of loyalty to employer, sister, or mother.

"I know, Mr. Clements," said Bergeron, her veneer of culture returning, her tone mellowing. "You and Ms. Marte are well-intentioned, if misguided. That's the only reason I let you in."

A phone rang somewhere else in the house. Bergeron sighed. "I should get that. Please excuse me for a moment."

When she was out of the room, Gus said, "Easy, partner. Don't take it personally."

"Don't take it personally that she thinks I'm a joke?"

"You mean, we're a joke," replied Gus. "I'm in this, too. Besides, if this case had a glaring hole, someone else would have found it by now."

Gus was right—not every ploy designed to trip up the bad guy worked, although the thought did little to reduce Rebecca's ire. She looked around the room, knowing she wanted to talk about recovering from this setback, but she was uneasy about doing that in the heart of Bergeron's lair.

"So, we get Ms. Bergeron's DNA from the state, swab the rest, and see who we can place at the scene," said Gus. "Right?"

It took her a moment, but she realized Gus was saying the game wasn't over. Bergeron thought the scheme was virtually hopeless, but so what? If they continued to play this one-in-a-thousand long shot, they could still stumble upon the father-daughter match in the profiles. They still had the leverage they needed to get Bergeron to panic.

"Right. And we won't need samples from anyone in the CODIS database, which will probably include a lot of the service people," Rebecca said just as Bergeron returned.

"Sorry for the interruption," she said, taking her seat. "Sounds like you're adjusting your strategy?"

"A bit," said Rebecca. "Gus was just suggesting we get your DNA information from the state like you mentioned. It'll take longer, but it can be done." That comment would cover anything Bergeron might have overheard or observed if there was surveillance in the room. "Your phone call? Not a problem, I hope."

Bergeron looked distracted a moment, then gave her head a shake as if trying to dislodge the image there. "Yes, it was a problem and, to be blunt, one you've caused." She held up a hand to forestall the reply forming in Rebecca's mind. "That was Lilith and Tony Fiedler. They're on their way over. Tony's calling your investigation an invasion of privacy and wants to get a cease-and-desist order. He's dragging Lilith along so I can tell her it's OK if she doesn't cooperate with you."

"Well, we'll get out of your way," said Rebecca. "It would be good, however, if you could ask Ms. Harrison to go along with us. Mr. Fiedler, too, if possible. It could help us flush out the person behind all this."

Bergeron got that faraway look again and held the pose for what seemed a minute. Finally, she asked, "Do you really have a plan, Ms. Marte?"

Oddly, Bergeron's gaze went to Gus's face with the question, then back to her.

"We do. It's like my partner said, nothing's guaranteed, but if we do this right, we can pare down the list of possibilities pretty quickly.

First, we can eliminate everyone in the government DNA database, since that comparison has been run and no one in it matched the blood on the altar. Of those left, many will have nothing to gain, letting us focus on the higher probability suspects, and so on. Yeah, I'd say the plan has a chance."

Bergeron stood and paced to the fireplace, then turned back. She released a long breath. "Please stay until my guests arrive. I'm going to tell them I'm going along with you, that I'm giving you my DNA so you don't have to wait on the state. And I'll encourage Lilith to do the same. Tony's going to be a tougher case, but we'll see."

Alarms went off in Rebecca's head. Had she and Gus become the hunted rather than the hunters? Why would Bergeron join forces with them unless she saw some way to turn it to her advantage? But how?

She needed some time with Gus away from the eyes and ears of Bergeron's home. "That would be great," said Rebecca. "We need to step out to my car, get some phone numbers, and make a few calls. We'll come back in when Ms. Harrison and Mr. Fiedler arrive."

Bergeron walked them to the front door. As they stepped out, she said, "I don't have a lot of faith that your methods can flush out a witch. But in some ways, you've given my beliefs a second chance. I'll do the same for yours."

"Thanks," replied Rebecca, and she and Gus started for the parking lot. About halfway there, Rebecca asked under her breath, "So, in her mind, it's still a witch we're trying to expose?"

"A murderer by any other name …," said Gus equally softly. It was the only paraphrase of Shakespeare Rebecca had ever heard from his lips.

2:03 PM, The Della Bergeron Residence

Rebecca reached into the back seat of her car and retrieved her notebook. She flipped through the first half-dozen pages, then pulled out her phone and started dialing.

"You really have calls to make?" asked Gus.

"No, but just in case she's watching."

Rebecca glanced at Gus in time to see him shrug. "Fair nuff. So, you think it's an act? She's going along because it suits her purposes?"

"That's what I was thinking inside—that we were walking into her trap, rather than her into ours."

Rebecca was still holding the phone to her mouth, effectively completing the ruse and making it impossible for anyone to read her lips. But she was also losing faith that such steps were necessary. "The thing is, now that I have a moment, I'm not finding any tells in her words or behavior. I think she actually believes ...." Rebecca pulled the phone down, chuckling. "That's what's wrong with this case. It's never, her alibi doesn't check out; she's guilty. Rather, it's our beliefs about what she's thinking with the complication that she might be thinking about something I believe but haven't said." Rebecca chuckled again. "Got that?"

"Clear as mud," said Gus. "You're starting to think she wants our help."

"Yes, strangely enough, I am," Rebecca said slowly. "On the surface, her claim about another witch screams 'lie' about as loudly as any words I've ever heard. But everything I hear in her tone and see in her body language says she believes it. You?"

"The same. Her upcoming acting job—convincing Fiedler and Harrison that she's 100 percent behind us—will tell us more. But so far, if I had to bet, I'd say she believes what she's saying. Which is not to say it's the truth. It's just reality as she sees it."

Both their heads turned at the sound of an approaching car. "That's Labadie," said Gus. They both exited the car to greet their client.

"Ms. Marte. Mr. Clements. Good to see you both."

"You, too, Ms. Labadie," replied Rebecca while Gus nodded his welcome. "Didn't we just see you leaving the property about an hour ago?"

"You did. The day got a little weirder, if that's possible, when Sis called to say she was going along with you. I thought Mr. Fiedler would have talked her out of it. But when she said she thought Lilith and I should go along, too, and that she and Fiedler would be here to discuss it? Well, I decided I had to crash this party."

"The more, the merrier," said Gus. "And now, maybe we should go inside where it's a little warmer and wait for the rest."

It didn't seem that cold to Rebecca, making her wonder if he was feeling all right. Unfortunately, she didn't know the symptoms of pancreatic cancer, but fatigue and a lack of energy were probably on the list.

As they were walking toward the front door, a third car with two occupants came toward the house, then turned through the porte-cochere toward the parking lot. "And it looks like the gang's all here," said Labadie. She didn't stop walking, which suited Rebecca. She didn't want to listen to the lawyer pontificate on the driveway, just to have to listen to it all again inside.

When they reached the house, Labadie pulled a key from her pocket but the door opened before she could use it. "I don't come here for weeks," she said, "and now it's twice in one day." The two women embraced.

"You should come over more often," replied Bergeron, stepping aside to let the trio enter. "Or better, I'll come to you." She waited as the other two approached. "Lilith, Tony, come in. Let's all go into the parlor."

No one said anything as they walked to the room. Crossing the threshold, however, seemed to signal an end to the peace, as Fiedler immediately launched into his denunciation of the PIs' stated plan.

"I have to object in the most strenuous terms possible anyone sharing their DNA with these investigators. And let me be perfectly clear. You are not required by law to support their investigations in any way."

"Nor are we prohibited from helping them, if we think it's the right thing to do," replied Labadie.

"No, you are not prohibited," replied Fiedler. "But I don't think you understand the risks, Ms. Labadie. Once your DNA data is out there, it's subject to theft and misuse. I'm sure Marte Investigative Services has state-of-the-art encryption on all their systems, but if recent history has taught us anything, it's that every system can be hacked. They could put it in the Pentagon, and it's still not safe. And in the wrong hands, your genetic weaknesses, physical and mental, are known. You could be blackmailed because you're a poor risk for that insurance policy or that new job."

"So, it comes down to the risk in my DNA record or the risk that my sister goes to prison?" Labadie said, her growing frustration with the lawyer starting to show. "I know which is greater to me, and frankly, I'm floored, Mr. Fiedler, that you don't feel the same."

"I don't want to risk the future of Ms. Bergeron either," replied the lawyer, "but this is not the way to help her. Look, I know it's normal to want the assistance you're providing to be the decisive factor." He subtly tipped a hand toward the chairs where Rebecca and Gus sat.

"How dare you!" snarled Labadie, her face turning red. "You think I want this to work because of my pride? I want this to work because people like you have done nothing for Sis. It's time to put up or shut up."

Fiedler, too, was getting agitated, but Rebecca's eyes didn't stay on him for long. She was looking at Bergeron. Why was the woman letting her sister fight this battle when the purpose of this meeting was to publicize her support and, presumably, get her daughter and sister to follow? But just when Rebecca thought she could hold her tongue no longer, Bergeron said, "Enough, both of you."

Bergeron turned to Labadie. "Rowena, I love you for what you've done for me and for what you're trying to do now."

She turned to Fiedler. "And you, Tony, are way out of your element. I'd want you to check the Terms and Conditions of an acquisition contract any day. But the laws surrounding the collection and use of DNA data and the risks involved? I doubt you've studied those issues even as much as I have. And after doing so, I agree with you completely. I have no intention of giving these two anything, and I encourage all of you to do the same."

"But I thought you told me you were going to cooperate," said Labadie.

A moment of uncertainty crossed Bergeron's features but was gone so quickly, Rebecca wondered if she had imagined it.

"I've had more time to think about it," Bergeron replied curtly. "Now, Tony, if you'd show them out?"

"Gladly." He walked over to where Rebecca sat, extending a hand. Rebecca stood, pulling her elbow from his grasp while resisting the urge to put it in the middle of his smug grin.

Rebecca glanced at Bergeron, still wondering what, if anything, she had just witnessed in the woman's face. The answer that came to her, however, was so foreign that she wondered if she dared to voice it. But then, there wasn't much of a case to worry about if they could only count on Labadie's cooperation. "I suppose keeping your DNA information out of everyone's database is the safest way to go."

"Exactly. My life. My DNA and it needs to stay that way. As for going forward on this case, that's up to my sister, but you're getting nothing else from me."

Rebecca nodded, and she and Gus walked ahead of Fiedler to the door. A phone rang somewhere deeper in the building, but it wouldn't be for them. They left.

Halfway back to the car, Rebecca said under her breath. "Forty-five minutes ago, she chews us out for asking for her DNA when the state has it? And now, she's keeping it out of everyone's hands?"

"Yeah. Strangest damn thing I've ever seen," Gus whispered back.

The sound of approaching cars interrupted their bewilderment, and Rebecca turned to see three police cars pull to the front of the home and stop. "This many cars could only be one thing." Then, Rebecca spotted an officer she knew. "Hank, what's up."

"Hey, Marte. Another death, another talk with the witch," he replied, then joined two other officers at the front door.

THURSDAY, OCTOBER 15

7:26 AM, A Farmhouse in Western Kansas

Perishables were a problem if you wanted to maintain the illusion of a dying world without electricity. But recently, nights had been near or below freezing, and food could remain edible longer. But despite that fact, Maggie's trips had become more frequent. And much shorter. Several times over the past few days, she had disappeared on a "foraging" trip, only to reappear a little over an hour later. She was going somewhere and it wasn't far from the farm.

The driveway in front of the house was rough and rutted, making the top speed on it perhaps 25 miles per hour. But for all Nicole knew, there was an interstate highway just over the ridge with a speed limit of 70mph. So, at that speed, Maggie could reach a town 35 miles away in a half-hour, leaving a few minutes for her business and a half hour to get back. It was a rough estimate, but Nicole was comfortable using it as a starting point.

What she wasn't comfortable with—what was slowly eating at her mind—was "the business" Maggie did when she got there. It seemed likely that it was related to her captivity or her impregnation, but otherwise, Nicole had little idea. Nothing like nursery furniture, toys, or baby clothes had appeared, but it was still early for that. And all she ever saw were bags and boxes that stayed locked in the truck's cab until Maggie personally carried them to her office.

And after Nicole gave birth, what then? Having completed her task, would she be killed, buried in a shallow grave somewhere on the endless grasslands? Maggie wouldn't want any witnesses to her atrocities, and Justin would accept anything she said. "Sorry, son, but childbirth was just too much for Nicole." Or if she was allowed to live, would she ever see the baby? Nicole would never harm her flesh and blood, but did Maggie believe that? How deep did her delusions go?

But at least, her place of honor in Maggie's perversion of reality was producing one benefit—her half rations had become somewhat more generous. But then, Nicole figured that was the result of practicality, rather than compassion. If she was pregnant, hunger could have negative effects on both mother and baby. Unfortunately, her reprieve didn't extend to freedom of movement. Nicole's ankles had been rubbed raw from the cuffs and now, every hobbling trip to the kitchen or the bathroom was filled with pain.

After many long hours thinking about her plight, Nicole had come to only one conclusion. She had to escape before she became pregnant, or failing that, before the child was born. She stood from the armchair, deciding that what passed for freedom in her world— a lap around the compound—was worth the pain it would cause.

"Where are you going?"

Nicole didn't bother to turn to look at Justin. "Getting some fresh air."

"OK, but stay away from the fence." Maggie had recently added that rule, saying it would keep them safe from any rodent that might nip them through the wire. The real reason, of course, was to slow any attempt Nicole might make to cut through it. Climbing it, as Maggie had guessed, was an impossibility.

As she walked toward the front door, Nicole glanced out through the picture window. It wasn't that long ago that she had thought this scene beautiful. But then, she had thought of the farmhouse as her life raft in a violent and deadly storm at sea. Now, it felt more like a dead weight threatening to pull her under the surface of the water.

As Nicole watched, Maggie's truck crested the rise about a mile from the farm. Nicole checked the clock on the wall. Almost exactly one hour and fifteen minutes, just like clockwork. She didn't know if these observations might someday prove useful, but any regularity she could find felt important.

She glanced out the window again and nearly gasped at the sight. Maggie's truck was still about a half-mile away, but behind it a second vehicle had crested the rise. And it looked like it had a light bar on the top. Could it be? Was it law enforcement?

At first, Nicole couldn't believe her eyes. She blinked several times as if she might dislodge the illusion from her mind's eye. But, no, it was real. She'd been trapped in the compound for months and had never seen another car. But now, there was one and it carried someone who would be able to help ... if she could only get word to the driver.

Maggie had stopped her truck and had gotten out to stand at the side of the road. She was still over a quarter-mile away, a mere speck against the rough brown background of the plains. She wouldn't want the other car getting closer. Too close and the officer might hear Nicole's calls for help. The police car stopped and someone got out. By movement and stance, Nicole felt sure the officer was male, and he was dressed in dark colors, probably blue and black.

"What are you looking at?" asked Justin from behind her.

"Nothing." But it was too late to stop him. He walked up to the window.

"Look! Mom found someone to bring back to the house. It looks like a policeman." Justin was grinning, shifting his weight back and forth between his feet.

Nicole had to do something; she might never have a better chance. But what? Going outside and yelling would do no good. The officer would never hear her. She couldn't get through the compound's fence, and even if she did, with the shuffle the ankle restraints permitted, it would be a half-hour before she was even within shouting distance. She could go out into the compound and wave her arms. Justin was excited enough he might even join in. But then, they'd just look like children at play, something Maggie could easily explain. 'Don't you wish you had all the energy those kids have?' she'd say, and the officer would chuckle and drive away.

Nicole's mind raced through the possibilities, but everything she considered turned out the same. Maggie would patiently answer all the officer's questions and lacking any official reason to search the house, he would leave. She had to do something to interrupt this inevitable sequence and then hope for the best. And at the moment, Justin was the only destabilizing influence she could find.

If Nicole could just get him to go meet them, there were plenty of things he might say in a casual conversation that would trigger an officer's suspicions. "You must be immune to the virus like my mom" came to mind. And if he said something like that, she had to hope the officer was quicker with his gun than Maggie was with her knife. At this point, Nicole was certain Maggie wouldn't let herself be taken.

"Justin, I think something might be wrong. I thought I saw something metal. I think the policeman may have pulled out his gun. Your mom might be in trouble."

Justin stopped fidgeting and stared at her, the grin now gone from his face. But after a moment, he said, "Naw, a policeman wouldn't hurt Mom."

"But we don't know he's a policeman. The man who owned that car might have died in the pandemic and this guy stole it. That way, he can get close to houses so he can rob the people who live there. It wouldn't hurt anything to take a look."

"You're right," said Justin, heading for the door. Nicole watched him leave, but when he neared the gate to the compound, he stopped, stood for a moment, and then turned back to the house.

Nicole opened the front door. "What's wrong?"

"Mom would be mad if I went beyond the fence," he said and walked back across the lawn.

"So, you're just going to let that man hurt her?"

"No," he said, then pushed past her into the house and started pacing. After a couple of laps, he went into the kitchen and returned with his rifle.

"Oh, my God, Justin. You can't just shoot him. We don't know for sure he's bad. Maybe he really is a policeman."

Justin's trot toward the front door didn't slow, but over his shoulder, he said, "I'm going out to listen. If Mom starts screaming, I'm shooting him."

"Justin!" Nicole's yell was enough to make him stop and turn.

Now that she'd upset the flow of events, she had to figure out how to get them back under her control. A call from a wounded officer would bring every law enforcement official in the county at a run, but even at this distance, Justin was a deadly shot. The officer might not have a chance to call. And if he didn't call, eventually his department would start checking, but that could take hours. By then, Maggie would have her tied and gagged in the trunk, and they'd be halfway to the next state.

"Justin, you have to be absolutely certain that your mom is yelling for help, not just laughing at some joke the policeman told her. She has to call for help because if you kill an officer, they'll lock you in jail forever."

Justin stood looking at her, his hand coming to his chin while he considered her words.

"Do you understand me?" Nicole asked sharply, not able to dismiss her panic until he agreed.

"Yeah, I got it. No shooting unless Mom yells for help." He turned and went outside.

Nicole dropped her gaze to the wooden floor of the farmhouse, heartened that she'd disarmed the situation but destroyed because she'd eliminated her chance at escape. Justin would wait for a cry that would never come, and soon, the officer would drive away. And she'd stay ... until Maggie discarded her.

Nicole raised two closed fists to her forehead, symbolically pushing back against her despair. The officer was still out there on the road; she couldn't give up now.

She limped into the kitchen. All the heavy cookware—cast iron ovens and skillets—were locked away. They could be used as weapons or, as in the current situation, struck together like a clapper hitting the lip of a bell. The sound could be heard for miles. In their absence, maybe something lighter would work well enough. But when she scanned the room, she discovered an option so startling, she could hardly believe her eyes. In his rush to protect his mother, Justin had left the gun case open. Two other rifles were sitting inside.

Nicole knew little about guns—only what she had learned watching and listening to Justin—but she knew these two rifles differed in the caliber of shells they used. If she wanted to attract the officer's attention with noise, the larger caliber would be better. But then, gunshots on the prairie were almost as easily explained as kids playing in the yard. She needed something more dramatic, something less easily ignored. Placing a shot near the car might do and the larger caliber round should be more noticeable when it hit. But could she hit a rock or a dusty stretch of the road when she could hardly see them? And if she didn't hit something like that and the slug went into the dead grass, it would be nearly imperceptible.

That left shooting into the police car. As long as there was only one officer—an assumption she could check through the gun's scope—she had the entire passenger side of the car for a target. A shattered windshield or a round into the radiator couldn't be ignored.

For this job, the smaller caliber rifle—the one that Justin called a twenty-two—seemed the better option. It was lighter and she could handle it more easily. And if things went badly and she hit someone, it would do less harm. She wasn't, however, certain about that. The bullets for the twenty-two were something called hollow points. She'd seen the tiny entry hole one made when he had shot a coyote. But when he turned the animal over, there was a gaping wound on the other side the size of her fist. A shot misplaced badly enough would kill the officer, even at this distance.

Nicole pulled the firearm from the cabinet. Justin kept his rifles loaded, but she wanted to be sure. She flipped the safety off and worked the bolt, making sure a bullet was in the chamber—

something she'd seen Justin do dozens of times. Once certain, she put the safety back on and went out the back door. Moving as quietly and quickly as the ankle bracelets allowed, she snuck behind the outbuildings until she reached the side fence. The officer and Maggie were still there in the distance, standing by the side of the road, talking. Nicole started forward in a crouch, moving slowly and staying near the fence.

When she was nearly even with the front of the house, she saw Justin. He had his face pressed up against the wire about ten yards from one corner of the compound. She dropped down to crawl, being careful to keep the muzzle of the rifle out of the dirt. The going was extremely slow as she checked the grass for twigs that would snap under her hands or knees. But even with her glacial pace, her heart was racing and her breaths were coming in shallow gasps. She told herself to calm down.

After what seemed like ten minutes but was probably less than two, she reached the fence at the front of the compound near the other corner. Justin was about 30 yards to her right with nothing between them except a few shaggy tufts of dead prairie grass.

She pushed the muzzle of the gun through the fence. Lying on the ground with the barrel resting on a strand of wire seemed perfect. She could relax and not worry about her arms that were shaking from fatigue and the extra adrenaline in her system. But when she peered through the scope, the wire above the muzzle was partially blocking her view. She would have to raise the gun from its rest. When she found the right spot, she placed her elbows on the ground to stabilize her aim.

Nicole checked the scene closely. The officer was indeed male and seemed at ease, his gestures sweeping across the horizon like he was describing the buffalo that had once roamed here. And he seemed to be alone; Nicole detected no shadows, no movement from within the car. But in the time it took her to assess the situation, the conversation ended, and he was getting back into the car. Nicole put the crosshairs just below the roofline on the passenger side and pulled the trigger.

She heard the crack of the rifle, felt a slight recoil against her shoulder, but saw nothing through the scope—nothing, that is, except grass. She moved the end of the gun to the left and the car reappeared in the crosshairs. Apparently, she'd jerked the rifle to the right rather than squeezing the trigger. And, unfortunately, no one in the distance had noticed her errant shot. The car had completed its turn and was slowly driving away as if nothing had happened.

"Nicole, stop firing. He's not hurting anyone. He's leaving."

Justin started toward her at a jog. Nicole could pull the barrel from the fence, turn it toward him, and force him to stop. But as soon as she went back to aiming at the car, he would overpower her. She had to take her shot now, figuring she had time for one more at a now moving target.

She chambered another round and then used a precious second or two to take a breath and try to calm herself. She aimed, then squeezed the trigger slowly. Again, she heard the crack of the rifle, then listened as the sound faded across the plains. The car continued to drive away. She quickly chambered another round, but it was too late. Justin grabbed the rifle by the forestock and pulled it free of the fence and out of her hands.

Nicole turned back to the road, expecting to watch her last hope disappear over the rise. But instead, the car's motion lasted only long enough for the officer to realize that someone had put a bullet through his rear window. The car veered sharply off the gravel and the roof lights began to flash. She couldn't see it, but Nicole imagined the officer bailing out of the other side while he called for backup. It wasn't necessarily going to be pleasant for her from this moment on, but her rescue now seemed assured.

"What the hell are you doing," Justin screamed. "They're going to haul you away to jail."

It took Nicole a moment to put herself back into Justin's world. In it, she had assaulted a police officer and was in big trouble. In hers, she'd saved her life and maybe his, as well. She could try to explain it to him, but events would soon make everything clearer than anything she could say. "I'll be fine, Justin."

He shook his head and then started toward the farmhouse with both rifles in hand.

9:44 AM, Marte Investigative Services

"I can't help wondering what the voice is like. Gruff and gravelly like Linda Blair in The Exorcist? No, I'm thinking more like the soft crooning of Mister Rogers. Never did trust that guy."

"Moron," Rebecca spat, hitting the off button on her car radio so hard her finger hurt. "If you could read, you'd know Della Bergeron doesn't hear voices."

Rebecca took a breath, knowing perfectly well why she felt so frustrated. After the police picked up Bergeron for questioning in the death of Mateo Sanchez on Monday, her investigation into the woman came to an abrupt end. It followed the same trajectory as the presumption that Bergeron was sane—it crashed and burned.

It had started during one of the initial police interviews about the Sanchez killing. Bergeron had admitted to some confusion during a meeting at her home in the hours following his death. It was something about an "inexplicable change" in her position on some issue. No one, save Rebecca and Gus, however, knew or cared about what that insight might mean. All everyone else saw was a second bout with delusion. And eventually, they believed, she'd recall being taken over when she murdered Goodwin as well, bringing the total of deadly possessions to three.

With this pattern of death following in her wake, the prosecuting attorney saw his responsibility clearly. He added the killings of Nicholas Goodwin and Mateo Sanchez to the charges against Bergeron. Those cases were not nearly as strong as Sims's murder, but they were in the first days of one investigation and the first hours of the other. And it was the pattern that was important. The judge agreed and bail was denied.

At the same time, a disagreement between Bergeron's criminal law team and her family surfaced. The rumor was it had been smoldering in the background all along and the events on Monday had just brought it to a blaze. At first, the lawyers had recommended a plea of temporary insanity. Though the chances of its success were slim, they argued that the strength and consistency of the circumstantial evidence against their client in Sims's death gave them few other options. Bergeron and her family disagreed. When Bergeron's story changed later and she claimed possession, the lawyers renewed their arguments. Harrison and Labadie admitted some doubt, but in the end, they stood with their kin.

The penultimate straw came when, against their counsel, Bergeron admitted another break from reality after the Sanchez killing. The lawyers called an emergency meeting of the family. The case was getting out of control. They might have swayed the group anyway, but during the discussion, they received a final piece of news. Forensics had detected trace amounts of gunpowder on

Bergeron's hands, and she claimed no memory of touching a gun in years.

With the possibility of death by lethal injection now seeming quite real, the family conceded to the law team—even the brother on the phone from Alaska, who had been a staunch opponent of their recommendations now concurred. The lawyers would argue that Bergeron was incompetent to stand trial, incapable of understanding the proceedings against her. If successful, she'd be found not guilty by reason of insanity and involuntarily committed for as long as her treatment required. It was a harsh decision they made but still better than death row.

Rebecca knew a great deal about what had happened behind the scenes because Labadie had told her when she came to fire the PIs. OK, perhaps they weren't fired in the traditional sense, but Rebecca still felt the case had been a failure. How else could she feel when she knew there was a chance that a sane—although peculiar—woman was going to be indefinitely committed for a mental illness she didn't have? The chance, of course, was slim, but in her mind, it existed.

Rebecca had voiced her concerns to Labadie during their meeting, and then, they involved Harrison over the phone. At first, Rebecca had felt uncomfortable suggesting to them that the High Priestess's possession might be real. And Rebecca was haunted by the woman's parting words from their first interview, "The answer you seek will be closer to the supernatural than you expect." How did the witch know she'd even consider that possibility, much less argue for it with her sister and daughter?

But in Rebecca's mind, her doubt about possession was balanced by Bergeron's verbal blunder during the argument at her home. One minute, she had called them out for overlooking the fact that the state already had her DNA. The next, she was claiming she was withholding a sample so no one would ever have it. It was like two people had been speaking, each not knowing of the other, and Rebecca found herself wondering if that could be true.

Labadie and Harrison both questioned whether the inconsistency had occurred; neither had been present when Bergeron talked about the state collecting her DNA following her arrest for the Sims murder. And when Rebecca had assured the two that there was no uncertainty about that statement—her partner had heard it, too—Harrison had said, "Unfortunately, just more proof that she's lost touch with reality."

Gus had told her to expect that reaction from the family. Damn, he could be infuriating when he was right.

Rebecca pulled into the parking lot for her office, shut off the car, and went inside. She wasn't looking forward to the day, although she had a half-dozen more background checks to run. At least business wasn't suffering, the infamy of the witch case bringing the clients to her door. She took the files from a locked cabinet, sat down at her desk, and then, pushed them aside. She wasn't in the mood.

At least Gus would be in soon. Maybe he'd have one of those ridiculous jokes of his. They seemed to invariably come from the 1960s, '70s, or '80s, and she often had to research the topic just to get the punchline. What the heck does "Where's the beef" mean? She needed to talk to someone her age, like Doc.

"Crap," she said to the empty room. How long ago had he said he'd be in St. Louis in a week? Was it six days? Eight? She decided to call.

"Agent Marte," he replied after the second ring. "To what do I owe this pleasure?"

"Hi, Doc. I wasn't sure you'd answer. Thought you might be driving?" That seemed a better way of asking than the question, "where the hell are you?"

"As always, your timing is perfect. I just pulled into a rest area in Kansas, maybe 30, 40 miles from the Missouri border. I should be back in St. Louis in five hours or so."

He sounded ... well, maybe not happy, but at least, not depressed. She decided it was the sound of being rested and resolved, and that was a great tone to hear from her friend.

"So, are you calling me to gloat, tell me you've solved the case of the witch of the St. Louis business world?" he asked. "I haven't had time to check the papers recently."

"I wish," Rebecca replied, a sigh preceding her statement. "It all went sideways shortly after we talked last time. And now, Della Bergeron is locked up, and only her lawyers and family are getting in to see her. Not that I have any business with her anyway."

Rebecca spent a few minutes reviewing the events of the last two days.

"That's unfortunate," Doc said when she was finished.

"Of course, I wouldn't need your condolences if you'd told me how Fiedler or Harrison killed Sims."

Doc was quiet a moment. "I did tell you. I sent a text almost a week ago." Rebecca started to check when he said, "Hold on a second."

After a few moments of silence, she heard the tone for an incoming message. Before she could switch applications, Doc came back on the line. "Sorry. I guess I didn't have any cell service and the message got stuck in my queue. It's theoretical, but it appears possible under the assumptions ...."

The sound of her outer office door being thrown open followed by "Rebecca" drowned out whatever Doc was saying. It was Gus shouting, and she was certain she'd never heard him so excited. He rushed into her office.

"We need to call Doc right now."

"He's already on the line," she replied and hit the speaker button. "Doc, Gus just showed up."

"Yeah, I know. I could hear him. Hey, Gus. You have something for me?"

"Do I ever," he started, then paused. He took a deep breath. "Now, this isn't definite," he said slowly. "It might be nothing."

"Nicole?" asked Doc softly.

"Yeah, maybe. I just heard. There's some sort of armed standoff in a little town, someplace called Granger. It's near ...."

"I know where it is," said Doc. "I've been through there a couple of times. What happened?"

"Someone took a shot at a deputy's car so they pulled up the property's owner, Maggie Ingalls. She's a dead ringer for Nicole's kidnapper. And the deputy spotted two others—a male and a female who could be ...."

"That's her," Doc said, interrupting again. "I gotta go."

"Wait," replied Gus. "You're not going to get within five miles of the place. They're already putting cars on all the back roads. They're taking no chances the shooter escapes. And that means, no one is getting in, either."

"Five miles away is a couple of hundred miles closer to Nicole than I am now." Doc was quiet a moment. "It sounds like this is still happening. How'd you find out so fast?"

"We've never really stopped looking," said Gus. "Especially my partner here. She tells me about all your calls, reminds me to keep my ears open. So, I set up feelers everywhere you went. Shots fired and a possible hostage situation, which is how this came out, caught the attention of an old friend at the Kansas Highway Patrol. He called me."

This time, Doc's silence was considerable. "I didn't know," he said softly. "I thought I was alone." He paused again. "I should have known better. Gus, Rebecca, thanks. I owe you."

"The least we could do," said Gus. "I won't try to talk you out of going because I probably couldn't. But make yourself known to law enforcement as soon as you get close. And don't do anything stupid like cutting across country to get to the house. OK?"

"OK, I'll play it by the book," replied Doc. He disconnected.

"Do you think he'll listen?" asked Rebecca. "I mean, he hasn't been all that discreet so far, what with the disturbing the peace and vagrancy charges he's racked up."

"And this last one in Nevada? Not so minor. It was breaking and entering, although apparently, some U.S. Senator got him some leniency."

"A senator?" asked Rebecca.

"Yeah, Senator Dempsey, I believe it was." Rebecca shrugged, not recognizing the name. "But Kansas ain't Nevada," continued Gus. "No guardian angel there ... well, none that I know of, anyway. So, I've done my good deed for the day. I think I'll take the rest of it off."

"OK," said Rebecca. "Go ahead and enjoy the time off. I'll just hang around here, check out his text that tells us how Bergeron was controlled."

Gus had started toward the door while she spoke but stopped in his tracks when she finished the sentence. He turned around slowly. "He came up with something?"

"He thinks he might have," replied Rebecca as she opened the text on her phone. "It says, check the research on the neuroscience of empathy." She lowered the phone, staring at her partner, "What the hell is that?"

10:22 AM, Marte Investigative Services

"What's it say?" asked Gus, again trying to read the computer screen over Rebecca's shoulder.

"Shush." It wasn't the nicest thing to say to her partner, but "just a minute" and "hold on" hadn't worked and she needed some quiet. Even the relatively nontechnical descriptions on the neuroscience of empathy used a vocabulary that was foreign to her. But over fifteen minutes or so, she had homed in on one specific area. And now, she hoped she understood it but doubted that she did. It was just too unbelievable.

"Sorry, Gus," she said when she turned from the computer to find him slouched in his chair. "Maybe you should have been doing the reading. Your background is stronger than mine."

"On neuroscience? You've got me mixed up with some other Gus Clements. So, tell me."

Rebecca took a deep breath, which, even to her, sounded unnecessarily dramatic. "First, there's a ton of research. The brain structures involved in empathy get a lot of coverage. And the differences between neurotypical individuals and psychopaths get quite a bit, too. At first, I thought that was what he wanted us to see, but I couldn't make anything match."

"Yeah, if Bergeron was the psychopath without empathy, how does that tell us anything about how she was controlled?" said Gus.

"Part of why it fell apart for me, too. And then I found these studies about how the brain reacts when someone feels empathy. It's not that the activity is only related to seeing. The brain's reactions are more like experiencing the situation. When someone says, 'I feel your pain' and they're empathizing, the reactions in their brain would look similar to their reactions if they were the ones being hurt."

"So, then ...." Gus paused, still considering this finding. "So, does this mean that Bergeron is the one who is empathizing? And she is being so strongly influenced that she can't tell someone else's pain from her own?"

"That's what I'm thinking. Your pain becomes hers ... literally. And your desires and your fears and all the rest. That certainly fits with her somewhat freakish ability to read people."

"Might even explain why she keeps some distance between herself and others," said Gus.

"Yeah, I skimmed a paper on that, too. If people take on too much of someone else's stress, anxiety, and anger—basically, if they're overly empathetic—they can become depressed. Bergeron might just be protecting herself."

"So, how comfortable are you with all this ... or even that we're looking at the right research papers?"

"On a scale of one to ten, seven that this is what he wanted us to see. But comfortable? How about a minus two."

"Yeah, me, too," replied Gus. "Let's call him back."

"I suppose we could leave him a message."

Gus frowned in response.

"He told me once that he debates every decision, big and small, but once he makes up his mind, that's it. And one of the things that he's decided is that talking on the phone and driving don't mix. He won't answer."

"It's Kansas. What's he got to run into out there?"

Rebecca shrugged, certain her prediction was accurate.

"OK, a message is better than nothing," said Gus after a moment. So, she called, he didn't answer, and she left a message.

"Yeah, you told me so," said Gus. "But, anyway, if we have zeroed in on the right area, picking up an emotion from another might explain how Ms. Bergeron came to feel hostility toward Sims ...," started Gus. "No, wait. She said the foreign emotion she felt later was omnipotence, not hatred. If she picked up a feeling of being all-powerful, she wouldn't have felt she was doing anything wrong. She'd feel that Sims was going to be fine. She might have even felt she was doing him a favor."

"OK," said Rebecca slowly, "but I'm still not sure how this would work. I mean, other than the one guard, everyone at the coven gathering was busy chanting. There was no one acting omnipotent ... whatever that would look like. So, who was Bergeron empathizing with?"

"Don't know," replied Gus. "although Doc thought it might be Harrison. I wonder ...."

The office phone rang with "Doc" showing on the display. Rebecca put the phone on speaker.

"Another rest area already?" Rebecca said in greeting.

"There are few people in the world who would warrant pulling off at an exit in the middle of nowhere. You and Gus do, but I'd love it if you'd make this quick."

"Sure. First, what part of the research did you want us to look at?" asked Gus.

"The part that says it's not just the visual cortex that's active when someone is empathizing. It's all the emotional and motor areas that would be activated if that person was in the situation they're observing."

"OK, so far, so good," said Rebecca. "We skimmed some of those papers. Now, the next issue. Later, when Bergeron recalled being possessed, she said she had been feeling omnipotent during the ritual. How could that have happened when there is no one there that night who was acting all-powerful?"

"I'd guess that Bergeron's susceptibility had to be developed over a long time, and the first part of the process is a whole lot easier to believe than the second. Initially, she wouldn't think that she is all-powerful, even as the High Priestess of her coven. No modern witch would if witches ever did. But she would know the myths surrounding her beliefs. She might have even fantasized about what it would be like to hold power over life and death. And someone close to her could make sure she was sensitized to these ideas by bringing them up in conversation, leaving books with that theme laying around, things like that. Bergeron still wouldn't consciously buy that folklore, but the notion would be there in her thoughts, connected to her practice of witchcraft."

"OK, I can see that," said Rebecca. "And the part that's harder to accept?"

"Well, first," said Doc, "if I was betting on who murdered Sims knowingly and in cold blood, I'd still put my money on Della Bergeron. There is simply too much evidence for that conclusion, and I have little but an extrapolation of theory against it. But if you want to consider it?"

Doc paused, perhaps waiting for or maybe even expecting her or Gus to balk. But when he received only silence, he continued. "OK, you two are all right with the idea that people can be more or less empathetic, right?"

"Sure," Gus and Rebecca said almost simultaneously.

"OK, then what if Bergeron is like the genius or the athlete with great eye-hand coordination but in terms of empathy? We know that the one-percenters in athletics can hit a 100-mile-per-hour fastball that most of us can hardly see. And one-percenters in intelligence do things like discover radioactivity and develop portable X-ray machines."

"Marie Curie?" asked Rebecca.

"Correct. So now, one-percent empathizers? I'm not sure what those people would be like, but by definition, they would acutely feel the emotions of others, and they would probably have some type of coping mechanism against feeling too much. Now, what if we're not talking about a one-percenter but a one-hundred-millionth of a percenter? Given the population of the world, there are seven or eight of them living today. And what if Bergeron is one of them? When her wall against others isn't raised, then a simple look might be enough to produce an emotional response, especially if all the groundwork had been laid in advance. All the casual mentions, the feigned slips of the tongue, the shared wild imaginings would add up over time. In this case, what we've been thinking about as a supernatural connection between Bergeron and an unnamed witch is actually a psychological one."

"It's a ... thought-provoking idea," said Gus.

"Thought-provoking meaning bizarre in this context, right?" replied Doc.

"Let's just say, I can't find fault in the reasoning, but it's probably an extremely difficult sell within the criminal justice system. Maybe it would work as a form of brainwashing if the experts get behind it. I can also see why you suspect Harrison over the others. The coven was there that night, but other than the daughter, they didn't have an opportunity to do the prep work. Fiedler and Putnam, on the other hand, might have had enough access to Bergeron, but neither of them was at the ritual."

"And from what Rebecca has told me," replied Doc, "if the lawyer could control Bergeron, it would end up in marriage, not murder."

Gus laughed. "Probably an even better reason it wasn't him."

Rebecca, however, wasn't laughing. She was too surprised—both by the strange possibility Doc had identified and by Doc's vocabulary. When had he started using her first name? Things had been so hectic that she hadn't noticed until now. But, somehow, she knew this wasn't the first time. She broke from her thoughts when he spoke again.

"So, back when you were on the case, I thought this might be a farfetched notion you'd like to check out when there was nothing else to do. Now that you're not, just chalk it up to my overactive imagination. And with that, unless you have something else pressing, I should go."

A quick look at Gus's shaking head and Rebecca said, "No, nothing else from us. And thanks for pulling over to give us a call. I'll just store your theory away with all the other minutiae I use to impress people who don't know me."

Rebecca could hear Doc's chuckling until he disconnected.

"Well, one case, the kidnapping of Nicole Veles is probably going to be over soon ... if not already. Even if it wasn't ours, I'm going to enjoy myself the rest of today. I'll pitch in on some of those background checks tomorrow."

"Sounds good. I'll get on them this afternoon."

But after Gus left, she said to the empty room, "Right after I see if there's any truth to Doc's notion."

At the Same Time, A Farmhouse in Western Kansas

If Justin hadn't considered her somewhat confused for attacking a law enforcement officer, Nicole would have asked him to leave one of the rifles so she could watch the situation unfold. But even without the aid of a rifle scope, she could see that Maggie had pulled over again and had gotten out of her truck. She started back up the driveway but stopped abruptly after a few steps. She was waving her arms in the air and yelling something back up the hill. The officer was answering, but Nicole couldn't make out any of the words.

After several minutes of shouted dialog, Maggie went back to her truck, got some papers from inside, and held them in the air. What was she doing, Nicole wondered? What plausible lies was she spinning that would cause the officer to drop his guard? But unless that happened very soon, it seemed like it would make no difference. Surely, the man had already called for backup, so even if she got the better of him now, the cavalry couldn't be far away. Not more than fifteen or twenty minutes, Nicole figured, since they'd be pushing their cars to the limit.

Nicole glanced at the farmhouse. Justin was standing by the door, rifles propped against the building. He was also watching the drama unfold.

This scene continued for another ten minutes or so, with Maggie probably suggesting it was just another errant shot out in the middle of nowhere. That kind of thing happened; it was just that one-in-a-million accident that made the national news. And besides, no one was hurt and she'd pay for the damages. But while the arguments Nicole was generating sounded convincing to her—at least, something to think about—the officer must have thought otherwise. He was keeping his car between himself and Maggie.

Eventually, Maggie must have decided her lies weren't going to work. She got back into the truck and started toward the farmhouse.

Nicole got up from the ground and started her ankle-iron shuffle across the compound. About halfway to the house, she turned back to check on the truck's progress. It was close. Much closer than she'd expected because it was moving fast. Perhaps Maggie had planned for a standoff with law enforcement and needed time to prepare?

The thought was unsettling. If Maggie was going to make a stand, it would mean she'd be trapped in the compound with the woman for hours, perhaps days. Nicole didn't think the situation would escalate. Justin was an excellent marksman and Maggie was average, but they'd have no chance against the dozens of officers that would soon be in place. More likely, no shots would be fired and the police would just wait them out. And when that started, Nicole suspected her half-rations would disappear. She wished she had stashed something to eat and drink when she had the chance.

That troubling thought ended, however, with the sound of screaming metal as the truck tore through the front gate. This wasn't the action of someone intending to make a stand; Maggie had just destroyed the first line of defense. And when the truck aimed at her, lining her up in the middle of the grille, Nicole recognized the action for what it was—the result of murderous hatred. Maggie was going to kill her, no longer caring who witnessed the deed.

It took only a couple of seconds for the truck to reach the spot where she stood, but it seemed much longer to Nicole as she waited. At the last moment, she dove to the left. The truck's crumpled bumper hit her left foot, and she screamed in agony. She rolled to her back, clutching her ankle and gritting her teeth. She wasn't sure she could stand. She was certain, however, that she wouldn't be lunging off of that foot again.

She struggled to her feet, putting most of her weight on her right leg. Maggie waited as if savoring the kill. The engine roared and the truck leaped forward, dirt and dead grass flying up in its wake. With cold detachment, Nicole decided to stand tall, stand motionless. To try to evade would only prolong her suffering. An instant death was the best she could hope for.

Nicole felt the impact, saw images of brown grass and blue sky tumbling in her vision. But it couldn't have been the truck; the blow came from the side. She landed hard and it took her a moment to catch her breath. Slowly, she sat up and looked at the spot where she had faced the truck. Justin was lying there. His head was twisted at an impossible angle. Blood streamed from a gash in his neck and oozed from his mouth. His eyes stared over her shoulder into an empty sky.

The truck had stopped about ten feet beyond Justin's body, smoke and steam coming from under the hood. Maggie got out. Her forehead was bleeding. She walked slowly over to where the young man was lying and got down on her knees. After a moment, she whispered, "You've killed him."

Nicole squeezed her eyes tightly in pain, partially from all that had happened to her, but mostly for Justin. He'd never had a chance, force-fed a twisted reality by a woman he called mother. And in his last act, he'd traded places with her in death.

"You killed him, you self-righteous bitch," Maggie screamed, glaring at Nicole. "And now, I'm going to send you to hell." She stood and started back to the truck.

Nicole looked back up the driveway. The police car hadn't moved. But then, driving into a fenced compound with people willing to shoot at law enforcement wouldn't be standard practice. She swung her gaze back to the truck. Maggie had just pulled her knife from the cab. She'd probably hidden it when she talked to the officer. Maggie wiped the blood from her forehead with a sleeve and started forward.

Nicole looked at the farmhouse, but she'd never get that far on her hands and knees before Maggie reached her. Between her and the house, however, she saw a glint. She looked closer. It was the reflection of the sun off the glass of the twenty-two's scope. Justin must have started back to her carrying the rifle before deciding it wasn't part of the solution.

Nicole stood but collapsed back to the ground from the throbbing pain in her ankle. She started crawling, Maggie closing in rapidly from behind. The two women reached the rifle at the same instant.

Nicole could hear the intake of breath as the older woman prepared to bury the knife in her back. Nicole grabbed the gun and rolled to the left. The blade of Maggie's knife hit her left forearm, cutting through the flesh to bone. Nicole screamed, dropping the rifle to the ground beside her to cradle her damaged arm.

Maggie drew back, intending to press the attack. Nicole knew the end was coming. She had fought the good fight. Again, it seemed time to end her struggle with quiet resolve. She rolled to her back, waiting. Maggie seemed to sense the change and slowed her advance to savor the victory.

"I should make you suffer, but I won't." She started to bend over, her arm coiled next to her shoulder, ready to strike.

But in the instant before the weapon started its descent, Nicole felt the cool of the rifle under her right hand. She grabbed the stock of the gun and brought the barrel up with all her strength. The blow caught Maggie under the chin, and the woman staggered back a step. Nicole brought the gun back down. There was no need to aim; Maggie was practically leaning against the muzzle. Nicole pulled the trigger.

At first, she thought she had missed, even though that seemed impossible. Then, a small red dot appeared on Maggie's shirt. Even so, the woman kept coming. She leaned over the muzzle of the rifle, bringing the blade down in a sweeping arch toward Nicole's chest.

4:37 PM, The Della Bergeron Residence

Rebecca pulled away from the home of Rowena Labadie, secure in the knowledge that her first step in gathering evidence on Harrison was going better than she had anticipated. The only problem now was that the doubts were starting to set in.

She had been able to accept Doc's description of the psychological leverage Harrison might have used against her mother. Yes, it was a lot to get your head around, but it seemed about the only way that Bergeron could have been tricked into killing Sims. But now, separated from the easy comradery of Gus and Doc, that speculation had started to crumble under the weight of her life experience. What if they were just fooling themselves? After all, even Doc had said in just about every call, Bergeron's probably the killer. Do daughters set up their mothers for murder? Do they kill again, twice and violently, to cover up the deed? Everything was inconsistent with what she knew about crime and criminals. For this to have happened the way Doc suggested, both Bergeron and her daughter need to be a one-hundred-millionth of a percenter, the former in feeling pain, the latter in delivering it.

Having worked through the dissonance-producing thoughts again, Rebecca told herself to relax. It wasn't like she was going to barge into Harrison's office, guns blazing. She was just going to do a bit of discreet snooping, starting with Bergeron's home. If Harrison had been extolling the fringes of the witchcraft folklore, there might be evidence of it in her mother's home. And there was also the question of how gunpowder had gotten on Bergeron's hands.

Rebecca had been to the witch's house twice before, but the roads were twisty and frequently blocked to through-traffic. It was the kind of area where you could spend an hour finding a home even after you were less than a hundred yards away and this street didn't look familiar. Spotting an elderly lady walking down the sidewalk, she stopped her car, picked up a slip of paper from the seat, and rolled down the window. "Everly Street?"

The woman gave Rebecca a look that she could only describe as "the evil eye." But eventually, the glare faded; Rebecca and her car must have passed muster in this quiet, upscale neighborhood bordered by less genteel areas. "Two streets up then left for two or three blocks."

"Thanks." Once the window was back up and Rebecca had pulled away, she muttered, "Damn phone." She wouldn't have to write down street names or ask for directions if the battery would hold a charge for more than a couple of hours. But then, by phone years, it was probably 210.

Once on Everly, she recognized her surroundings; it was a straight shot to the front gate of Bergeron's home. She rolled down the window at the guard station. "Rebecca Marte. Someone is supposed to meet me at Ms. Bergeron's home."

When at Labadie's house, Rebecca had claimed she had lost a family heirloom—a locket with pictures of her grandparents—and she thought she might have dropped it when she was interviewing her sister. Of course, the family wasn't going to let her into the mansion alone, and Rebecca had hoped that her escort would be her former client. The trust they had developed would have given Rebecca a freer hand to search the building. Labadie, however, was busy but said it was no trouble to get someone from Meteor to come out; she had made similar arrangements on occasion. So, Rebecca would just have to do her best with a stranger in tow.

"Sure, you're the PI. Your partner, Gus Clements, talked to me about ... about the death of Mr. Sims."

"He's had nothing but good things to say about the work your company does."

"Thanks. It's Lamont, by the way."

"Nice to meet you, Lamont."

Rebecca wondered if this was his transition to flirting and how she should handle it—it was never a good idea to get on the wrong side of security. But that possible problem disappeared when he said, "You can go on in, Ms. Marte. You'll be met at the front door."

Rebecca thanked him and drove to the house, finding an unfamiliar car parked in the lot. She walked around to the front, but before she could push the doorbell, the door opened. There stood Harrison, a handgun raised in front of her.

"Whoa. What's going on?" Rebecca didn't have to act to sound surprised.

"Get in here," Harrison snarled, stepping back into the house and gesturing with the gun.

Rebecca did. After she had walked past, Harrison closed the door.

"Open your jacket."

"I don't know what's going on. I just wanted to look for my missing locket. I think the chain might have broken when I was here speaking with your mother."

"Drop the act, Marte. After Mother's mind cleared, she knew she'd contradicted herself. And you noticed the slip since you're here searching for evidence. Now, open your jacket, take your gun out with your left hand, thumb and one finger only, and put it on the table. I see anything different and you're dead."

The odds Rebecca could flip the gun up into a full lefthanded grip or toss it into her right hand quickly enough to defend herself were extremely remote. She did as told.

"Move away." Harrison took the pistol in a gloved hand and placed it in a pocket. "You can have it back later. Raise your jacket and turn around."

"I only have one handgun."

"Forgive me if I don't believe you. Now, do it."

After confirming Rebecca had nothing tucked in a waistband or hidden under the legs of her pants, Harrison had her remove her phone. It went into the pocket with the handgun.

"So, you trade in your shotgun?" Rebecca surprised herself with the somewhat irreverent remark because humor was an emotion she wasn't feeling. Maybe some could laugh looking into the business end of a pistol, but she doubted it. There was nothing funny about dying painfully. But to focus on escape, she pushed that thought to the back of her mind.

"Yes, poor Sanchez. He was clever enough to spot the embezzlement, which surprised me. But he wasn't smart enough to pick the right culprit. And when he wanted a meeting with Mother, saying only it was important company business ... well, of course, she called in the acting CEO."

Rebecca doubted Harrison had any training on subduing someone with a firearm—that is, other than what she would have seen in the movies or on television. But so far, that was sufficient. She was staying far enough away that a lunge for the gun would be foolhardy and yet, close enough that she could hardly miss. She also seemed quite calm, given that she was about to murder someone. But then, she wasn't a novice.

"So, let's go look for your missing locket, shall we? Where did you meet with Mother?"

"That room," said Rebecca pointing to the second set of pocket doors on the right.

Harrison released a single laugh. "Nice try, Marte. You played me for the fool once already, asking for everyone's DNA when you had no use for it other than to shake me up. Now, look where that bit of deceit got us." She held up the gun as if to prove her point.

Rebecca felt no need to admit that the request had been based on a hypothesis that proved wrong—that Bergeron was avenging her rape. The mistake had, after all, exposed the criminal.

"Since you're curious about that room, go—take a look," Harrison said.

Rebecca did, revealing a home office with state-of-the-art automation. "Mother would never meet with anyone in here. But on the other hand, it would be the perfect place for you to look for evidence after you distract me by asking for a cup of tea. Start with the desk. Open a few drawers."

Rebecca casually surveyed her surroundings for a possible means of escape as she walked to the desk. There was nothing except windows—not even another door—and those were probably modern replacements. Crashing into one of those panes of glass at a full run would probably leave her stunned and bleeding at best. She opened a drawer and shoved it closed.

"Easy," said Harrison. "You wouldn't be slamming things like that. I might hear. And push some of the stuff around inside the drawers."

"So, your mother picks up on your emotions? Enough that it overwhelms hers?" Rebecca was finding nothing in the drawers that she could use as a weapon. Throwing something like a staple puller might give her a fraction of a second longer to reach her assailant, but Harrison was now standing a couple of feet farther away. The added distance increased the likelihood that the shot would miss, but the odds still weren't good.

"Yeah, it's almost like the supernatural crap she puts so much faith in. I feel something and she reacts. How's that for weird?" Harrison paused a moment. "You know what's even stranger about

Mother's beliefs? She wouldn't have them, except for me. I was just a kid—ten, twelve, something like that—when I got interested in the occult. Even went with a Goth look for a while. Then, all of a sudden, Mother's into it, too. I thought perhaps my emotions had affected her before, but this was so far out of the norm, I was certain. And her strange attraction to Sims? My doing, too. That's good. Now, the file cabinets, though the one on the left is locked."

Nothing but papers inside, Rebecca saw as she opened a drawer. A handful thrown in the air would be distracting, but probably only for an instant. And because she was standing between the file cabinets and a table and chairs, a quick drop to the ground and roll wouldn't get her far. And it wouldn't provide any cover.

"The gunpowder on your mother's hands? That was a nice trick," said Rebecca.

"Rummage through the drawers," said Harrison sharply. "For a PI, you certainly don't know anything about searching for evidence." She released a single laugh. "It seems that if you wrap a gun with a rag and fire it several times, it'll pick up some residue. I just happened to use the one Mother wipes her hands on after gardening. I wasn't sure it would work but those tests must be something else."

After a few moments of opening a drawer, rifling through it, and moving on, Harrison said, "That's good. Now, let's go to the room where you actually met Mother. After all, you would have searched there while we chatted and before I left to make you a cup of tea."

Rebecca went through her mental inventory of that room, coming up with little besides another set of windows, heavy tables and chairs, and lots of books. And then, she recalled the fireplace tools on the hearth. Would Harrison have overlooked them? They seemed somewhat obvious. After all, a poker seemed to be the impromptu murder weapon in about every fourth movie she watched.

When she pushed the doors open, she saw Harrison hadn't missed the tools; they were gone. She kept her gaze from the fireplace, not wanting to give Harrison a reason to gloat for her foresight.

"Check behind the chair cushions."

Rebecca did while gazing around the room for other possible weapons. Unlike the office, the parlor was decorated in antiques—old pictures, an antique Victrola, a clock on the mantel. Why couldn't Bergeron have been interested in broadswords and crossbows? They wouldn't have been out of place in this room.

"Run a hand through your hair," commanded Harrison.

"What?"

"You heard me. Now do it." Rebecca did. "You're frustrated, or faking frustration anyway, because the locket's nowhere to be found. Now, get down on your hands and knees beside each chair. I don't expect a full forensics examination of Mother's home, but it never hurts to be prepared."

"Aren't you going to join in the search?"

"I'm much too cultured to go crawling around on the floor. You would have done all of this to sell your cover. But when I go to make your drink, you search the office, then come back and check the library table and the bookshelf before I return. So, get to it."

The woman's planning to make this search look real was impressive. But the question it raised was, why hadn't Harrison let her search for real and leave? Then, the woman could have waylaid her elsewhere. There must still be some evidence left in the house. But what and where?

"You know this isn't going to work, don't you?"

"Do tell, but keep moving. I want to get this over with before dark. I don't want to have to pick my way back to the house in the middle of the night."

"You're going to kill me on the grounds?"

"This area is very interesting," said Harrison like she was commenting on the weather. "Stately mansions with manicured grounds like Mother's within a stone's throw of some heavy woods, rugged cliffs, and small houses that have seen better days. People are shooting off guns along the bluffs all the time. No one's going to notice another shot or two. So, kill you on the grounds? No, but nearby. Then, I walk the mile or so back through the woods, put everything in place, and drive away after a nice long chat with the guard about our unsuccessful search. Now, time for that cup of tea you requested. Sorry, but it might be a bit cold since I made it an hour ago."

"What's still here that you're afraid I'll find?" Rebecca asked as she picked up the cup and took a sip.

"Good girl. Now, take the cup by the body and set it back on the coaster. That should leave some nice fingerprints. As for what's here? Not much, really—a few pictures of occult rituals, several books, things like that. But all this evidence adds up. And besides, I didn't want to chance you texting a picture to yourself or something like that. It could raise questions about what you were really doing here. OK, out to the car."

"One week," said Rebecca, as they started toward the front door. She was hoping to draw Harrison into a discussion that would increase her doubts, make her think about risk rather than each step she'd carefully choreographed. A moment of hesitation might be enough for Rebecca to overpower the woman. But when Harrison said nothing, Rebecca continued, "I give you a week before the police knock down your door. It'll be a simple matter for them to review my case files, talk to my partner who knows all about this."

"Case files? You don't have a case. But even assuming you made some notes and told Clements about your hunches, it changes nothing. You have no proof. And Mother's slip? Just the ramblings of a certified looney. Nobody but you would care."

Rebecca opened the door and stepped out, followed at a safe distance by Harrison. They headed for the parking lot.

"Gus will care."

"Perhaps, but he's not going to be around long enough to do anything about it." Rebecca flinched, surprised at the woman's revelation. "Oh, yes, I know all about your partner's cancer. It's amazing what a grieving spouse will say to a sympathetic listener. You, on the other hand, were tougher. You don't seem to have a friend in the world. Well, none longer than one night anyway. Now, open the driver's side door, roll down the window, and get in."

Rebecca did. Harrison slid into the passenger seat behind her.

Rebecca could see three possibilities for gaining her freedom, although none of them looked that promising. She could run the car into a tree or a ditch. The trouble was, if she hit something hard enough to knock herself out, it was unlikely Harrison would get anything more than a bloody nose. The physical evidence might be enough to convict her abductor eventually, but she'd be long dead by then.

On the other hand, she could just turn toward the freeway rather than the bluffs or pull over at the guard station. How would Harrison handle a little disobedience? If she attempted to physically subdue her, even from behind, that might work in Rebecca's favor.

Almost as if the woman was reading her thoughts, Harrison said, "I don't want to shoot you in the car. Or worse, have to kill the guard, too. It complicates the story a bit, making it a carjacking gone wrong. What I have planned is so much more apropos, but if you insist on dying early …."

Rebecca was down to her last option for escape during the drive and the time for it was fast approaching. She could see the guard station just ahead.

The driveway from the road to Della's home split at the guard shack with an entry lane on one side of the structure and an exit lane on the other. Both lanes had retractable gates. The gate on the exit lane had always been open when Rebecca visited, probably because the guards didn't care about departing traffic. It was open now. But even so, she would be expected to slow down when she approached and Lamont would turn to wave. Guards always did, perhaps to show they were on the job but more likely just to break up the monotony. And when Rebecca casually returned the gesture, she'd make a slitting motion across her neck, then bring her hand up to wave where Harrison could see it, then point downward when her hand dropped back out of the woman's line of sight. She just had to hope those two signs would make Lamont curious enough to check.

"Wave back when the guard waves at you," whispered Harrison from her hiding position in the back seat. It seemed the first break Rebecca had gotten—permission from her would-be killer to implement her plan.

Right on cue, Lamont turned toward the window and waved. The flicker of hope that Rebecca had lit grew a bit brighter. But before her hand got even as high as her throat, Lamont looked back down at a book he was reading. Rebecca waved anyway, not wanting Harrison to shoot her for failing to complete the useless gesture.

Mentally, Rebecca kicked herself. Why the hell hadn't she flirted with the man?

4:54 PM, The Missouri River Bluffs

Rebecca had often wondered why, in the finale of so many fictionalized accounts of crime, the perpetrators would answer all the hero's questions about the who, where, and why of their transgressions. The bad guys had been asocial throughout the book or movie, robbing, killing, and raping, but now, they felt compelled to put the hero's mind at rest ... before they put the hero to rest. Why would they do that? But in Harrison's case, the woman liked to gloat, and Rebecca was going to use that desire to get as much time as she could. Hopefully, she'd find a way out.

"So, why'd you kill Sims?" asked Rebecca glancing in the rearview mirror at her passenger. "Or should I say, put your mother up to it?"

"Killing a lover is just a small part of what I owe her for the way I was raised. Skin a knee and get a drop of blood on a dress and it was a day without food. Two days if the dress was new. But the physical abuse was nothing compared to the contempt in her eyes. I think she saw her rapist every time she looked at me."

If that was true, then college must have been a sanctuary for her. In all the photographs Rebecca had found of those days, keeping off an extra ten pounds seemed to be the biggest worry Harrison had. "Seriously?"

"Bravo, Marte. I figured you for one of those open-minded dilettantes who wants everything tied up with a cliché. No, I wasn't abused, though Mother could have been warmer, less involved with herself. There was no dirty uncle who wanted to diddle me after school. I didn't join a gang and succumb to group-think. I didn't torture small animals growing up. I didn't play violent video games. Got any more favorite stereotypes that you want me to deny?"

"So, why did you do it then?"

"You wouldn't understand," replied Harrison. "Turn left at the next street." To emphasize her directive, Harrison pressed the gun barrel to the back of Rebecca's neck.

"Try me." Street lights were becoming scarce and the road, winding. Rebecca slowed down further, not in a hurry to see this journey end.

"OK," said Harrison after a moment. "Basically, I got tired of being frustrated. I'd become very good at manipulating Mother. After all, I had twenty plus years to practice. But eventually, she'd spot the changes, wonder how it had happened, and take everything away. She has such wealth while she keeps me doing menial labor so I'll appreciate my position later. To hell with that."

"You're willing to kill your mother over a little money?"

"First of all, it's not a little money. It's a lot. And second, I'm not killing her. All I did was put her in a position so compromising that she couldn't possibly free herself. And believe me, without something like a death, she'd find a way out. I have the experience to prove it. Pull over here."

Rebecca did, checking her surroundings. It didn't appear to be anything more than a slightly wider spot in the road. Heavily wooded terrain rose steeply on the left and dropped off more gradually on the right. Then, she noticed a crude path leading down the hill.

"But she could end up on death row," said Rebecca.

"Highly unlikely. Women like Mother don't get executed. They get let off with a slap on the wrist if that. And truthfully, I thought she had a great dodge going, her lawyers working the technicalities and her playing the witchcraft card. Then, she pushed it too far with all the blackouts and possessions, and now it looks like the first part of her unplanned retirement is going to be in a mental ward. That wouldn't have been my choice, since now she has the emotions of the deranged as well as confinement to deal with. That could be a little tough on her, but she's made her bed."

As the woman talked, Rebecca considered her options. Overpower her? Harrison had consistently maintained her distance to this point, so that was probably out. Talk her out of it? Rebecca hadn't spotted a crack in the woman's resolve so far and that seemed unlikely to change just because of the new setting. Duck and run? Maybe. If she could put some of the thick brush between herself and that gun, she liked her chances.

"Have you been here before?" asked Harrison, breaking into Rebecca's thoughts.

"No."

Harrison smirked. "First, you can't conduct a decent search, and now you don't know about your own case? You aren't much of a PI, are you? This is where Nicholas Goodwin was killed."

"Don't you mean where you killed him?"

"No, I said it correctly. I had nothing to do with his death." Given everything else she'd admitted to, Rebecca tended to believe her. "Down the hill is an old shack that some street gang used in the past. After Goodwin died, the police showed a lot of interest in it, so it makes sense you'd come here for a look. Who knew the gang was still active and you happened to stumble onto them?"

Harrison rolled down her window. "Get out." Rebecca did.

"Move back from the car." Rebecca complied as Harrison followed her progress with the barrel of the handgun.

"A little more." Rebecca took another step back. "Now turn around."

Rebecca glanced over her shoulder but didn't turn. Instead, she faced Harrison, plastering a smirk on her face she didn't feel. "It's going to be a bit suspicious when they find powder residue in my back seat."

Hopefully, Harrison took the comment as an insult to her planning—she hadn't thought of everything. The alternative was for her to wonder why anyone would help in their execution, and that thought would lead to the real reason for Rebecca's statement.

There was, however, a third option. Harrison stuck her whole arm out of the open window. "Now, turn."

Rebecca shrugged and prepared to spin and run. But before she could, Harrison shook her head, then reached down to open the door with her left hand. It was the moment Rebecca had been waiting for.

Sometime during high school, Rebecca's rebelliousness had become more social—drinking, joyriding, skinny dipping. But before that, she'd been pure tomboy, joining the boys on the athletic field rather than in a car or someone's basement. She knew all about the elusiveness of a football player in the open field. Or the fake shot and jab step of a basketball player before a drive to the bucket. Later, those rough skills had been sharpened by her FBI training. Now, she had to hope that was enough.

The moment Harrison pulled her arm back through the window to exit the opening door, Rebecca lunged right, then spun to her left in a sprint. Harrison fired. And again. The second shot had been close, hitting a branch to her left—an overcorrection to her movement. The next shot, however, might find its mark except that Rebecca had reached the edge of the brush next to the path. Without hesitation, she leaped.

The drop was more than she had expected, and the branches, though small, were stiffer than she had hoped. They tore at her clothes. They scratched her arms and legs. One lashed her across the face and Rebecca tasted blood in her mouth. But the injuries were minor ... until she landed on a large rock sticking up a couple of feet from the forest floor. She felt a pop in her ribcage, followed by waves of searing pain with each gulp of precious air. The scream she trapped in her throat came out as half gasp, half grunt. Even that probably told Harrison she was hurt and that was a problem.

After several moments enduring the anguish to get the air she desperately needed, Rebecca's breathing slowed and she sat up. Carefully, she probed her ribs, wincing with each touch. She twisted to look up the hill but that, too, sent stabs through her chest. Clearly, making a run for it on the path was no longer an option. Ten yards in a sprint and she'd be doubled over in wheezing agony. And pushing through this underbrush, even if she could manage the torture, would make so much noise it would be like wearing a neon sign that said, "Here I am, shoot me."

Harrison was coming, taking the path, of course, rather than plunging into the undergrowth. Rebecca could hear her. But she heard something else. Water. At first, she thought it was the Missouri River, but the sound was too close. Peering through the brush, she saw a small stream. And then she smelled it—the odor of decaying life and discarded trash trapped in stagnant pools. Even so, with the promise of quiet escape that it represented, Rebecca wouldn't have cared if it smelled like an open sewer.

She stood. A small stone that had come to rest against her back now tumbled down the larger rock, its clattering descent giving the hunter an update on her position. Harrison fired into the brush, missing to the left, but if Rebecca continued to make noise, the shooter would home in on her all too soon. Searching the ground, Rebecca found a small stick and tossed it into the brush to her right, hoping enough gunfire would bring the police. But Harrison didn't fire, perhaps suspecting the first noise was a mistake and the second, a distraction.

Rebecca sat down, buttoned her jacket, and turned up the collar around her neck. Even though the woods were getting darker, her white shirt could still give her position away. The blue of her blazer, though not a hue found naturally in the woods, was at least dark.

The ground was covered with dead leaves and twigs that had been composting over a long winter, spring, and summer. She dug her fingers through the top layer, bringing up a handful of dark, damp soil. She rubbed some on her forehead and cheeks. Then, she ran both hands through her light blonde hair. It wasn't the face paint of football players, but hopefully, it would reduce her body's reflection from the patchy light of the woods.

She lay down on the ground. Harrison wouldn't be expecting the lower profile, and hopefully, any more shots would be over her head. She began crawling forward on her stomach, careful to keep her upper body straight and her breathing shallow.

The going was slow. Even though the creek was only about twenty yards away, the brush was thick, requiring her to slither over the smaller plants and around the bigger ones. Several times she found herself surrounded by saplings of a half-inch or more, and she had to back out and try a different tack. The decaying vegetation collected in the neck of her jacket and the waistband of her pants as she belly-crawled. From time to time, she could swear she felt things moving around in her clothes, and she'd pause to wipe the worst of it away.

Eventually, she reached the edge of the stream. The path from the road split there, going both up and downstream. Harrison had been here already—Rebecca knew from the noise the woman had made. She had probably tried both directions before deciding she'd passed her prey and returned to the road. She had either given up, which Rebecca didn't believe for a second, or she was retracing her steps. So, with no time to lose, Rebecca slipped into the water.

The creek was warmer than the air and shallow. It was perhaps a foot in the slow-moving pool where she now lay, while it appeared to be only a few inches where the channel was wide or it was partially blocked with rocks. Downstream, Rebecca would find the Missouri River, but probably not people. If she floated on the river, she'd find some type of commercial operation eventually, but bobbing along on the slow-moving current would leave her exposed. She had no idea what lay upstream—homes, roads, a park, nothing but more woods?

Harrison fired again. It sounded like she was at the top of the path, firing down the hill. Had she seen something or was she just trying to flush her out? Either way, Rebecca needed to get moving. She turned upstream, taking advantage of a sharp turn in the creek bed that would put her out of sight after about ten yards. But when she rounded that bend, she found that the path had made the same turn. Of course, it would. Whoever came down here would be following the water.

Rebecca could hear Harrison coming back down the hill again. In fact, the woman was making no secret about her location, stopping every few moments to pick up a rock or limb and toss it into the brush. The tactic was the same as the one she had used but with one important difference. Rebecca had intended to hide her position;

Harrison intended to drive her into a killing zone. Rebecca could feel her pulse surge as the objects landed closer and closer. Her gut was saying fight or flee; her mind argued otherwise, trying to keep her movements measured and quiet.

At first, Rebecca carefully slid her hands and knees over the creek bed, testing their placement before transferring her weight. But as the situation deteriorated, she had no choice but to reduce her caution in favor of pace. The price of her haste, however, came payable within moments as one of her hands landed on something sharp. When she raised her arm, she saw the blood flowing down her wrist, waves of bright crimson and dark red in the dappled light of the thicket. Rebecca could see a tetanus shot and a regime of antibiotics in her future, but there was nothing she could do about it now. She hurried on.

After a few more minutes, Rebecca decided she had pushed her luck as far as she could. Harrison could come striding down the path at any moment, leaving her sitting in a pool of dirty water with the woman smirking down at her. But if she crawled off into the brush, she could hide until dark. Harrison wouldn't continue after sunset, and even if she did, Rebecca would see her light coming from a distance.

Then after dark, she'd continue her crawl upstream, emerging only when she was a safe distance away.

* * *

The couple of hours until sunset had seemed interminable. Another hour or two until the night deepened felt endless. Rebecca had tried to relax, but even letting her head loll to one side brought her rudely back to her painful reality and she'd tense again. By now, that cycle had repeated so many times she was exhausted. Her damp clothes were in tatters. She was shivering uncontrollably. She hadn't eaten since breakfast, and then, only a small container of yogurt. Right about now, she'd give fifty bucks for a big greasy cheeseburger and fries.

She looked around ... or tried anyway. There was a moon, but it was mostly covered by clouds, leaving the forest in darkness. But that was to her advantage. Harrison would need a flashlight to walk the path, but she didn't need light to navigate the creek. She had the sound and smell to get her to the bank and the feel of water to keep her on course. And, besides, her eyes had fully adjusted to the night, and she could make out vague shapes in the woods around her. It was time to get moving and maybe the exertion would warm her up.

Rebecca crawled to the edge of the stream, afraid she might lose her footing if she tried to walk. When she reached it, she changed her mind about reentering. Even though the water was tepid, the temperatures were dropping and she'd never warm up if she kept getting wet. She started picking her way along the path upstream.

The going was excruciatingly slow. The path was littered with rocks and roots, each a potential stumbling block that could send her sprawling onto the ground. Every few minutes she had to stop; pain and her fight to control it were robbing her of her last reserves of energy. But after what seemed hours, Rebecca saw the vague outline of a bridge. She moved closer. By its width, it was a road rather than a footbridge.

The path continued under the bridge alongside the creek, but enough people had scrambled up and down the bank to clear the way. Even so, Rebecca could hardly negotiate the steep incline to the road. "So, how long till rush hour?" she mumbled to herself when she stood beside the pavement, only to be answered by the high beam of headlights that cut through the darkness.

"Ah, Ms. Marte," said a voice that could only be Harrison's. "I wondered when you'd show up. Four hours to go what, 50 yards? You're not going to win any races that way."

Pinned and helpless in the middle of the beam of light, Rebecca saw no options for escape. She could hardly move, much less run. She prepared herself, waiting for the moment of pain and the oblivion that would soon follow. In those few precious moments, she wondered if she should have done something differently? Downstream instead of up? Make a stand at the house? Try to waylay Harrison in the woods? But at each point, she'd played the odds correctly. That, however, was the unfortunate thing about odds; even the best of them didn't guarantee success.

"Lower the weapon and put your hands up," came a shouted command from the darkness to Harrison's left. It was Gus. It made sense that Harrison had guessed where she was going, but Gus? How had he found them?

But in the split second of Rebecca's thought, Harrison also made her decision. She spun to her left, firing three shots into the darkness. Gus returned fire and Harrison fell. That quickly, it was all over.

FRIDAY, NOVEMBER 6

8:08 AM, Marte Investigative Services

Rebecca stood from her office chair, wrapping her arms around herself as she walked to the window. The morning commute was still in full swing, filling the street below with drivers intent on making the next light or finding that perfect parking space. Pedestrians crowded the sidewalk, sipping their morning coffee, talking animatedly with a friend, or checking their phone. The scene was teeming with life.

Rebecca, however, had never felt more alone.

She turned from the window to look into the reception area, completely from habit rather than by necessity. Gus wasn't there. Gus would never be there. His last place on earth was a cold, dark street on the Missouri River bluffs. She cursed the memory of that night.

But as much as she missed the man—the long hours working cases, the priceless advice and endless aid he gave freely, the pretend bickering—she was even more devastated by the way he had died. It was the one-in-a-million chance that no one ever took seriously. It was literally a shot in the dark—or three of them if she was to be precise—but one of those slugs had found its mark. There had not even been time for last words; he was gone by the time she got to him. At least for his lack of suffering, she was thankful.

Fate had been cruel, but what was even more painful to Rebecca was the nagging question of why Gus had tempted fate at all. In his final moments, he had ignored everything he had taught her. He had approached to within ten yards of Harrison, but he was a better shot than that. He had stood in the open with no cover save the blackness of the night, while the location had no lack of trees. He had forced a situation in which both he and Harrison had died. But why?

That Gus's days were numbered might have been part of the reason he'd acted so uncharacteristically but not all of it. If Gus wanted to die, just about any other option would have been more reliable. By all accounts, Harrison should have missed. And if she didn't miss, she should have only wounded him.

After turning these questions over in her thoughts endlessly for days, Rebecca decided Gus had exposed himself to the vagaries of chance because he had no time to do otherwise. Though an excellent shot, his sight was slowly deteriorating. Though in good shape for his age, his knees wouldn't handle a prolonged footrace. So, he had positioned himself close to the killer in the dark; he couldn't risk making a mistake. Then, when Rebecca appeared on the bank of the stream, Gus would have sensed that Harrison was about to fire; she had certainly felt her end was coming. So, he had risked the final days of his life to give her more days of her own. Rebecca had felt she owed her friend and mentor before, but now it was a blood debt—one she could never repay.

Rebecca turned to go back to her desk, deciding to bury her pain in work. But after only a couple of steps, the door into her reception area opened. She looked into the adjoining space to find a familiar figure—well, mostly familiar. The eyes were sunken in a face that was too gaunt, too pale. The khaki pants bunched up under a belt tightened three notches more than usual. Even his movements seemed tentative, almost as if it was difficult to raise a hand or move his feet. But it was the face of a friend, and at the moment, that was exactly what she needed.

"Doc! When did you get in?"

She rushed forward, intending to give him a hug. For the emotional comfort the embrace would provide, she'd ignore the twinge from her still mending ribs. But as she neared, Doc retreated. The movement itself was slight, less than a half step backward. But his gaze went to the wall behind her as a hand came up to his face to rub his chin. He was about as closed to her approach as he could be without crossing his forearms over his chest. She stopped a step away, hurt.

"Two days ago," he replied. "I wanted to see if I still had a job and find a place to live. And I do ... have both that is." He paused. "I just dropped by to say how sorry I am about Gus. I saw the story a few weeks ago and meant to come to the funeral, but things got away from me."

Doc saying that things had gotten away from him was like oil saying to water, "we mix well." The statement contradicted everything Rebecca knew about who he was. His measured, calculated approach to life had to be struggling against ... what? She wasn't sure.

By the time the violence at the Kansas farmhouse ended, there had been at least seven sets of eyes watching from the hill, some through binoculars, some unaided. And each of those witnesses, it seemed, had spoken to one or more newspapers. All of those accounts said Nicole had been stabbed at least twice. And all of the later accounts—after Nicole had been identified—included statements like, "We thought it was a falling out among criminals. If we'd known who she was ...." But they hadn't and Nicole was left to fight for her life. Fortunately, she had survived.

But now, Rebecca wondered if the physical injuries described in the papers were less crippling than the emotional ones that weren't. The papers had said nothing about her captivity.

"Are you OK?" Rebecca asked. "You seem a little tired."

"Yeah, I'm fine." She waited, but that only caused him to add, "I probably should get going."

"If you want a rundown on the witch case, I can do it in five minutes."

Doc hesitated, but then agreed, and the two went into the office and sat. Keeping to her promise, she wrapped up her summary quickly. When she was done, Doc said, "It's a tragedy but at the risk of sounding callous, Gus may have died exactly the way he wanted — bringing down one last bad guy."

"Yeah, his wife said basically the same thing, but it's still tough."

"Of course," replied Doc, nodding slowly. "And how'd your client take it? I mean, Bergeron's still guilty of Sims's death even if she was emotionally coerced into doing it, right?"

"Correct. Labadie appreciates knowing what made her sister act so out-of-character, as well as the fact that she'll face a lesser offense because of diminished capacity. But she's not so happy with her sister's incarceration. At least her lawyers think they may get some accommodations because of Bergeron's unique mental gifts. Or would that be her unique mental curse?"

"I suppose that depends on context," said Doc. He paused a moment, rubbing his chin. "So, you didn't tell me how Gus found you."

"Just like you'd expect—a bit of old-school detective work. My phone was on the fritz, so I'd written Bergeron's address on a slip of paper. He found the pad and evidently read the indentation in it. The blank page was in his car."

"So, who's old school now?" asked Doc, a slight smile coming to his face. "Gus for using a well-worn trick or you for resorting to pen and paper?"

It was good to see something besides exhausted resolve in Doc's manner. "Terrible what we have to do when technology lets us down, isn't it?" she replied, returning the smile. "Anyway, Gus went to Bergeron's house. The guard told him I had been there but had left. He had the guard call the house, but of course, they got no answer. I understand that they got into a bit of an argument at that point, Gus insisting on going in while the guard refused. Eventually, he called his supervisor, and his boss agreed to send someone out to check the house. After that, it's just guesswork."

"Gus drove around the area," said Doc. "Saw your car or maybe even Harrison driving it. He watched her until you showed up. That about what you're thinking?"

"Pretty much. Or maybe he went to the spot where Harrison took me. It was where Goodwin was killed."

"Oh, yeah. How's his death tie in with all this?"

"It doesn't. Four kids stole a car and accidentally hit him while they were joyriding. One of them confessed a couple of weeks ago. So, while the timing, the location, and his identity made it suspicious, Goodwin's death had nothing to do with the Sims case."

"It happens," Doc replied with a shrug. "And the strange thing about no fingerprints in blood on the knife? I suppose that's just an oddity of how Bergeron stabbed Sims."

"Unless you think Bergeron's empathy extends to mirroring actual physical movement. In the research I scanned, there was some mention of the motor cortex being involved."

Doc's eyes narrowed. "Picking up someone else's emotional response is one thing, but picking up an unfamiliar movement when Harrison wasn't doing it? I think that's a stretch." But even with his disclaimer, Rebecca could tell he hadn't completely discarded the idea. Then, Doc grinned. "But that would make one helluva training method if we could bottle it."

Doc was starting to relax. The talk was helping, although Rebecca was concerned that shifting to his problems would end that trend. But what kind of friend acts like nothing is wrong when clearly, something is. One offhand question couldn't hurt. "So, is Nicole back in St. Louis, too?"

"No. She's not coming. And like I said, I should be going." He stood.

"I'm sorry if that was too personal."

He closed his eyes a moment, sighed, and then slowly sank back into the chair. "No, her location isn't a secret. And besides, I need to learn how to say this, even if I can never accept it." He released another long breath. "Nicole is not coming back because our life together is over. The kidnappers destroyed a lot of her memory including most of the time we were together."

"What? That's not possible, is it?"

"Unfortunately, it is. There's research on different chemicals that can be used to erase traumatic memories, providing a possible cure for things like depression. But the techniques aren't perfect; they tend to affect every recollection, good and bad. And used indiscriminately, as the kidnappers did, prior associations among events are broken and suggestions are added to become a new reality. The kidnappers planted the belief that the world had seen another, even more lethal, pandemic. Nicole's not going to try to escape if there's nothing to escape to."

"They know that's what happened?"

"Yeah. Nicole told the detectives. And at the farmhouse, they found canisters of a gas, xenon, that's used in this memory-erasing research. There's no doubt that they destroyed a couple of years of her life."

"That's awful," said Rebecca. "You'll just have to start working on new memories with her."

The look of pain that crossed Doc's face was so palpable that Rebecca winced, not sure what she had said. Doc rubbed his forehead, looking down at his lap for a moment. His eyes glistened when he looked up.

"If her mind was a blank slate, then that might be possible. But she remembers me ... or believes she does anyway. She remembers all the times I beat her or yelled at her. She remembers me raping her. She remembers me leaving her for dead alongside a road. Her folks were able to find out that much and told me."

Rebecca raised a hand to her throat. "But .... But she knows that's wrong, that none of that ever happened."

"Logically, yes. Emotionally, not at all. And even if she was going to try to recapture what she had, she's going to start with what was most important to her—things like her career and her family. There is some pain in these distorted recollections, too, but looking further into the past, she knows that these things mattered. They defined her.

"But me? Her recollections of me are all vile and there are no memories from the distant past to correct them. And if she decides to find a life partner, does she start anew with a man she doesn't know? Or does she deal with all the anguish associated with me just because someone says that at one time we were close? The choice is obvious, even if I wish it wasn't."

"Doc, I am so sorry. Maybe her memories aren't totally gone. Maybe they'll come back. Things like that happen, don't they?"

"Possibly." His statement, however, lacked all conviction.

"Look, if you ever need to talk, I'm here. Friends, right?"

Rebecca had angered a few men by suggesting they had a friendship, but she wasn't surprised when Doc said, "Of course. Always. But now, I really do need to get going."

Rebecca walked Doc to the outer door, wondering if this was the last time she'd see him. She'd thought of Nicole's kidnapping as a nearly insoluble problem, and it had nearly destroyed him trying to find the answer. But that issue seemed almost insignificant compared to the barrier he now faced in the mind of his former love. Would he become consumed in a fight against Nicole's mental demons? Would she become a constant reminder of his failure to get Nicole back whole?

Doc stepped into the hallway, then turned back. "You'll call me next time a case looks like it has something I could help with? Something with a psychological context?"

She smiled, her worries answered. "Assuming I can tell because this time I evidently had psychology confused with the supernatural."

ACKNOWLEDGMENTS

This book would not have been possible without the help of a number of talented individuals.

First, I'd like to thank Ms. Janet Harrison for reading and providing numerous helpful comments on an earlier draft of the manuscript. (And no, she's not related to any of the fictional Harrisons in the book.) A special thanks go to Dr. Liz Gehr for helping me watch my technical Ps and Qs. Any inaccuracies in the technical content are mine; hopefully, they're all intentional to build the fiction.

The diligence of my editor is greatly appreciated. This time, it was cumulative adjectives and their order ... not to mention all the other slipups that are so easy to overlook when you know a story by heart.

Finally, thanks go to my talented daughter, Ms. Courtney Perrin, for the design and creation of the cover art. Maybe I can build a picture with words, but I could never do what she does with graphics software and a computer ... not to mention pens, paint, and all the other media she uses.

ABOUT THE AUTHOR

Bruce Perrin has been writing for more than twenty-five years, although you will find most of that work only in professional technical journals or conference proceedings. After receiving a PhD in Industrial/Organizational Psychology and completing a career in psychological research and development at a major aerospace company, he's now applying his background to writing novels. Not surprisingly, most of his work falls in the techno-thriller, mystery, and hard science fiction genres, examining the intersection of technology and the human mind now and in the future. Besides writing, Bruce likes to tinker with home automation and is an avid hiker, logging nearly 2,500 miles a year in the first eight years of Fitbit ownership. When he is not on the trails, he lives with his wife in St. Louis, MO.

Thank you for reading From the Mind of a Witch. If you'd like to help others find this story, please consider leaving a review on Amazon, Goodreads, or the website of your favorite bookseller.

For all the latest on my new releases, promotions, and book reviews, please subscribe to my blog: BruceMPerrin.blogspot.com

www.ingramcontent.com/pod-product-compliance
Lightning Source LLC
Chambersburg PA
CBHW021125190726
48288CB00008B/2499